Vincent, Survivor

O.L. Eggert

Cover illustration by Diego Rodriguez
Cover design by Kit Foster
Edited by Jessica Nelson & Eliza Dee
Formatted by Polgarus Studio

ISBN: 978-0-9973752-1-3
eISBN: 978-0-9973752-0-6

*Thank you to everyone who supported me along the way.
Especially you, Megan.*

www.OLEggert.com

Chapter 1

It was a dim Sunday morning in Oakwood—the last weekend the old city would ever have.

Nestled between a laundromat and dirty salon, a neon sign buzzed lazily over a grimy brick building, announcing it as Granny's Liquor. Through its barred front doors, at a lone table in the far corner, next to a shelf of condoms, sat a dark-haired man. His almost-black eyes darted across the pages of a crisp paperback in one hand, and a cigarette nub dangled from the fingers of the other.

"Have you been keeping up with the news, Vincent?"

He turned his face up, revealing pronounced cheekbones and a sharp chin that intensified his serious expression. "No," he said.

A woman frowned at him from behind the front counter. She could have easily been mistaken for a frail old lady with her petite frame, wispy locks of gray hair, and stick-thin wrists that looked like they might break under a strong wind. But behind her glasses, sharp blue eyes—attentive and alive—dared any well-meaning youth to treat her as such. "Take a look at this," she said, holding up the front page of a newspaper: "Murder Rates Double; Missing Persons Cases Triple. Still No Comment from OPD Chief."

"It's probably just a bad turf war going on with the gangs, Grandma."

Grandma snorted. "You aren't worried?"

"Just keep your head down and stay out of their business. Then they won't bother you."

"Don't give me that shit, Vincent Li. It's not me I'm worried about. You still have that gun I gave you a couple years back?"

"Yeah, it's in my closet."

"Maybe you should start carrying it with you, just in case."

"You're being paranoid," he scoffed.

Grandma slapped the newspaper down on the counter. "Don't be an asshole, Vincent. I'm serious. Something about this doesn't feel right."

"I'm a grown man, Grandma. I'll be fine."

She pointedly opened up her paper and mumbled, "Grown man, my wrinkled ass."

Vincent rolled his eyes with a soft chuckle before getting up and walking over to her. He put out his cigarette in an overflowing ashtray next to the register, then motioned to a shelf of cigarettes behind Grandma. "Give me two packs."

Grandma's eyes flicked up over the rim of her glasses. "Whatever happened to quitting?"

He raised an eyebrow at her, then pointed to the ashtray.

"You're one to talk. That's not all mine."

Grandma sighed, but put down two packs of cigarettes on the counter. "That's completely different," she replied. "I'm old, with bad arthritis, cataracts, high blood pressure, diabetes, and a whole bunch of other crap I'm sure the doctors haven't found yet. I think in the grand scheme of things, shaving off a few years of my life isn't that big a deal."

Vincent scrunched his nose as he paid. "Can you not talk like that? Thinking about you dying is depressing."

She flashed him a wolfish grin, then motioned at the book in his hand. "What're you reading this time?"

"It's called *Gallant's Quest.*"

"More of that fantasy garbage? Let me guess, the hero overcomes an evil wizard to save his kingdom from certain doom."

Vincent lit a cigarette and sucked in a deep breath before answering. "Seems like it so far."

"Hunh. What's the point if you already know what's going to happen? The hero always wins. There's no fun in that."

"I guess that's what I like about them." He shrugged. "Anyways, I better get going. See you tomorrow, Grandma." He waved goodbye and headed out the door.

Outside, the distant wail of a siren and the cawing of crows overhead greeted him. Vincent placed his cigarette loosely between his lips and started the short walk home, admiring the city he'd called home his whole life—twenty-two shitty years to be exact. He always found Oakwood to be an odd name, given how few oak trees there actually were.

The only greenery consisted of sporadic patches of life on stiff, dead lawns, the occasional bush, and resilient tufts of weeds in the cracks of the sidewalks and roads.

Vincent turned onto his street and walked toward a narrow seafoam-green house. Years of neglect gave it the same run-down and sad look as all the homes around it—peeling paint, streaks of dirt, and barred windows and doors. He hurried up the front steps, lost in his thoughts, when he noticed something strange. A loose rock lay upturned on his front porch; a quick look aside showed a dark patch of dirt where it had been.

The stone was a fake. Vincent picked it up and flipped it over in his hand. Someone had guessed the combination to open it and gotten to the spare house key inside. He looked up at the front door, eyes narrowed to suspicious slits. It wouldn't be the first time someone tried robbing him, but how had they figured out the combination?

"Son of a bitch," he muttered. Vincent pushed the door open with a drawn-out creak. "Hello? You assholes still in here stealing all my shit?" His neck bristled at a noise from the back of the house and he whipped out his cell phone. "I don't want any trouble. If you just leave, I won't have to call the cops on you."

A dark figure appeared at the end of the hallway and lifted its arms. "Relax, Vincent. It's just me," a deep voice replied. A man with a shaved head and a strong resemblance to Vincent walked into the living room. Large, corded muscles bulged underneath his plain white shirt, giving him an overpowering "don't fuck with me" look.

Vincent blinked hard to make sure he wasn't seeing things. "Dante?"

The man gave him a weak smile. "I was just passing through to pick up some of my things." He lifted a duffel bag as evidence.

Vincent ignored his words and took a few steps forward. "What are you doing here? You still have a couple years on your sentence."

"I'm out on parole for good behavior."

"Really?"

"You think I just broke out of prison?" Dante asked incredulously.

Vincent's brain sputtered, trying to play catch-up. Dante looked so different; he'd packed on at least forty pounds of muscle since they last saw each other.

Dante looked down at his feet and tried walking around, but Vincent stopped him. "What are you doing?"

"I should go," Dante said.

"Go where?" Vincent said. "I haven't seen you in . . . shit, at least four years, and you think you're just going to leave?"

Dante shook his head. "Sorry, I don't even know what to say. I was hoping to get in and out before you got home."

Vincent's voice rose as he spoke. "That's all you have to say? I haven't seen or talked to you since you went to prison. You never took my calls, never returned my letters—do you know how many times I tried going to see you?"

"Look, I'm sorry for what I did, but I needed to be alone."

"So you were just being an asshole," Vincent spat.

"I shouldn't have come here." Dante pushed past and headed for the front door.

"Stop!" Vincent's voice softened. "Let's not make this complicated."

Dante's big shoulders drooped, and he turned back slowly.

"Four years is a long time. Are you going to at least give me a hug?" Vincent asked with his arms out.

Their lips pricked up, mirroring each other's lopsided grins before the men met in a crushing bear hug.

"It's been too long," Vincent said over a joyous laugh.

"I know, little brother, I know," Dante replied.

Vincent pulled back and looked him over. "You got real big."

His brother shrugged. "There wasn't much to do besides work out and read. How have you been holding up?"

"Just living." An awkward silence fell between them. Vincent opened his mouth to say something, but nothing came out. His brother had become a familiar stranger to him over the years. "Are you thirsty or something? I got some beer in the fridge."

"You really think I want alcohol after what happened with Tommy? I'm never touching the stuff again for as long as I live."

Vincent shrugged. "Fair enough." He studied Dante's face, which seemed to have put on an extra twenty years. He looked worn out. "Now that you're out on parole, what're you going to do?"

"I was planning to stay at a cheap motel somewhere until I find a job," Dante said. "I need to find one pretty soon. It's one of the conditions of my parole."

"Why don't you stay here with me, Dante? Your room's exactly the way you left it. It'd be like old times."

He looked uneasy. "Are you sure? Even after what I did to get myself thrown into jail? If you don't want me around, it's okay. I get it."

"You're my fucking family. You get that, right?" Vincent's fist thudded gently against Dante's shoulder. "I don't know what went through your head these last few years, but quite frankly, I don't care anymore. Whatever it was—all that's behind us—I'm glad you're finally back." Vincent tried taking the duffel bag, but Dante pulled away.

"What about the old crew? Are you still hanging with Roach and those guys?" Dante asked. "I can't get back into that kind of shit."

Vincent shook his head. "Don't worry. I cut ties with everybody not long after you left. They were always more your friends anyway." He motioned to a large TV on the wall and multiple shelves of fantasy and sci-fi movies and books he had collected over the years. "This is how I pass the time nowadays."

Dante blew a relieved breath, and his expression softened around the edges. "You really wouldn't mind me staying here?"

Vincent grabbed the back of Dante's head and bumped foreheads with him. "Grandma's going to rip you a new asshole when she finds out you're back in town."

A genuine smile spread across Dante's face, and he relaxed. "How's that tough old bitch doing now?"

"She just turned sixty-six last month and is still kicking and cussing."

"I'm glad some things haven't changed." Dante smirked.

Vincent pulled back and looked his brother square in the eyes. "It's good to have you home."

Chapter 2

Vincent woke peacefully the next morning, an unusual occurrence. He turned over and saw he had even beaten his alarm clock by a whole half hour. The usual lethargy he felt before work wasn't there, and he slipped out of bed effortlessly to start getting ready. It wasn't until he was adjusting a tie in the mirror that he noticed the faint smile playing at his lips; the smile widened at the sound of a cabinet closing down the hall. Vincent finished up and joined his brother in the kitchen.

"You ready to see Grandma?"

Dante looked up from a bowl of cereal, a crease in his brow. "You think this is a good idea? She's going to be so pissed when she sees me."

"The sooner you do it, the sooner it'll be over." Vincent sat across from him with his own breakfast. "Don't worry. She's going to love having you back."

Dante mumbled something under his breath, then motioned to Vincent's tie. "What's with the getup?"

"I'm a manager at the Shoe Emporium now—got to look the part," Vincent said.

"You aren't talking about the place that always had the going out of business clearance sale?"

Vincent grinned. "That's the one."

"No joke, huh? No one ever goes there," Dante said. "The pay must be terrible."

"At least it's honest work," Vincent said. "Speaking of which, what were you thinking of doing?"

"I'm pretty good with cars. Maybe one of the car shops around here could use a mechanic."

Vincent barked out a short laugh. "You must be confused. Stealing and fixing are two different things."

Dante gave him a playful tap on the arm that made it go numb, and then stood up. "I'll wait for you outside."

Vincent finished his breakfast and joined his brother on the front porch a few minutes later. He squinted up at the sky. The clouds swirled overhead, dark and angry as a brisk wind blew by. "It's going to rain again."

"That's weird." Dante shivered. "It's usually pushing past a hundred this time of year."

Vincent nodded. "The weather's been acting up since last month. Colder than it should be, and it's been raining on and off—it's like summer never came." He lit a cigarette and offered it to his brother.

"I quit that stuff years ago."

Vincent shrugged in a "suit yourself" gesture and stuck the cigarette between his lips. "Why would you go and do that?"

"That shit'll kill you, Vincent."

Vincent stopped mid-puff and cast his brother a sideways look. "You used to go through almost two packs a day."

"People change, I guess."

"I guess so." Vincent took another drag and watched a pickup truck pull into the driveway across the street.

A thin man practically spilled out of the driver's-side door, collapsing on his hands and knees. He scrambled onto his feet, blinking bloodshot eyes as his rickety hands fidgeted with the belt of an oversized bathrobe. The man's hair clung in wet clumps to his forehead—though it probably wasn't from a recent shower, given the dark circles of sweat in his armpits and around his collar. The man gave up trying to tie a knot and darted around the truck to the passenger door. Before opening it, he surveyed his surroundings with a suspicious eye and noticed Vincent and Dante watching.

Dante gave a slight wave, but that seemed to spook him.

He threw open his truck door and pulled out a paper bag of groceries with a grunt, and then scurried into his house like a cockroach caught out in the open. He reemerged a minute later and ran back to the truck, pulling out another bag of groceries. Vincent watched with growing curiosity as his neighbor did this a few more times.

On his fifth trip, the bag in his arms broke, spilling canned goods all over the driveway. "No, no, no!" the man croaked, dropping down and attempting in vain to scoop them into his arms.

A woman walking by noticed and moved to help him, but the man's eyes bulged at her and he shouted, "NO!"

"I can give you a hand picking those up," she said.

Vincent's neighbor swatted her back. "Get away from me! You're not getting me, you understand? Nobody's going to get me!" The woman tried getting a word of reason in, but he continued his tirade. "I know you've been watching me. During the day, at night, for two weeks now—you always watch. I know! *I know*. What do you want from me?"

Vincent chuckled. "Jesus, this guy's crazy."

"Drugs?" Dante suggested.

"Probably."

"Do you know that guy?"

"He moved into the neighborhood a couple years ago," Vincent said. "I've never seen him cause a scene like this, though. He keeps to himself mostly."

His neighbor chased the woman off his driveway, then sprinted back to the house, his bathrobe fluttering like a cape. He slammed the front door behind him with a tone of finality.

Vincent dropped his cigarette and ground out the nub under his heel. "Well, that was a fun little show." He nodded at a rusted hatchback parked on the street. It was a piece of crap with dings and scratches from its previous owner, but it reliably got him around town. "Let's get going."

A bell jingled when they walked through the front door. Grandma didn't bother looking up from her morning paper. Vincent caught a glimpse of the front page headline: "Husband and Wife Killed. Arson Suspected."

Grandma motioned to a pot of coffee simmering next to

her. "Just finished brewing," she said.

Vincent grabbed a stained mug off the table and exchanged looks with his brother. "We're going to need another cup."

"What the hell are you—" Grandma's mouth went slack when she saw Dante standing before her.

Dante smiled sheepishly. "Surprise?"

"Dante Li," she whispered. "Dante *fucking* Li, is that you?"

"He's out early for good behavior," Vincent explained.

A mean look snaked its way onto Grandma's face as she walked around the counter. She jabbed a bony finger into Dante's chest. "You son of a bitch. You got some nerve showing your ugly mug around here, especially after what you put me and your brother through!"

Dante bowed his head in shame.

She thumped her arm against his chest, flushing deep red. "You selfish little shit!"

"I'm sorry, all right?" Dante said.

Vincent smirked at the sight of the little old lady berating such a huge man.

"You're sorry?" Grandma mocked. "Do you know how many times we tried visiting you after the trial? God damn it, you can't even begin to understand how stressful it's been for me. You know how bad my blood pressure gets when I'm stressed, and that's not even considering how your poor little brother felt during the whole ordeal."

Vincent tried interjecting. "Grandma, it's okay. We already talked about it."

"Knowing you, 'talked about it' means you just cussed him out a bit," she said.

He rolled his eyes. "Gee, I wonder where I got it from." Grandma glared at him, and he pressed his lips into a tight line, miming locking his mouth shut and throwing the key away.

"So?" Grandma turned back to Dante. "What do you have to say for yourself?"

"I . . ." Dante trailed off, obviously unprepared for the question. "I don't know, it's hard to explain."

"Shut up!" Grandma yelled. She started pacing, muttering obscenities under her breath and occasionally casting Dante dirty looks.

His brother looked to him for help, but Vincent could only shrug.

Finally, Grandma stopped her raving and turned her full attention to Dante. She wiped some tears from her eyes and held her arms out expectantly.

"Come on, bring it in," she huffed.

Dante gave her a big smile and picked her up in a tight embrace; Grandma's feet dangled a foot off the floor for a full minute. When he set her down, she gave him a peck on the cheek, then stepped back.

"Don't you ever pull a stunt like that again," Grandma said. She put a hand on both brothers with a sad smile. "Take it from me, kids, don't ever turn your backs on one another, no matter what happens. If you stick together you can get through anything."

A pained look crossed Dante's face. "But—"

Grandma cut him off with a stern scowl. "Dante, I've been around the block more times than I'd like to count. Facing your demons alone is a road best avoided." Dante tried protesting again, but she shushed him. Grandma went behind the counter and came back out with a plate of cookies. "You're in luck. I happened to make these last night. They're your favorite: cinnamon and sugar."

Vincent eagerly grabbed one with each hand, but Dante hesitated. Grandma pushed the plate into his stomach, scowling. "Take one," she demanded.

Dante grinned and popped a whole cookie into his mouth with a satisfied moan. "God damn, Grandma. I missed these so much."

Vincent wolfed down one of his own. It practically melted in his mouth and brought back warm memories of when they were kids, hanging out with Grandma after school. A smile crept onto Vincent's face, working muscles he hadn't used in a long time. The three quickly fell back into familiar conversation, and for a brief moment, it felt like Dante had never left in the first place.

An hour later, Vincent reluctantly left Dante and Grandma to head into work. He was in such a euphoric daze he barely noticed the unusual quiet. There were few cars on the road and even fewer people on the sidewalks. He pulled into an empty parking lot of mom-and-pop shops and found a spot in front of the Shoe Emporium. Vincent hurried into the canary-yellow building to open shop, passing by a faded clearance sale sign with curled edges in the window.

His good mood was dampened when, at half past nine, he was still the only person in the store. Vincent went into the back room and checked the work schedule—as he'd thought, another employee was supposed to be with him.

Bill was a forty-something guy who lived alone on the other side of town. He was a bit on the slow side, with a strange affinity for useless trivia, like knowing cat pee shows up under a black light. However dumb he was, though, not once in his two years of working with Vincent had he ever come in late or called out sick.

Vincent dialed Bill's cell phone, but it went straight to voice mail. "Hey, Bill, it's Vincent. You got a shift today and you're not here. Call me as soon as you get this."

When lunch came, Bill still hadn't shown up or bothered calling in, much to Vincent's annoyance. He locked up the store and crossed the street to a burger joint he frequented, Donald's All-Star Patties; the smell of greasy heart attacks wafted into his nose as he entered. He expected a busy lunch line, but it was a ghost town except for a pimply teenager at the register and a mother with her child, ordering their food.

Vincent waited patiently behind the woman and glanced down at the little girl by her legs, babbling childish nonsense. The girl noticed and gave him a pudgy-cheeked smile. He returned the smile, making her blush and rub her face into her mother's pants. Vincent chuckled, and then looked up to find the mother staring at him. He gave her a small nod, but she blanched and scooped up the child in her arms.

The woman turned to the cashier. "Cancel my order."

She shot Vincent an accusing look. "Stay the hell away from us, you hear? I have pepper spray, and I swear I'll use it!"

Before Vincent had a chance to process what the hell happened, she dashed out the door, leaving him dumbfounded. Vincent gave the teenager a perplexed look. "What was that all about?" he asked.

The cashier gave a slight shrug. "Haven't you been keeping up with the news? Folks dying or going missing. Something's happening in Oakwood, and people are freaking out." He leaned forward and in a hushed whisper added, "It's not just here. It's happening all over the world."

"Don't be stupid, kid. If people all over the world are really disappearing there'd be more news about it, don't you think?"

The boy threw his hands up in a placating gesture. "Hey, man, I'm just telling you what I read on the Internet."

"Of course you read it on the Internet. Look, just get me a chicken sandwich combo."

Vincent received his food in short order and finished it without further incident. On his way back to work, he happened upon a vending machine for the local newspaper. He rarely read the paper, but on a whim grabbed a copy.

Back at the Shoe Emporium, he opened it up and began reading.

"Mother Found Dead in Home."

"High School Student Kidnapped by Unidentified Men— No Leads!"

"Police Department 'Swamped' with Cases. Mayor to Address Funding to Expand Police Force."

Vincent called Bill again, and again it went straight to voice mail. Vincent didn't bother to leave a message. He glossed over the newspaper headlines and the hairs on his neck pricked up. He started dialing 9-1-1, but stopped before hitting the call button. He let out a frustrated growl, irritated with himself for getting so worked up over nothing. The newspapers were just trying to stir shit up to sell more papers.

"This is stupid," he muttered, crumpling up the paper and tossing it into the garbage. "Missing one damn day doesn't mean anything." Vincent pushed any paranoid thoughts out of his head and went about the rest of his work day.

But he couldn't shake the uneasy feeling scratching at his insides, and he caught himself on more than one occasion going for his phone to call the police.

When Vincent closed the store, an uninviting night had already fallen. The moon was almost entirely hidden behind black, brooding clouds. Vincent loosened his tie and walked a little faster than usual to his car, locking the doors once inside. Shadows crept around him, scurrying away from the occasional slip of moonlight.

Vincent hurried home and didn't feel at ease until he walked through the front door and bolted it shut.

His brother was watching the news on the couch. "How was work?" he asked.

Vincent opened his mouth, but a knock at the door interrupted him. He whirled around, startled by the sound.

Dante lowered the TV volume. "Who'd you come back with?"

Vincent frowned. "No one."

Dante looked at him expectantly. "Well? You going to get that?"

Through the peephole, Vincent saw a squat, overweight man on the porch. Long greasy strands of brown hair fell limp over his face, obscuring beady eyes and framing a strangely squash-shaped nose. The man peered at the door, a nervous jitter to his movements, and rapped his knuckles against it.

Vincent cracked the door open, but left the security screen closed. He peered out into the night to make sure the man was alone before looking down to address him. "What are you doing here?"

"I've been waiting for you all fucking day. I was getting worried I'd run out of time before you got home."

"What the hell do you want? I told you multiple times I don't have anything for you to fence. I don't do that shit anymore," Vincent said.

"I know, and it's a damn shame. You were one of my best."

"Who is it?" Dante called.

The man's eyes practically popped out of their sockets. "Is that Dante in there?" he asked, clumsily jumping to try and get a look over Vincent's shoulder. His eyes lit up when he saw Dante. "Hey, man! It's me, Roach!" he shouted.

Dante was behind Vincent in a matter of moments. "What the hell are you doing here, Roach?" He turned to

Vincent, shaking his head. "Don't tell me you're still stealing for him. If my parole officer finds out, my ass is going right back to jail."

"I'm not," Vincent growled. "Like I told you yesterday, I cut all ties with the guys."

"And it was damn cold of you to turn your back on all of us like that," Roach said. "I thought we were closer than that."

Vincent rubbed a weary hand down his face. "What are you doing here?"

"Let me in." Roach jiggled the security screen handle. "It's not safe to talk out in the open."

"You're okay right where you are," Dante said. "Our hearing is fine."

Roach wiped sweat from his brow with an impatient whine. "Okay, fine. Listen, I came to save you, Vincent." He flashed a greasy grin, making his chin crease in two. "Lucky you're here too, Dante. I can probably save you as well."

"Save us from what?" Vincent demanded. "You're not making any sense."

Roach checked over his shoulders, then pressed his face near the screen. "You must've been seeing all that shit on the news lately, right?" he whispered in a low, secretive tone. "Let's just say things are about to get a lot worse." He hesitated, concern etched into his face. "I'm just trying to do some good before it's too late."

"Are you talking about the disappearances?" Dante asked. "What do you know about that?"

Vincent's eyes hardened. "No, whatever bullshit you're

trying to pull us into, we don't want any part of it." He began to shut the door, but Roach slammed his hand into the screen.

"Wait! I'm not fucking around this time, guys. This is serious. If you don't come with me, you aren't gonna make it in the new world." He looked between the brothers for some kind of answer, but got nothing. "Just put this on and come with me." Roach produced a necklace with a smooth lump of silver dangling from it.

Dante gave him a pitying look. "Good night, Roach."

"No, wait!" Roach's voice became a muffled rant as the door shut in his face. "Fine! See if I give a shit! I tried, I really did!" His footsteps padded off into the night, leaving Vincent and Dante to ponder in silence.

"What are you thinking?" Vincent asked.

"I wouldn't worry about him. Roach was always a little dramatic," Dante replied.

Vincent nodded, but their former fence didn't look like he was acting. There was real fear in Roach's eyes.

***

The mousy lawyer had a pencil mustache and a bad comb-over. He peered over tiny round spectacles, squinting at the legal paperwork in his hands. "I don't understand," he drawled. "Your name isn't mentioned here, Bo."

"I'm not surprised," a haughty voice replied.

"You must understand, Mother never liked our brother much," another person chimed.

Bo watched his sisters in sullen contemplation. They

both mirrored their mother in her younger years: long, severe faces, sharp noses, and a perpetual glare. They wore expensive-looking suits with huge, puffy hairstyles that were all the rage. Compared to them, he looked like a homeless man in his cheap secondhand suit; it had cost him an arm and a leg, but he figured it was the respectful thing to do for his mother's funeral.

His older sister, Chun, turned her nose up at him and sneered. "Why are you even here?" Her voice was a broken violin, erratic and fluctuating between painful screeches and unbearable yelling.

"You didn't seriously think Mother would leave you anything, did you?" Fung, the youngest of the siblings, daintily put her hand over her mouth and giggled.

He shrugged and played with the rough calluses on his hands, choosing silence as his answer.

"What's the matter, too good to talk to us?" Chun barked.

Fung waved her down. "Don't bother. You know how it is with him." She leaned toward the lawyer as if disclosing a big secret. "He's an idiot, never bothered to take school seriously. Raising him was so hard on mother."

"He's an ungrateful pig and pushed her to an early grave," Chun spat.

Bo wondered what it would be like to punch them both right in their smug noses and shatter their shit-eating grins. Imagining their cartilage crunching beneath his knuckles brought a smile to his face.

The lawyer shifted uncomfortably in his seat and cleared

his throat. "Let's stay on topic, yes, ladies?" He gave Bo an apologetic grimace. "You don't have to be here if you don't want. Your mother left you nothing in her will."

Bo pushed his chair back and got up to leave. He felt all the pieces click together in his mind and his next step became clear. "Have a nice life, sisters." He left them at a loss for words, and a smile played at his lips as the office door shut behind him.

He had cobbled together enough money from his job at the docks to move far, far away from Hong Kong, and he would never look back.

Chapter 3

"Wake up. Wake up!"

Vincent groaned and waved his hand in a shooing motion.

"Seriously, get your ass up!"

A strong hand grabbed him by the shoulder and shook. Vincent's bloodshot eyes popped open, and Dante's blurry form came into focus. He propped himself up on an elbow. "What are you doing?" he asked, voice throaty.

"Come with me, and be quiet," Dante said.

"What are you—"

"*Shhhh*. Trust me," he hissed.

The urgency in his tone silenced any further objections from Vincent; he followed his brother into the living room, where they crouched by the front window. Dante carefully lifted a corner of the curtain enough for Vincent to peek out.

"Look."

Vincent squinted into the night. "What am I looking for?" he whispered.

"There." Dante pointed across the street. "Do you see that?"

The faint outline of a black SUV materialized, haphazardly parked on the lawn of the house opposite them.

"You woke me up for this?" Vincent mumbled irritably. "So the crazy druggie has equally crazy friends that don't know how to park. So what?" He tried standing up, but Dante grabbed him with a strong grip.

"Stay down!" Dante whispered. "I was job searching on the Internet when I heard that car pop the curb. When I came to the window, I saw Roach and another guy force their way into that house."

The fog of sleep quickly dissipated from Vincent's head. He grabbed the curtain from Dante's hand and forced it shut. "Did they see you?"

"No, but that's not the worst part." Dante produced Vincent's cell phone and held it up to his ear.

Vincent heard a looping automated message: *"Oakwood Police are currently experiencing a high volume of calls. Please try again later. If your emergency cannot wait, please come to the police station to file a report."*

"What in the fuck," Vincent muttered. He grabbed the phone from Dante's hand and confirmed he had dialed 9-1-1. "What's that supposed to mean? They're too *busy?*" Vincent's throat went dry as he recalled Roach's words.

Dante lifted the edge of the curtain again. "They're coming back out."

Two figures left the house across the street. Vincent immediately recognized Roach, and the other person with him carried a limp body over his shoulder. A small orb of white light glowed dimly from each of their necks.

"Oh shit!" Vincent fell back and scrambled away from the window. "They're kidnapping him!"

Dante hurried to the back of the house.

"Where are you going?" Vincent hissed. He dared another peek and watched as Roach and the other man dumped his neighbor into the back of the SUV. They were so nonchalant about it he wondered if they had done this before. Vincent heard movement behind him and turned to see Dante fully dressed; his brother tossed a pair of pants and shoes by his feet. "What's this for?" he asked.

"We have to go after them," Dante said.

Vincent threw his arms up. "Are you serious?"

"You heard the message. The cops are too busy to respond."

"And? Why the hell does that mean we need to do something?" Vincent fired back.

There was a desperate look in Dante's eyes. "If you don't want to help, that's fine, I'll do it myself."

An engine roared to life, and powerful halogen lights swept across the edges of the curtain as the SUV made a screeching U-turn.

"How do you plan to chase them?" Vincent snapped. "You have no car."

"I'll take yours."

"Like hell you will. I'm not giving you the keys."

"It would only take me a minute to hotwire it." Dante stepped out the front door and watched Roach drive off.

"Come on, Vincent! We don't have time to argue about this."

Vincent crossed his arms. "Hell, no. I'm not sticking my nose in places it doesn't belong."

"Fine. If that's how you want it." Dante's jaw tightened, and he ran out.

"God damn it!" Vincent threw on his pants and shoes and hurried after his brother. "Wait!" he called.

Dante froze with a rock in his hand, ready to smash in Vincent's driver's-side window. "Did you change your mind?"

Vincent nodded and disappeared into the house, reappearing only moments later with the keys. He watched the SUV make a left turn at the end of the street. "All we're doing is following them. No superhero crap."

"Okay," Dante said impatiently. "They're getting away, we have to hurry!"

Vincent kept his headlights off and caught up to Roach's car with ease; it wasn't difficult, despite the other man's lead, since he was the only other vehicle on the road. Vincent followed a safe distance behind Roach's taillights, which glowed like evil red eyes in the night. Slowly, the suburban homes around him gave way to large warehouses and factories made of corrugated metal, a cheap and rusted mosaic of reds, browns, and intricate graffiti.

Vincent recognized where they were headed—Oakwood's shipping docks. He pulled onto the side of the road as Roach's SUV drove through a rusted gate toward the waterfront.

He scanned the shadowy outlines of shipping containers and operating cranes in the docks. "What kind of shady shit has Roach gotten himself into?" The car door opened in response, and Dante darted across the front of the car.

"You lying asshole!" Vincent killed the car's engine and went after his brother, catching him at the gate. "I thought you agreed we were just going to follow them?" he whispered, eyeing their surroundings for danger.

Dante shook Vincent's hand off. "I still am," he replied.

"We know where they are now. Let's go back," Vincent said.

"We can't just leave now. Look where we are. Who knows what Roach is going to do to that guy?"

"That's exactly *why* we need to leave. I'm not going to end up dead in a ditch for someone I barely know. I don't even know his fucking name," Vincent said.

"Then leave!" Dante shoved him back.

The outburst caught Vincent by surprise, and he didn't react.

"People have called me mean, selfish, violent—and they might be right about all that—but I am not a *bad* person. Someone in there needs help, and I'm not going to sit on my ass if I can do something about it."

Vincent recognized the resolve in Dante's narrowed eyes. It was a look he had seen so many times growing up, and he knew there was no arguing the point. He tilted his head up to the sky and took a deep, invigorating breath of cold air.

"You don't have to come," his brother reiterated.

"And let you go in alone? Screw off, of course I do."

Vincent ran his hand through his hair. "Let's get this over with."

Dante pressed his forehead into Vincent's and grinned. "That's what I'm talking about." He spun around and led the way through the dilapidated docks. Most of the lights had blown out, providing them excellent cover as they snaked through the maze of containers and buildings. The smell of salty ocean water grew stronger with every step, accompanied by the faint lapping of water.

They found the black SUV parked in front of an open warehouse door; soft orange light flickered over the concrete.

Vincent hadn't skulked around in the dark in years, but like riding a bike, it was all muscle memory. He crouched low and padded silently over to the car, where a quick look through the windows showed it empty. The hairs on his neck stood on end when his ears picked up hushed, incomprehensible whispers slipping out from the warehouse. Vincent crept forward and carefully poked his head in.

Old junk and bits of garbage cluttered the floor and dusty shelves, and the smell of oil hung heavy in the air. To his left, a staircase led up to a walkway overhead. Vincent beckoned for his brother to join him, and without any verbal communication, they crawled up the stairs.

From their perch, they had a bird's-eye view of the whole floor and easily spotted their targets in a small clearing in the middle of the warehouse. Roach and his partner stood beside a steel drum with a crackling fire inside it, each with a submachine gun hanging from his shoulder. Vincent's neighbor was tied onto a chair between them, still wearing pajamas and with a sack over his head. The man wasn't moving, and Vincent feared the worst.

Roach's eyes darted from one corner to the next, nervously fidgeting with his silver necklace that reflected the fire's light.

Wait, no. Vincent squinted at the lump of silver. It wasn't reflecting light at all, but emitted its own pale, white glow. Roach's partner wore an identical necklace, and it, too, glowed.

Vincent nudged his brother. "Well?" he mouthed.

"We wait," Dante silently answered.

Vincent clenched his jaw and nodded his understanding, but in the back of his mind he was terrified. Any hope of rescuing this guy evaporated with the introduction of the guns.

"Hello, Roach."

All eyes turned to a young boy who emerged from the shadows; he was gangly, all arms and legs, and barely filled out his clothes. Based on his height, he was probably still a preteen. Vincent's nose wrinkled at an overbearing, woody cologne emanating from the boy; the scent mixed with a horrifying smell of rotting meat, and the combination almost made him gag.

Roach and his partner in crime both dropped to one knee and bowed their heads as if addressing a king. "We found the last Gatekeeper just like you wanted, boss," Roach said.

The boy folded his arms behind his back and walked up to Vincent's neighbor to inspect the body. "Is he still alive?"

He turned around and the fire lit up his face.

Vincent's breath caught in his throat. Pale skin stretched taut over the bony features of his corpse-like face, and black marbles for eyes glinted deep inside their sockets. The horrifying image clashed with the childish superhero shirt he wore.

Roach chuckled nervously. "You know how I am, boss. I don't got the stomach for it."

The boy reached up with skeletal fingers and played with a glowing necklace of his own. "Give me your gun, then," the boy said.

"Y-yes, Kojo." Roach's hands trembled as he handed his weapon over.

The boy, Kojo, hummed. "What's the matter with you?"

Roach wiped nervous sweat from under his chin. "You're starting to smell, Kojo. I think your body's gone bad."

The boy reached into his shorts and pulled out an amber bottle of cologne. He released a new blast of fresh-cut wood into the small warehouse. "Better?"

Roach motioned at Kojo's head. "Your face is going bad, too."

Kojo felt his face, only mildly surprised by his cadaverous visage. "Sorry about that. I've been meaning to switch, but with all the work, it slipped my mind. One moment."

Kojo held his fingers to the sides of his head and made a gentle tugging motion. His face contorted grotesquely as something rose beneath it, and the skin stretched and contoured around a foreign object. But just when it looked like his face was going to split, it instead melted away. The pale skin receded to the sides of his head, but instead of bone, a wooden mask emerged, carved to look like an old man. Wrinkles were etched beside its eyeholes and white hairs hung from its chin beneath a disconcerting little smile.

Kojo's muffled voice asked, "Is this better?"

"Yeah, sure," Roach said.

"Good." Kojo lifted the gun with his thin arm.

Vincent's brain was still playing catch-up when shots exploded in the small warehouse. The man tied to the chair yelped, then was drowned out by gunfire as bullets tore through his body. He convulsed horribly and fell over, and then . . . nothing. He lay dead in a growing pool of his own blood.

The glowing light vanished from all three silver necklaces.

Vincent stared wide-eyed at the fresh corpse, and his stomach dropped out from under him. His knees buckled, and his vision blurred. He grabbed onto the handrail to steady himself and pressed his eyes shut to stop the world from spinning. Stomach acid tickled the back of his throat, and it took everything he had not to throw up right there on the spot.

Roach ran off to a corner and unloaded the contents of his stomach, retching sloppy chunks all over the floor.

Kojo tossed the gun aside and walked over to Roach to put a comforting hand on his back. "What's wrong?"

Roach wiped the back of his hand across his mouth, then shook his head. "Christ, do we have to—do you gotta kill them like that? They're still people."

"There's no way around it," Kojo said. "The Gatekeepers have to die, and at least his was a fast and painless death. Besides, you didn't know him. In a few months you won't even remember what he looked like. You'll be fine, Roach. Just focus on the future and the rewards coming your way. You'll have your own fortress, your own servants, and you'll never have to scrape the gutters of society for scraps anymore. You'll be a king."

"I-I guess," Roach muttered.

"Good. I'm going to open a Gate now." Kojo lifted his shirt and revealed a simple sheath strapped to his tiny chest. He pulled out a crystalline dagger, its jagged blade refracting light in brilliant iridescent bursts. "Both of you, pay attention," Kojo said. "You'll salute with your right hand in a closed fist over the heart. Hold that position and let me do the talking. Minotaurs have strict traditions, and I don't want you accidentally dishonoring him."

Kojo lifted the dagger over his head and, with a grunt of effort, plunged it forward. The tip of the blade disappeared as if lodged into an invisible wall. Holding tightly on to the hilt, Kojo jerked his body down and brought the dagger with him. There was a tearing sound as the blade left behind a line of sparkling light in the air, which gradually flattened out into a shimmering pool. Vague shapes and colors shifted erratically beneath its surface while it hummed with power.

A moment of stunned silence passed, and then the shimmering pool birthed a massive bull's head. The creature grunted as two powerful arms emerged behind the head, followed by a torso, and then hoofed legs. The bull stood to his full height on his back legs, easily reaching eight feet tall. Imposing bronze armor covered his muscled body, and linens of deep red and gold hung loosely beneath it.

Vincent immediately recognized the creature from fantasy books he had read. A minotaur—there was no mistaking it.

Kojo straightened up and placed his right fist over his heart, as did Roach and the other man.

"Stratigos Steelhorns," Kojo said.

The bull mirrored the salute and spoke in a deep, rumbling bass. "Kojo."

"The Matriarch is giving you two days to clear out the city. Afterward you're to head south and join the goblins on their march east," Kojo said.

"Of course. Are the Gates ready?"

"They're all open."

"Then I will prepare for the assault," the minotaur said, turning back to the magical pool he came from.

"Also, Stratigos, make sure to leave me some survivors. I know how your soldiers can get carried away during battle," Kojo said.

"I will consider it," the minotaur replied.

"That wasn't a request."

The minotaur turned back to Kojo, a dangerous change to his demeanor. "Watch your tone when you speak to me," Stratigos said. "My King may be working with your Matriarch, but I do not work *for* her."

Kojo bowed ingratiatingly. "The Matriarch's tasked me with summoning her twin thunderbirds. The magic I'll be using is complicated enough as it is, so I urge you not to make it more difficult than it has to be by purging the city and taking all the humans as slaves. I'd hate to have to tell her you delayed their arrival."

"You dare threaten me?" The minotaur bellowed and made an abrupt motion. Steel flashed and before anyone could react, a sword was pointed at Kojo's face.

The boy glanced at the blade before speaking, unflinchingly calm. "Don't be stupid and act in anger. If you kill me now, the Matriarch's deal with King Minos will fall through. You and I both know how badly your people need this new land."

Stratigos reluctantly relaxed his grip. After a moment's hesitation, he sheathed the sword. "You are a shrewd creature."

The tension dissipated and Kojo wagged a finger at him. "You really should learn to keep your temper in check. The brightest candles are the first to burn out."

The minotaur made a noncommittal sound. "We will meet again." He squeezed himself back through the shimmering pool and was gone.

Kojo spun on his heel and made a swirling motion with his finger. "Let's go, people. It's finally starting." He marched out with his men, and a moment later, the SUV drove off, leaving the brothers to stew in silence.

Muted seconds seemed to stretch into hours.

Vincent slowly turned to his brother. "What the fuck did we just see?"

They both regarded the thing the minotaur had come

through; it sparkled as waves pulsed along its surface. Kojo called it a Gate, and it just allowed a fictional creature of myth to step into their world. From the sound of it, there were more coming.

Dante sprang to his feet. "We need to go . . . now!"

Vincent nodded as a torrent of questions hit him. How could minotaurs possibly exist, who the hell was Kojo, and what was about to happen to the world?

Chapter 4

Vincent floored the gas pedal, and his old hatchback peeled out of the old docks, sputtering and rumbling in protest at being revved so hard. His knuckles were a ghostly white against the steering wheel as his eyes darted between the road and Dante. "Did we—did *I* really just see what I think I did? There's no way, right? Tell me I'm hallucinating all this!"

Dante's stared ahead, eyes unfocused. "I was hoping you could tell me the same thing."

The horrible image of his dead neighbor projected itself before Vincent—his blood-soaked pajamas, the leaking holes, the way his body fell to the floor like a rag doll. "We couldn't save him . . ."

"What are you talking about?" Dante asked.

Vincent slammed his hand against the dash. "They just murdered him in front of our fucking eyes, and we didn't do a damn thing about it!"

"There wasn't anything we *could* do," Dante said, his tone apologetic. "They had guns—at least we tried." He knitted his eyebrows together and pressed his lips into a line. "I got a bad feeling about all this—*look out!*"

A police cruiser sped across the intersection, sirens flashing and wailing. Vincent barely slammed on the brakes in time, and the car came to a screeching stop.

"We should get the cops and tell them what happened," Dante said.

Vincent laughed bitterly. "Tell *them* what happened? Someone better tell *me* what the fuck happened before we do that."

A booming explosion cut him off, rocking the car violently and rattling its windows; in the distance, a mushroom of fire momentarily ignited the night sky.

"What was that?" Dante roared.

Vincent had no intention of finding out. Fear stuck its icy fingers into his heart and spread rapidly through his body. He started driving again, his mind humming with only one thought: getting as far away as possible. From the corner of his eye, he saw a figure dart into the street; he gritted his teeth and swerved to the side, barely missing a panicked woman.

"Slow down!" Dante hollered.

Vincent looked in the rearview mirror. Something leapt from the shadows in a flurry of motion and pounced onto the woman's back. They were swallowed up by the night before he could make out any more details. *What the hell was Roach trying to warn us about?*

"Too little, too late," a jeering voice echoed in his thoughts. "Too little, too late! Too little, too late!"

It took Vincent some time to realize his body was taking him back home on autopilot. The people of his neighborhood were wide awake, standing in their yards, shivering in tight circles while talking among themselves. Others fled from some unseen threat, fathers and mothers clinging to their frightened children. And every dog in the city seemed to be barking their panic.

Vincent felt a modicum of relief when he saw his street, but before he could turn onto it, a muscled man sprinted in front of the car. Vincent hit the brakes and narrowly avoided an accident. It took him a second too long to realize an armored minotaur stood before them, blinking under the car's headlights.

"Vincent!"

A bellowing battle cry from the minotaur drowned out Dante's voice. The great beast lifted a spear and threw it. Vincent had a brief moment of detached clarity in which he realized how massive the minotaur's arms were—they may as well have been tree trunks attached to his torso.

The two brothers screamed together as the spear punctured the windshield and flew between them, burying its tip into the backseat.

"Run it over!" Dante roared.

The minotaur dove into the hood of the car as Vincent floored it; tires squealed and smoked, but the car didn't budge an inch against the minotaur's strength. The minotaur roared and Vincent suddenly found himself upside down in the car, held precariously in place by his seat belt. The car jostled and metal groaned as the car buckled and spun on its head.

Vincent heard three loud pops, and his world finally stopped spinning long enough for him to see the minotaur's legs stumble away from the car.

"Drop, you son of a bitch!" Grandma shouted.

Two more pops and the minotaur's heavy body collapsed next to Vincent's broken window with a meaty thud. He let out a startled yelp, but noticed several bloody holes in the bull's thick skull.

"Get out of there, boys!"

They unbuckled their seat belts and hit the ground at awkward angles, their bodies crunching over shattered glass. As Vincent crawled out the window, a cacophony of screams and panicked shouting greeted him. Plumes of smoke rose from unseen fires while gunshots echoed around him like a constant alarm. The people who had been calmly talking only moments before were running in every direction. It was absolute chaos, with people shouting to stick together and screaming for help. A woman's shrill shriek grabbed Vincent's attention.

He watched in frozen terror as a group of armed minotaurs marched down the street in a tight line, shoulder to shoulder, round shields the size of dinner tables forming an impenetrable wall before them while spears struck down anyone unfortunate enough to be in their warpath.

"Vincent, Dante, over here!"

Grandma waved them over, a gun in one hand and a young woman beside her in awestruck terror. Grandma and the woman started running down the street, and Vincent and Dante chased after them. The Li brothers shoved their way through the dense crowds and eventually caught up to Grandma in front of her store.

She ushered them all inside, then bolted the locks behind them, muffling the chaos outside. In the relative silence, Vincent's heart thundered like a drum in his ears while punching against his ribs to break out.

"Come with me," Grandma ordered.

They followed her to the storage room in the back of the store and navigated a small maze of overstock. She stopped them at a small bare space, then traced her finger along the square-patterned floor; she flipped up a loose tile to reveal a cleverly hidden latch, and then hoisted a trapdoor. A set of stairs led into a basement area Vincent had never known existed.

"Get the fuck inside," Grandma hissed impatiently.

The young woman hurried down, followed by Vincent and Dante. They entered a concrete room. A single lightbulb hung from the ceiling, dimly illuminating a bed in the corner and a couple shelves of canned food and water. Grandma closed and locked the entrance to the hidden room, abruptly cutting off all sounds from outside.

The girl in front of Vincent turned around, dressed in polka-dotted shorts and an oversized North Oregon University sweater. Dark brown locks of wavy shoulder-length hair framed her thin face and contrasted sharply against her pale skin. For a brief moment their gazes met. Her gray eyes reminded him of a gathering storm cloud, and there was a sense of familiarity about them.

Vincent turned his focus back on Grandma as she came down the stairs. "What is this place?"

"It used to be a bomb shelter. I converted it to a panic room when I bought the place, but I never thought I'd actually have to use it." Grandma's wide eyes focused on him. "Do you know what's going on out there? I was watching my antique shows one minute, and the next there was an emergency broadcast telling everyone to stay inside and lock their doors. But then even that cut out!" She slumped to the floor in a tired heap. "And then I started seeing those cow-people running around, cutting people down. I just don't . . ." Grandma looked up, her eyes pleading. "Please tell me I'm not fucking crazy, and I didn't just shoot a man."

Vincent shook his head. "That was a minotaur, like from Greek mythology." It was odd hearing himself say "minotaur" as if the answer were obvious.

Grandma screwed up her face. "That's what I thought."

"But that's insane! Minotaurs aren't real."

Vincent regarded the young woman beside him with a prick of annoyance. "Then what the hell is killing everyone out there? That's real enough for me."

"Oh my god, I am freaking out right now." The young woman gulped. "Is this really happening?"

She sounded on the verge of a nervous breakdown, which annoyed him immensely. Vincent looked from her to Grandma, then asked, "Who is she?"

Grandma sighed and holstered the handgun in her belt. "This is my granddaughter, Elise. Elise, the big guy is Dante, and that's Vincent, his younger brother."

Vincent and Dante both stared.

"Granddaughter . . . as in you had a kid, who then had another kid?" Vincent asked.

Grandma rolled her eyes. "What else do you think *granddaughter* means, you idiot?"

"Grandma, you always told us you had no family," Dante said.

"She did what?" Elise said, balking. "Of course she has a family! Why would you pretend you don't, Grandma?"

"I don't have to explain myself to you," she spat.

Elise's wounded look quickly turned to irritation. "Why are you being so difficult?"

The two women stared each other down with matching glares of enmity. The tension crackled in the air, and a part of Vincent was curious, but he knew better than to stick his nose where it didn't belong.

"What're we going to do?" Dante asked. "We can't stay down here forever."

Grandma folded her arms. "Of course not, but we're sitting our asses down right here for as long as we can. You saw how bad things are out there. Going back up now would be suicide."

The room rumbled and shook some cans off their shelving, but the tremor passed quickly.

Vincent watched the lightbulb swing ominously from its cord, and gulped. "I'm with Grandma."

"What about the rest of the city?" Elise asked, frowning. "We could be out there helping."

Dante nodded slowly. "We should be, but how much of a difference are we really going to make? We all saw how strong they are. One flipped Vincent's car like it was nothing. Plus, they got weapons, and we don't."

"Besides," Vincent said, "the people I give a shit about are already here, so I don't see any reason to leave. Not to mention we don't even know what else Kojo brought into the world."

Grandma arched an eyebrow. "Who the hell is Kojo?"

Vincent and Dante recounted what happened at the docks. The boy with the wooden mask; the Gate; the necklaces; all that talk between Kojo and Stratigos. Of course it sounded ridiculous in hindsight, but Grandma and Elise sat through the whole story without interrupting.

When they finished, Grandma was the first to speak.

"I knew it," she said with a conspiratorial whisper. "Didn't I tell you, Vincent? I told you something was happening."

"I thought Dad was just being paranoid when he made me bring a pocketknife, whistle, *and* pepper spray." Elise sat on the bed and pulled her knees into her chest.

Grandma's head perked up. "How is Philip doing?"

"If you'd call once in a while, maybe you'd know," Elise snapped. Even as the words left her mouth, she looked regretful. "I'm sorry."

Grandma waved her back. "Don't apologize, girl. I haven't been the best grandmother to you."

"You know," Elise began in a hopeful tone, "you can still come back home. When we make it out of here, there's an empty bedroom in the house waiting for you. I know you and Dad haven't been on speaking terms, but—"

"No," Grandma said bluntly. "I've said it a thousand times before, and this is the last time I'm going to repeat myself. I'm not going back." An uncomfortable silence fell between the two women.

Dante cleared his throat. "Elise, what were you saying about your dad being paranoid? What did you mean by that?"

"He almost didn't let me make the drive down here," she replied, looking grateful for the subject change. "He mentioned something about people going missing in Portland and the cities around it. I just thought he was doing his usual overprotective dad thing."

"An increase in missing people? That's exactly what happened here," Grandma said.

Dante hummed thoughtfully. "We might not be the only city under attack."

A sound piqued Vincent's ear, a faint stretching and tearing of material. All heads turned to see a glittering line magically appear in the corner of the room. Vincent opened his mouth, but only managed a faint rasp in his throat. He watched in muted horror as the line wavered, then slowly expanded into a shimmering pool of watery material. It was much smaller than the one he had seen at the docks, but the resemblance was undeniable.

Vincent pointed. "It's a Gate!"

They gasped in unison as a small bipedal creature jumped out and landed facing away from them. It stood a couple feet tall, its body and features obscured under a black robe with a hood; two tan-colored paws and a tail stuck out from under the hem.

"W-what is that?" Elise whispered.

Two furry hands reached up and pulled the hood down, revealing a pair of floppy ears.

"Is that a dog?" Elise took a hesitant step toward it. In the same moment, the Gate quivered, then disappeared with a pop.

The creature whirled around at the sound, and the flattened face of a pug looked to where the Gate had been with a look of dismay. "The Gate!" the pug exclaimed. "How did it close?" He sniffed at the air quizzically, but froze when his buggy eyes finally registered the others in the room. "Oh my."

"Christ, it can talk," Grandma said.

The dog frowned. "Foolish troll runts. Have you never seen a wizard?" He spoke with the kind of refined dignity Vincent would have expected from a guy wearing a powdered wig. The pug's chest swelled under his silken robe. "I am Sorceress Epoch's personal assistant, handpicked and enchanted through her very own powers."

"Sorceress Epoch?" Vincent echoed, more curious than terrified.

"Surely you've heard of her? She is the greatest sorceress of our time."

Grandma muttered out the side of her mouth, "What do I do? Do I shoot it?"

The pug's ears twitched. "Shoot me? Shoot me with what? What's that primitive contraption you are holding in your hand? I warn you, I will defend myself if I must." He pawed at his side, and dread swept across his face. "Oh no," he moaned. "I left my staff back in the lab."

Grandma took aim with her gun. "That does it, I'm killing it."

"So this is how I am to end? Killed by insignificant trolls—the shame! Why couldn't my death at least be by a dragon, or something indicative of my powers? What will the other wizards and sorceresses think?" the pug lamented.

Vincent gently pushed Grandma's arm down. "Relax. Nobody is going to kill you."

"Are you sure we shouldn't?" Grandma asked. "That's a talking dog, and last I checked, dogs aren't supposed to talk."

He shrugged. "Look at it. It's an ankle-biter at best."

"How dare you. Why would I bite anyone's ankle? That's barbaric," the dog protested.

Elise kneeled beside the pug. "What's your name?"

"My name is Flea." The pug sniffed and folded his arms haughtily.

"That's it?" Elise prodded.

"Yes. Just Flea."

Dante scooted closer with an air of caution. "Is it dangerous, though?"

Flea scoffed. "Hah! I am not the one threatening to kill you."

"Look how cute he is," Elise added, reaching out to pet him.

Flea swatted her hand away, indignant. "I am not your

pet to be played with. I am a full-fledged *wizard*."

"What does that even mean?" Vincent said.

Flea rubbed his forehead with an exasperated sigh. "Forbidden arcana, I forget how you trolls have such a limited understanding of things."

Vincent interrupted him. "We aren't trolls. We're humans."

"Hu . . . man? What is that, an offshoot of a troll?"

"We don't have anything to do with trolls," Vincent said irritably.

"No need to lose your temper," Flea mumbled. "If you do not wish me to address you as trolls, then perhaps you should tell me your names?"

Vincent introduced everyone.

Flea bowed with a flourish of his robe. "A pleasure."

Dante eased his defensive posture. "How did you get here?"

"I was trying to get to Crossways to pick up alchemical ingredients, so I made a Gate." Flea regarded his surroundings. "I must have miscalculated it, however, since I am most certainly not in Crossways right now. Speaking of which, where am I?"

"You're in Oakwood," Vincent said.

"Oakwood?" Flea pawed at his flabby chin. "That doesn't sound familiar. Are we near the Ignis Islands?"

"Where the hell is that?" Vincent wondered. "Oakwood's in California."

Flea cocked his head like a curious pup.

"As in the United States?" Vincent expected some kind

of recognition, but saw only more confusion on Flea's face. "North America ringing any bells, what about planet Earth?"

"Planet Earth?" Flea repeated. "No, you must be mistaken. Our planet is called Terra Mater."

Grandma snorted. "You're mistaken, you little freak. This is most definitely Earth."

"Could it be?" Flea hummed thoughtfully. "Have you ever seen an elemental? What about imps, golems, kobolds, or even qilins?"

The others stared blankly.

"I've read about those things, but none of those are real," Vincent said. "They're just myths."

Flea paced in an excited circle. "So what you're telling me is that those things don't exist *here* on Earth?"

"Not in real life," Vincent said, and the others nodded their heads in agreement.

Realization dawned on Flea's flat face. "Forbidden arcana, don't you see? We must be from two different worlds. Do you understand the implications of such a discovery? Somehow I created a Gate bridging our worlds— this is the discovery of a lifetime. I've read of such things being possible in theory, but never successfully done. I'll be heralded as one of the greatest wizards!"

Dante held up his hand to stop Flea's excited jabbering. "Wait a second. Does that mean minotaurs come from Terra Mater?"

Flea wrinkled his nose at Dante, annoyed by the interruption. "Yes, yes, minotaurs do indeed live on Terra Mater. What does that have to do with anything?"

"Minotaurs are murdering us out there!" Dante snarled. He stormed forward and picked Flea up by the collar of his robe. "Why are you doing this?"

"What are you talking about?" Flea sputtered, kicking his short legs out.

Grandma joined Dante's side. "You better start talking, Flea. What are you *creatures* doing here on Earth?"

"Stop it!" Elise shouted.

"I don't know anything," Flea choked. "This is a misunderstanding."

Elise pried Flea from Dante's hands and pulled him close to her chest in a protective cocoon. "He obviously doesn't know anything about what's happening!"

"You don't know that. He could be lying," Grandma countered.

Flea cleared his throat and adjusted his robe with a venomous glare. "I don't know what you're trying to accuse me of, but minotaurs couldn't possibly be here. They don't have even the most basic magical understanding to create Gates, let alone one that transports between different worlds. Don't make such preposterous accusations."

"So you admit you know something," Grandma said.

"Everyone calm the hell down," Vincent shouted. "I don't think Flea's lying. He's just an innocent bystander in all this."

"Exactly, you imbecilic brutes!" Flea barked.

"But," Vincent added, "and this is a big but. You definitely know things. You're from the same world as those minotaurs. We don't know what's happening outside this room, but I bet you could help us understand. Your information is going to be invaluable to us."

"You speak as if I have already agreed to assist you. What if I refuse? I could simply go back to Terra Mater," Flea said.

"Can you?" Vincent prodded.

"Of course I can." Flea paused, ears drooping. "No. No, I cannot at the moment. I have no staff to channel my magic, not to mention I don't even know *how* I managed to create a Gate here in the first place."

"So you're stuck in a foreign world you know nothing about."

"It would seem that is my predicament," Flea admitted.

Vincent held his arms out in a placating gesture to both parties. "Well, there you have it: a mutually beneficial arrangement for everyone. You help us out, Flea, and we'll help you out."

Dante and Grandma exchanged looks and nodded their agreement. Sensing the danger was over, Elise set Flea back down.

Vincent held out his finger. "What do you say?"

Flea regarded the offer with a dubious glare, but relented and reached up with his small hand; as Flea gripped his finger and shook, Vincent noted with mild curiosity that the dog had five fingers. He smirked at the absurdity of the situation. From minotaurs to wizard-pugs, it had been a terrifying and strange night.

***

Bo sat alone in a dingy noodle shop, staring into an untouched bowl of food that had grown cold and soggy. He was doing . . . *all right*, he supposed. He knew enough English to get by and had found work as a janitor in a middle school. It paid just enough to leave him a few dollars after all his bills were taken care of.

The poverty didn't bother him, though. It was the loneliness of living in a strange land all by himself. He was invisible; no one spoke to him unless they needed something. He stirred his noodles absently, cursing his stupidity for moving here in the first place.

Someone tapped his arm, startling him from his thoughts.

"I'm so sorry! I didn't mean to scare you," a soft voice said.

When he turned and saw the young woman speaking to him, his jaw almost dropped. She had a food-stained apron on, and her hair was greasy from cooking, but something about her ensnared Bo's attention. He stared in stunned silence—a little too long, perhaps. She brushed a few locks of hair behind her ear and blushed.

Her pink lips moved, but Bo heard nothing, lost in his own thoughts. He shook his head and blinked. "What did you say?"

She giggled girlishly. "I asked why you came in here for food if you're not even going to eat it. Seems silly, doesn't it?"

"Yeah, silly . . ." Bo looked down at his bowl and chuckled.

An old man hollered from behind the counter. "Get back here, Xifeng! We have orders to fill!"

"Be right there!" She gave Bo a playful wink. "See you around."

Her voice carried a melodic quality to it, like honey to his ears, and he wanted nothing more than to hear it again. "Xifeng," he murmured.

Chapter 5

The panic room was well stocked, a testament to Grandma's preparedness—or paranoia, Vincent couldn't decide which. They had enough food and water to last a week, despite the demands of three people and a dog, and there was a box of crosswords and old magazines to help pass the time. Grandma had also installed a landline telephone and even thought ahead to keep an emergency radio.

They tried the phone first, but the line was dead silent. Vincent and Elise tried their cell phones next, but couldn't get a signal—if there was even one to be had anymore. They then tried the radio, taking turns every few hours to search through the stations; each attempt yielded only static, and as the hours passed, their hopes of making any kind of contact dwindled.

Sometime during the second day, the lightbulb blinked out without warning. Grandma replaced it with a backup bulb, but it was no use, the electricity was out. Luckily, she had a box of candles, but it did little to settle the gnawing fear that the world was falling apart outside their concrete box.

Vincent looked up from his hundredth crossword puzzle and threw it aside with disgust. "I can't do another one of these goddamn things."

Grandma made a chiding sound. "Don't be an ungrateful little shit."

Vincent rolled onto his back with a big stretch. "You should've packed some alcohol down here. Christ, what I'd give for a glass of whiskey right now."

"You really think now's the best time to be getting drunk?" Elise asked.

He scoffed at her naiveté. "Are you kidding me? We're probably the only people alive still. I can't think of a better time to get shitfaced."

"You don't know that," Elise said.

"You don't know I'm wrong either," Vincent sneered.

"*Cada martes tiene su domingo.*"

Vincent glowered at her. "What'd you just say to me?"

Elise chuckled. "All I said was, 'each Tuesday has its Sunday.' It's a Spanish saying that means good times will always come after the bad. I heard it from a farmer while I was in Bolivia."

"When the hell did you go to Bolivia?" Grandma asked.

"I went last summer with some of my friends. We volunteered with local water and sanitation projects there."

"Oh, you're so noble," Vincent mocked.

"Is your brother always such a pessimistic jerk?" Elise asked Dante.

He grinned in response. "This is Vincent on a good day. Don't pay him too much attention."

Elise returned the grin with a toothy smile of her own. "What about you, Mr. Dante? Are you as pessimistic as he is?"

Dante thought it over before answering. "I hope for the best and prepare for the worst."

Elise chuckled, and then turned her stormy eyes back on Vincent. "A little optimism goes a long way."

He rolled his eyes. "If you're so sure everything's fucking peachy up there, why don't you prove it by trying the radio again?"

Elise's eyes narrowed to angry slits in an almost perfect replica of Grandma's signature death glare. "I think I'll do just that," she said hotly.

Vincent waved her by. "Be my guest."

She grabbed the radio off the shelf with a huff, defiantly looked him in the eyes, and turned it on.

A broken voice crackled over static. "George—come—Chi—"

Elise dropped the radio with a startled cry, and for a brief moment, everyone looked at it in stunned silence.

"A refuge—food—" the static voice continued.

"Someone tune the damn thing!" Grandma shouted.

Vincent came to his senses and scooped the radio up with excited hands. He licked his dry lips and carefully turned the knob, afraid he would somehow lose it if he went too fast.

The radio squealed and screeched as it honed in on the signal. He gave it a couple more tweaks and a man's gruff voice poured out from the speakers, loud and clear.

"This is George Garcia, Police Chief of the Oakwood Police Department. A refuge has been established on Blossom Island. We have food, medicine, and weapons."

It was a prerecorded message and looped back to the beginning. Vincent listened to it a few more times before switching it off, satisfied there was nothing else to the message.

A deep furrow formed in Grandma's brow. "He used the word 'refuge.' It must be pretty bad out there."

"But they have food and guns," Dante said.

"And other people have probably heard that broadcast," Elise said excitedly. "Which means there are people going there right now. We're not alone!"

"What are we waiting for?" Grandma asked. "Let's go."

Flea let out a grateful moan. "Yes, please. I cannot stand another moment in this accursed box."

"Blossom Island is on the other end of town, though," Vincent said. "Who knows what we'll bump into between here and there?"

"We have to leave this place eventually," Dante said.

Grandma shuffled past them. "Out of the way. I'm making an executive decision here."

"What are you doing?" Dante asked, grabbing her arm.

"I'm going to go up and make sure it's safe," she said.

"You can't, Grandma. You're almost seventy. Let me go," Dante replied.

"Ha! Like hell you are!" Grandma held up her handgun. "If anything happens, it's got to be me."

"But—"

Grandma silenced Dante with angry eyes. "Let me explain something to you, Dante. I don't like being talked back to by little shits, especially one who doesn't understand that he still has his whole life to live."

"Grandma, you can't be serious," Dante muttered.

Vincent pulled his brother back, knowing there was no arguing with the cantankerous old woman. "Just let her do this," he said.

Grandma gave him a sympathetic smile. "Thank you, Vincent. I'm glad someone around here isn't a complete idiot."

Everyone crowded at the bottom of the stairs and watched Grandma go up alone. She undid the lock and cracked it open, and then, after a moment of deliberation, stepped out.

A painstaking minute dragged by before she returned. "It's empty up here," she said.

The back room had been trashed. Shelves were torn from the walls, scattering overstock onto the floor in haphazard piles. The storefront was even worse. It looked like a wrecking ball had smashed through the front wall and crushed everything to pieces.

Grandma sifted through some of the debris and tried picking up the mess, but gave up when she realized how pointless it was. "My store," she moaned.

Flea made a disgusted sound and covered his nose. "It reeks of death."

"Damn, what happened here?" Vincent noticed a box of cigarettes by his feet and picked it up; they were mostly crushed, but he managed to find one only slightly bent at the tip. He waded through the rubble and debris to the front counter for a pack of matches to light it.

"Guys, you need to see this," Dante called.

Vincent joined his brother outside, blinking hard against the daylight and bringing into focus what little remained of Oakwood. Homes and stores lay in ruins as if hit by bombs, exposing their foundations like bones in a half-eaten carcass. The cars that were usually parked alongside the street had been smashed in or flipped, scarred by deep gashes and punctured by spears.

Vincent stumbled back in sheer awe; he hit a piece of rubble and it clattered over the street, echoing.

Elise muffled a shriek and stepped away from the laundromat next to Grandma's store. "Oh my god," she squeaked. "There's—there's—oh god." She turned away and collapsed on the sidewalk, dry-heaving.

Vincent and Dante went up to the building's broken window, swatting away an annoying swarm of flies buzzing around their heads.

A sickening smell, like old meat, hit Vincent's nose and twisted his stomach into a tight knot; he spat his cigarette out, sputtering, and clamped his nose shut. "Fucking hell," he muttered. He squinted into the shadows and saw the dark outlines of people tucked in the corner. He leaned through the window to get a better look, but an open hand below him caught his attention.

Vincent found the body it connected to. A man stared back, his skin blue and veiny in death, and the lower half of his body gone. Bloody entrails spilled out over the floor into a dark pool of blood. Vincent recoiled in horror and joined Elise on the sidewalk, fighting back the urge to throw up.

Dante pulled his shirt over his nose and went inside the laundromat. Grandma made to go after him, but one look inside made her turn away in disgust. He reappeared in the doorway moments later, grim, and tossed a heavy sword onto the ground. "I found this stuck inside one of them," he said.

Flea studied the sword from a safe distance. "That is minotaur-made, a standard-issue short sword. But I don't understand, why is King Minos's army here? What purpose does this slaughter serve?"

A jolt of fear shot down Vincent's spine. They were standing out in the open without protection. "We need to get off the streets," he said. "We can figure out a plan at my house . . . if it's still there."

No one argued such sensible advice.

Bodies littered the path to Vincent's home. They were sprawled out on the streets, slumped against houses and cars, and scattered across the lawns, where their blood fed the dead grass. Someone, or something, had even thrown a few bodies into an unceremonious pile. Vincent tried to avoid looking at them, but death was everywhere he turned.

Puffy faces, pale blue skin, maggots festering in open cavities, blackened pools of blood—he didn't understand how there were so many bodies. It felt as if there were far more in death than there had ever been in life. Discarded swords and broken spears left a record of how they died.

Vincent, lost in his thoughts, ran into his brother, who had stopped abruptly.

Dante pointed to someone's yard a few houses down. "What is that?" he whispered.

Vincent saw something hunched over the remains of a dead woman, its face buried in her chest. It almost looked like a naked human, but its skin was blistered and blackened like a fresh burn victim. Yellow pus and bloody discharge seeped from open sores and trickled down its emaciated body, running along the contours of its skeletal frame and sinewy muscles.

"Jesus H. Christ, it's eating that woman," Grandma stammered.

Elise, already pale in the face, swayed on her feet; her eyes rolled up into her head and she fainted. Fortunately, Dante reacted quickly and caught her in his arms, throwing her over his shoulder with ease.

"Hey!" Grandma called out. "Get the hell away from her!"

The creature pulled its face out of the woman's chest cavity, tearing away stringy flesh as it did. Perfectly round, unblinking yellow eyes looked in their direction as it chewed its food with sharp little teeth.

"What in the actual fuck is that thing?" Vincent muttered.

"A ghoul," Flea explained. "Wherever there is death, there are sure to be ghouls. It's unusual to see one during the day, however. They are nocturnal creatures."

Grandma aimed her gun at the ghoul. "I won't ask you again. Get away from her!"

It screeched angrily and raked the air with long fingers that ended in bony points.

"Don't antagonize it," Flea warned. "Ghouls hunt in packs, so there are sure to be others nearby. They won't attack the living unless they are hungry or feel threatened." He glanced at the corpses around them. "I don't think it's hungry, so if we leave it be we can pass by unharmed."

"But it's *eating* that woman's body," Grandma said. "That isn't right."

"Grandma, that lady's dead. I don't think she cares too much at this point," Vincent said. "Let's not piss this thing and its friends off."

Grandma cussed under her breath and lowered the gun.

The ghoul sensed the danger had passed and returned its attention to its meal. It grabbed her hair and prowled away on all fours, dragging her body alongside it.

Vincent breathed a sigh of relief when the ghoul disappeared behind a house, and they ran the rest of the way. To his immense relief, the little seafoam-green house had survived intact. Vincent hurried up the front steps and threw open the door without thinking, but when he stepped inside he froze. He didn't see anything, but after everything he'd experienced, his house felt foreign and dangerous.

Grandma nudged his ribs. "Let's make sure nothing's hiding in here."

Dante gently laid Elise down on the couch while Vincent

and Grandma checked the house for threats. By the time they finished, Elise was stirring awake.

Elise clutched her head and groaned. "What happened?"

Grandma kneeled beside her and brushed her hair to the side. "You passed out, girl. You'll be fine, though. Just give it a minute."

Vincent double-checked the locks before finding a spot by the window. He watched a crow peck at a corpse, and a wave of exhaustion washed over him.

"We have to get to that refuge. It's our best bet," Dante said.

Vincent rubbed his eyes, weary. The thought of going back out was exhausting. Dante, on the other hand, was thriving under the stress; his eyes were wide, clear and attentive as he conversed with Flea in hushed whispers.

It wasn't too surprising. Ever since they were kids, Dante had fared better under extreme conditions. That very fire had kept them both alive.

Vincent pulled himself away from his thoughts and emptied his mind, instead enjoying the relative peace and quiet he had here and now. He had an awful feeling that peaceful moments would be a rarity in the coming future.

Chapter 6

After Grandma was sure Elise had fully recovered from her fainting spell, she stood up and barged into the kitchen.

Vincent made a face at her as she rummaged through his cabinets. "Just snoop through my stuff, Grandma. I don't mind at all," he said sardonically.

"Ah, shut up," she replied, with a dismissive wave. Grandma opened the cabinet door over his fridge and pulled out an amber bottle of whiskey. "Bingo, baby." She didn't bother getting a glass and put the bottle to her lips.

"Hey! Don't drink it all!" Vincent protested.

Grandma lowered the whiskey with a satisfied belch. "I needed that."

Vincent snatched the bottle from her hand and glowered at her before finishing what little was left.

"Where are your smokes?" Grandma asked.

He went to his stash nearby and tossed her a pack.

"When did you start smoking?" Elise asked from the living room. "I don't remember ever seeing you with a cigarette when I was a kid."

Grandma lit a cigarette in her mouth and took a deep breath, holding the smoke in her lungs a moment before breathing out. "I've been a smoker since I was twelve," she said, the smoke curling around her words. "I stopped for a bit after you were born, Elise. Philip wouldn't let me babysit you until I promised to quit."

"Why would you start back up after quitting?" Elise folded her arms, frowning. "Those things will kill you."

Vincent smirked, lighting one for himself. "Really? After what we've seen, you're worried about these little things killing her?" As he spoke, he could feel the nicotine's calming effects on his nerves, a much-needed, albeit momentary reprieve.

"She's my grandmother," Elise scolded. "I want her to live a long and healthy life."

"You sound just like your father. It's always cancer this, poison that." Grandma put out her cigarette on the counter with a grunt. "Look, I'm stopping for now, okay? No need to get all worked up about it."

Elise gave her a warm smile. "Thanks, Grandma."

Grandma nodded at Dante. "You and Vincent go find whatever supplies you think we'll need. I'll gather up the food you have here." She shook her head. "The sooner we get to that refuge on Blossom Island, the better."

Vincent nodded his understanding and followed his brother back toward their bedrooms. He went straight to his closet and dug up a shoebox hidden under some clothes. Inside it was the gun Grandma had gifted him a few years ago—nothing special, just a basic 9mm pistol. He ejected the magazine and checked the bullets before sliding it back in and stuffing the gun under his belt.

Flea padded into his room a moment later. "This is where you sleep?" He picked up a discarded sock in his fingers and held it at arm's length. "It's filthy in here."

Vincent stopped rifling through his dresser long enough to give Flea a mean look. "Is there any particular reason you're bothering me right now?"

Flea shrugged and meandered about the room. "I am simply curious about this new world I am trapped in." He picked up a book sticking out from under the nightstand and blew a cloud of dust off its cover. Flea opened the book to the first page and began flipping through it rapidly. "Interesting." The dog barely gave each page a glance before turning to the next.

"What are you doing?" Vincent asked.

"I'm reading, what does it look like?" He stuck his nose back in the pages and thumbed through the rest of it.

Vincent watched in amazement as the pug turned the last page and shut the book only a few minutes later. "Did you just read through the whole thing?"

The dog set the book down with a slight nod. "Of course I did. It was a short read."

"That was a full-length novel. It took me like four hours to get through."

"Sorceress Epoch enchanted me with the highest level of intelligence her power could muster. She needed a competent assistant, given the complexity of her experimental magic. One of the ways the enchantment manifested was in my ability to read quickly."

Vincent's eyes flicked to Flea's humanlike hands. "And those freaky little sausage fingers? Did she give you those on purpose, too?"

Flea puffed out an indignant breath that flapped his jowls. "You aren't very pleasant to be around, did you know that?"

"I might have been told that a couple times in my life," Vincent said.

Flea folded his hands behind his back. "If you must know, yes. She gave me hands as well. How else was I supposed to help her with potions if I couldn't even pick up a simple vial?"

"So is enchanting animals to talk a common thing where you're from?"

"Mostly among the sorceresses, but not all are created equal. You can usually tell how talented a sorceress is by how sophisticated her assistant is."

Vincent rubbed at his chin thoughtfully. "It sounds like Sorceress Epoch put some work into you, then. Won't she come looking for you since you're missing from your world—what was it called again, Terra Matters or something?"

"*Terra Mater*," Flea corrected. "And no, unfortunately she won't be coming after me. I haven't seen her in over a year."

Vincent raised an eyebrow.

"Some time ago she was supposed to meet with a client

interested in magical artifacts. She created a Gate to travel to him, but when she stepped through, she simply . . . disappeared. She never came out the other end. I tried searching for her, but found no traces. After a while, I gave up and returned to the lab. I didn't really know what else to do, so I continued her work, hoping she'd come back one day." Flea made a dejected sound. "It's been a terribly lonely existence without her."

"Damn," Vincent muttered. He felt a kinship with Flea's plight.

"I try not to think about it too much," Flea said. He reached inside his robe and pulled out a mahogany pipe. He snapped his fingers and created a few fleeting sparks, then studied his hand, perplexed. "That's odd. Something is blocking my magic."

"I got you." Vincent kneeled down with a lit match and helped get Flea's pipe smoking.

The dog leaned back, puffing contently. "Thank you."

Elise appeared in the bedroom door. "Hey, Vincent."

"What do you want?"

She tugged at her shorts. "I never got a chance to change into actual pants before Grandma dragged me to that panic room. She said you might have a pair that would fit me."

He glanced at her bare legs and noted how thick and sculpted they were, like those of a runner. "Try these on," he said, tossing her the first pair of blue jeans he found in his dresser.

Elise caught them, but remained in place with a distant look in her eyes.

Vincent glared at her. "Did you need something else?" he asked irritably.

Elise blinked as if awoken from a daydream. "Oh, sorry."

Flea puffed smoke out the side of his mouth and patted her leg. "Are you all right?" he asked.

She hugged herself and leaned against the door frame. "I've just been thinking about how messed up everything is. We all saw the bodies. It's really starting to sink in that we could die out there. I'm scared, Vincent, aren't you?"

Vincent absently flicked the ash off his cigarette. "No."

She studied him briefly. "You're a terrible liar, you know that?"

Vincent's eyes narrowed to slits. "There's a bathroom in the hallway you can use to change," he said, ignoring her comment.

"That came out wrong. I didn't mean—what I was trying to say was—" Elise stopped and nodded, a sympathetic expression on her face. "Never mind. Thanks for the pants."

Vincent watched her leave, swallowing a lump that had formed in his throat.

Half an hour later, Vincent and the others stood around the kitchen table with the supplies they had gathered. They had a first aid kit, a book of matches, cigarettes, some spare clothes, two handguns with exactly twenty-two bullets, a switchblade, a faded baseball bat, and various boxes of dry food and bottled water.

Elise picked up the box of cigarettes. "Really, Vincent? This is an essential?"

He grabbed them from her hand. "As a matter of fact, yes. Be happy I ran out of hard liquor, or else I'd be bringing that too." He put his cigarettes next to his copy of *Gallant's Quest*. Vincent had every intention of finishing the book, apocalypse be damned.

"Looks like we're set, then, guys. Let's do this," Dante said.

They packed up their gear into two backpacks, one for Dante to carry and another for Vincent. Dante opted for the baseball bat while Elise put the switchblade into her pocket; Vincent and Grandma took the guns since they had experience shooting them.

Vincent checked the front window. It was disconcertingly quiet. The domestic squabbles and sirens he had come to expect from Oakwood were absent, leaving only overpowering silence. "It looks clear to me," he reported.

Dante moved behind him and searched the streets. "There," he said, pointing to one of the few intact cars. "We'll use that one."

Flea appeared under Vincent and peered quizzically over the windowsill. "What is that metal contraption?"

"A car," Vincent replied.

"Ah yes, of course . . . What is a car?"

"It's a machine."

"But what does it do?" Flea probed.

Vincent rubbed his forehead impatiently. "What is this, fucking twenty-one questions? A car is a machine that's used to transport people fast, okay?"

Flea threw his hands up in a placating gesture. "You must

understand, this is all so new to me. Sorceress Epoch once told me I have an inquisitive spirit, perhaps even to a fault . . . what is *twenty-one questions*?"

An irritated growl rumbled in Vincent's throat.

"Well, no need to get violent about it," Flea said.

"We ready to go?" Dante asked. His question cut through their idle chatter with a leader's razor-edged tone.

Vincent pulled out his gun and nodded. Elise took a shaky breath, but nodded, as did Grandma and Flea. Dante gripped his baseball bat and opened the front door.

The rotten smell of death wafted past their noses to remind them of the stakes.

Vincent and Grandma wasted no time taking up positions on either side of the group while Dante led them on a short walk down the street. The white car he had picked out was old and definitely pre-90s, which was to their advantage.

"How are we supposed to start the car without the keys?" Elise asked.

"Like this." Dante smashed the driver's window with his bat and sent the glass tinkling to the pavement. "Elise, give me your knife."

She did, but with a heavy dose of skepticism. "What can you do with this?"

Vincent gave her a smug smile while his brother went to work. Dante got in the car and popped the ignition cover off, exposing the wires underneath. His fingers moved deftly, cutting and stripping the necessary wires. He then removed the steering wheel covers and, within several minutes, detached the steering wheel locking mechanism.

Vincent nodded as he watched his brother work, impressed he still remembered how to do it after such a long time in jail.

"All done, get in, guys," Dante said.

Grandma jumped into the passenger seat while Vincent, Elise, and Flea piled into the back.

"Do I even want to know how you learned to do this?" Grandma asked.

"Probably not," Dante said, shrugging. He touched the stripped wires together and the engine sputtered to life.

Elise looked Vincent up and down as if seeing him in a new light. "You steal cars?"

Vincent grinned fiendishly. "That's not even the worst of it." His smile widened at her horrified reaction.

Dante regarded her through the rearview mirror. "Don't listen to him. We always avoided hurting anybody, and that was a long time ago."

Elise didn't seem convinced. "If you say so."

Dante threw the car into gear and hit the gas.

****

"You little fuckers! I'm gonna murder you when I catch you!" a hoarse voice yelled.

Vincent checked over his shoulder, his young heart beating hard and fast. The threat wouldn't be an empty one if they were caught, and he had no intention of dying at the tender age of thirteen.

"Come on, Vincent! Keep up!"

Vincent turned his attention back to Dante; his brother was only a few steps ahead, his scrawny legs pounding against the pavement as they fled their pursuer. Vincent clutched his throbbing eye, which had swollen to the size of a golf ball, and swore he would kick his brother's ass if they made it out alive.

The man chasing them loosed a bestial roar that urged Vincent's legs on, and he followed Dante around the corner of a dilapidated house.

"In here," Dante hissed, crouched by an open window leading into the house's basement.

Vincent slid through it in one fluid motion with his brother only inches behind. Dante carefully shut the window behind him before ducking into the shadows with Vincent.

A hulking man pounded past them seconds later.

Vincent didn't dare breathe, holding on to his breath for dear life until his lungs forced him to let it out. He sucked in haggard gasps, slowly regaining his composure while he waited for the danger to pass. When he finally felt safe, he turned to his brother and swung at his face in a fit of anger.

Dante sidestepped the punch with little difficulty. "Calm down!" His own cheek was swollen and bloodied, and his nose might've been broken, too.

"You idiot," Vincent gasped. "I told you that was a bad mark. You never listen to me!" He tried hitting Dante, but missed again. "Now what do we do? We didn't get anything!"

"Listen to me—Vincent, seriously—hey, would you

stop—seriously, stop trying to hit me!"

Vincent stopped swinging, but not because he wanted to; his body was just too exhausted to go on. "What?" he grumbled.

Dante gave him a toothy grin. "The guy was too busy beating us up to notice I snuck this from him." He pulled a bulging wallet from his pocket and shook it victoriously.

Vincent's good eye widened. "No way. How much is in it?"

"Let's find out." Dante pulled a thick fold of bills out and began counting it with an increasingly greedy fervor. "*Jackpot.*"

Vincent fidgeted anxiously, unable to see the bills being counted. "Well? How much did we get?"

"Eight hundred dollars," Dante murmured. He grabbed Vincent's head and gently bumped their foreheads. "We'll be okay, little brother. This is going to buy enough food for at least two months!"

Chapter 7

Big cities are much like the human body. The roads are its arteries and the people its lifeblood. So what happens when a city with a population of almost one million tries to evacuate all at once?

They clog the arteries up and the city dies.

Oakwood was no exception. What should have been a thirty-minute drive turned into a three-hour one, and they weren't even halfway there. Dante pulled up to another congested intersection, where a junker of a station wagon had been turned onto its side, blocking half the street. He started to steer their car around it, but braked abruptly on the other side.

Elise forced her eyes away. "Oh my god," she muttered.

A row of bodies were lined up against a wall, strung together at their feet by iron manacles and lying in a veritable river of their own blood and organs.

Vincent wanted to look away, but couldn't. His eyes fixated on a small boy at the end of the chain, slumped over in a kneeling position, his arms frozen in a frantic attempt to hold in the intestines splayed out over the pavement. "What the hell happened here?"

Flea gulped as he surveyed the gruesome scene. "Forbidden arcana, such barbarism."

"What happened here?" Vincent hollered.

"I-I can only guess," Flea squeaked, shaking under his robe. "It seems minotaurs disemboweled these poor things."

"Minotaurs did this?" Elise sniffed. "What possible reason could they have? This is beyond cruel."

"The minotaurs have a long history of aggressively conquering their neighbors' lands. They were well known for taking slaves and killing those deemed unfit for manual labor." Flea shook his head. "But this was all centuries ago, before they were forced to sign The Fourth War's Treaty."

Vincent's cheeks flushed, red and hot. "These bastards think they can just walk into our world and take it over?"

"It looks like it's working," Dante said, grim.

A low, cavernous wail blared in the distance, reminiscent of the foghorn on a large ship.

Dante looked back, searching for the sound through the windshield. "What was that?"

"That's a war horn!" Flea exclaimed.

"What the hell's a war horn?" Vincent didn't like how that sounded.

Flea darted from one side of the car to the other, climbing over Vincent and Elise's laps and pressing his nose against the windows. "Minotaurs use war horns to communicate when engaging in combat."

The war horn blew again, close enough that they pinpointed its direction a few blocks back.

Grandma smacked Dante's arm. "What are you waiting for, boy? Drive!"

Dante motioned at the blockade of cars and bodies around them. "Where? The only direction I can go is back!"

Vincent threw open his door. "There's no way we're getting through all this shit in the streets. We need to move on foot."

For a moment, the others hesitated, but the war horn blew again, practically upon them.

"Don't just sit there like slack-jawed idiots. Move!" Grandma jumped out of the car and pointed to a paint store. "We can hide in there."

The unpleasant smell of paint filled their nostrils, but the place was otherwise deserted. They scrambled behind a packed shelf of cans and peered out the windows, without a moment to spare.

Two people came to a labored stop outside, a woman with straw-colored hair and an older man with a prominent belly.

The man propped himself up on his knees, wheezing and coughing violently. "They got Anthony! Fucking hell, they just gutted him!"

"We can't stop here," the woman said, panting. "We need to keep moving, Charles."

From the corner of his eye, Vincent saw Elise open her mouth: "In here—mmf!"

Vincent clamped his hand tightly over her mouth. "Shut

up. You trying to get us all killed?" he whispered.

She muffled something back, eyes flashing angrily, but Vincent refused to let go. She struggled to make contact, but the two strangers gathered themselves up and took off running. Elise made a harsh noise in her throat and, without warning, bit down on Vincent's finger.

He bit down on his lip to hold back a scream. "What the fuck," he growled, inspecting his bleeding finger.

"Be quiet," Grandma barked, silencing them both.

Heavy footsteps plodded around the building, and two minotaurs appeared in the store window. They seemed even bigger in daylight, practically bursting out of their shining armor. Vincent's muscles tightened, and he instinctively reached for his gun, but the creatures were oblivious to their presence. They inspected their surroundings, and then took off in the direction of the people they were hunting.

Elise spun on Vincent the second they couldn't hear the minotaurs' hoofed stomps. "Why did you do that? They could have hidden in here with us!"

Vincent balked. "Are you stupid? We literally had seconds to get them in here. The minotaurs would have seen and killed us, too."

"We could have tried!" she countered.

"Don't be so naive. He made the right call," Grandma said.

Elise sputtered her protest, but Dante agreed with Vincent. "There was no other choice. If the minotaurs found us in here, we wouldn't have stood a chance."

"Exactly," Vincent proclaimed victoriously.

"We can fight them in the open, though," Dante said. "Let's go. We can still catch them!"

Vincent did a double take. "Wait, *what?*"

Dante jumped to his feet before Vincent finished his thought and bolted out the front door.

Elise chased after him a second later, yelling "Wait for me!"

You've got to be kidding me. Vincent hurried outside and caught a glimpse of Elise as she disappeared around the corner. He yelled for her to stop, but she was already gone. A stream of curses trailed from his mouth as he went running after her. He caught sight of Dante and Elise going down a straightaway in the direction of gunfire, precious seconds ahead of him. He quickened his pace into a dead sprint and caught them at the entrance to a small cul-de-sac.

The two minotaurs stood in the middle of the street, unperturbed by their arrival. The man with the beer gut lay dead at their feet, a spear protruding from his back. The woman, however, was still alive a few yards away, her bloodied face set in a defiant snarl. She cradled her shoulder, which stuck out at an odd angle, and a gun lay discarded on the ground next to her.

The minotaurs regarded Vincent and the others with mild amusement.

One of the minotaurs lifted an onyx horn to his mouth. "Shall I sound the war horn?"

The other shook his head. "There is no need. These puny things pose no threat." He looked them over and spoke in a deep, rumbling bass. "I am feeling generous today. Leave us, and we will spare your lives."

Vincent's eyes flicked over to the wounded woman and felt a pang of guilt. "You heard him. We can still get out of here in one piece," he said to Dante. "They just want her. We don't have to get involved."

"No. I'll lure them away and one of you can get her out of here," Elise said. "I'm fast. I did track in high school."

Dante shook his head. "It's too dangerous. Let me do it."

Vincent felt a vein pop on his forehead. "Have you both lost your damn minds?"

"Leave, now," the minotaur commanded.

"How about *you* leave and we'll spare *your* lives?" Dante countered.

The minotaur banged the butt of his spear on the concrete. "Such insolence! Do you truly think yourself our equal in combat? You insult me!"

Vincent looked at his brother like he'd lost his mind.

The second minotaur stepped forward. "Your bravery is admirable, human, so I offer you this deal: kill or be killed. Here, take this weapon."

The minotaur's heavy spear clattered at Dante's feet. The weapon was unwieldy, at least twelve feet in length, requiring both hands just to hold. The minotaurs snickered between themselves as Dante took a couple slow and clumsy stabs with it.

"What the hell do you idiots think you're doing, running off like that?"

Vincent turned around and saw Grandma and Flea slow to a stop.

Grandma took in the scene, then gave a weary but expectant sigh. "God damn it, of course you went and found the minotaurs," she groused.

"No more delays. Let us end this!" the minotaur roared. He lifted an enormous shield and pointed his spear forward, while the other one drew a sword.

Vincent blew out a shaky breath. *This is really happening,* he thought miserably. The minotaurs were huge and armored, so there was no way they would win a fair fight. Vincent's hopes perked at a wild and desperate plan forming in his head.

"Wait!" he screamed.

The minotaurs stopped their advance.

"You aren't both going to fight us at the same time, are you?"

The minotaurs exchanged looks, and then nodded. "Of course," they said.

"Well, that doesn't seem fair to me," Vincent said. "You only gave us one weapon, and he doesn't even have armor on, unlike you two."

"Then you were foolish to come unprepared," one of the minotaurs said.

Dante whispered out of the corner of his mouth, "What are you doing?"

Vincent swallowed his fear and continued. Either this worked, or it would just make two very angry minotaurs. "Are you really such chickenshits that you need to gang up on us like this? What are you afraid of, that we'll kick your ass?"

The minotaurs bristled at his words. "We fear *nothing*."

"Could have fooled me," Vincent goaded. "Look at yourselves, cowering behind all that armor."

The minotaur holding the spear puffed his chest out indignantly. "You dare?"

"Put your money where your mouth is. If you're really so strong, then fight us fair and square. One on one. Man to man—er, man to bull."

"Enough!" The other minotaur unclipped his helmet and tossed it aside.

His partner gasped. "What are you doing?"

"The weakling is right. There is no glory to be had in this slaughter," the minotaur said, undoing his breastplate next. "We could use a decent fight." He lowered his shield, then stepped forward with his sword at the ready. "I will fight them myself."

"As you wish."

Vincent exchanged looks with Grandma, who nodded her understanding, then turned to Dante. "It's all you."

His brother stepped forward to meet the challenge.

The minotaur charged them with a bestial roar that shook Vincent to his very core, shaking out the last flecks of bravery he had.

Vincent reached behind his pants and pulled out his gun. "Now, Grandma!" He screamed out a bloody battle cry and unloaded the whole clip.

The minotaur realized his mistake too late. As big as he was, with as much muscle as he had, none of it mattered without his armor. The minotaur's mouth opened in muted surprise as bullets found new homes in his chest and head. His charge came to a stuttering stop, and he stared silently at Vincent, his fury palpable. He then dropped to one knee and, with a final gasp, died.

The surviving minotaur's eyes became unfocused, and he lifted his head up in a bellowing howl that sent a chilling fight-or-flight response through everyone. "In life you were trapped by the Labyrinth, so in death you are free! I will avenge you, brother!" When he turned his eyes back on Vincent they showed only murderous intent.

Vincent gulped. "Ah, shit."

The minotaur raised his shield and charged him.

Dante tried stabbing the minotaur, but the berserk warrior easily parried his spear and sent him spinning to the ground. A split second later, the minotaur was upon Vincent. He jumped high into the air and stabbed down with his spear.

Vincent sprang to the side, narrowly avoiding the attack, but before he could recover, the minotaur slammed his shield against him. His body bounced off it with a metallic clang, and he flew through the air, eventually hitting the ground hard and rolling into a heap, the breath knocked out of him. Vincent tried getting up, but his brain and body weren't connecting anymore, and everything was spinning and muddled.

Elise's shrill scream pierced the fog momentarily. "Vincent, look out!"

His eyes came into focus long enough to see the minotaur charging him from the other side of the cul-de-sac. *How far did that fucker launch me?*

Something glinted in the sunlight and glass shattered against the minotaur's helmet, splashing a green liquid through his helmet and all over his face. He pawed at his head with an angry snarl. "What did you do to me?" he roared. The minotaur stumbled in place and managed a few, rigid steps.

Vincent blinked in disbelief as the minotaur's body stiffened and his brown fur took on a gray tinge; flesh gradually turned to stone, and within moments, the minotaur had transformed into a solid statue. Vincent shook his head and stared hard at the minotaur. "Am I seeing this right, or did I just get a really bad concussion?"

Dante gave the statue a curious poke with the spear. Its metal tip rang against rock. "What did you do to it, Vincent?"

"It was me," Flea corrected firmly. All heads turned to him, and he held up a small vial containing a bubbling green concoction. "Medusa's Serum," he said matter-of-factly.

Grandma sniffed. "What in the hell is a Medusa's Serum?"

"It turns whoever it touches into stone." Flea studied the stone minotaur. "Judging by the minotaur's size, I would estimate the effect to last approximately one hour."

Vincent rubbed at his aching head. "You couldn't have done that sooner?"

"I forgot I had some in my pockets," Flea said with a slight shrug. He lifted the flap of his robe and peered inside. "I wonder what other potions I brought with me—oh look, half an Everburn Elixir—that could come in handy."

The woman they had all come to rescue groaned weakly.

Vincent watched the others run to her aid while he nursed a throbbing headache. "No, no, I'm fine. It's just a little brain damage, but thanks for asking," he muttered darkly. When he finally stopped seeing double, he lit a cigarette and staggered over to them.

Everyone gave Elise a wide berth while she worked on the injured woman, using their first aid kit. There was so much blood smeared on the woman's face it made Vincent a little woozy.

"Is she going to make it?" he wondered aloud.

"My face hurts like hell," the woman rasped in a Southern drawl. "But I'm not dead yet."

"Try not to talk so much, I need to clean this thing out." Elise ripped off a piece of her shirt and gently wiped the blood from the woman's face, revealing a deep cut that ran the entire length of her right cheek. "That's going to leave a scar."

As the rest of the blood was cleaned off, the mystery woman's features came to light, revealing blue eyes to go with her blond hair. Thick but tidy eyebrows squirmed like tiny caterpillars as she struggled to sit up.

"I wouldn't do that if I were you," Elise warned. "Your shoulder needs to be popped back into place."

The woman groaned. "That's just freakin' great."

Elise took out a bottle of iodine solution and a roll of gauze; several minutes later, the wound on the woman's face was cleaned and bandaged. "That's the best we can do," Elise said, frowning. "We should suture this shut, but this kit doesn't have anything we can use for that." She leaned forward and gently took the arm hanging from the woman's dislocated shoulder. "This is going to hurt just a tiny bit."

The woman arched an eyebrow. "How much is a tiny—ah! Son of a whore, that hurts!"

"All better," Elise said, beaming.

"Where'd you learn all this?" Vincent asked.

"I took first aid courses a few years ago. I figured it'd be useful when I volunteered at places without hospitals or doctors." Elise smiled. "I guess it finally came in handy."

Elise's patient sat up with a muted wince. She massaged her shoulder and gave them a grateful smile. "There must be a God up there looking out for me. Y'all saved my life. I owe you one."

Elise offered her a bottle of water and a couple pain relievers, then did the same for Vincent.

The woman swallowed her medicine before offering her hand. "My name's Natalie Bell."

Dante took Natalie's hand and pulled her up. Introductions went smoothly until it was Flea's turn.

The little pug offered his hand. "My name is Flea. A pleasure to meet you."

Natalie rubbed her eyes. "Is anyone else seeing this?"

"He's exactly what you think he is," Vincent said. "We sort of found each other, but he's harmless."

"And he helped fight off those minotaurs," Dante added.

Flea pshawed bashfully. "It was nothing, really."

"I'll take a talking pug any day of the week over those

bastards," Natalie replied, motioning to the minotaurs. "What're you folks doing out here alone?"

"We heard a radio transmission saying there's a refuge over on Blossom Island," Elise said.

"Hmm, I don't know anything about a Blossom Island." Natalie limped over to her dead companion and shook her head sadly. "Poor Charles. At least it was quick." She looked over her shoulder at them. "If you want, you can come with me. My group's got a little base set up near here. We have food and water."

Elise's eyes lit up. "Really? There are others with you?"

"Oh sure, there's a bunch of us holed up nearby," Natalie said.

"What about guns, you got those?" Vincent asked.

"We've got plenty."

Elise gave him an exasperated sigh. "Guns? Really? That's what you're concerned about? She just told us there are other survivors."

"Who cares how many people there are if they can't defend themselves?" Vincent snapped.

"Both of you shut up," Grandma ordered. "You can argue until you're blue in the face once we get off the streets."

Dante nodded at Natalie. "Lead the way."

Chapter 8

As Natalie led them through side alleys and backyards, skulking from one building to another, the gray afternoon gave way to night. They eventually reached their destination at the outskirts of downtown Oakwood, which had a perfect view into the heart of the city. Dark outlines of skyscrapers stretched up to the sky like dead giants, reaching for the star-encrusted blanket that night had draped over them.

"Who'd have guessed the stars could look so nice from here," Dante said.

Without the constant barrage of lights from Oakwood, the stars finally had their chance to shine. Thousands upon thousands of them twinkled overhead. A marvelous sight to behold.

Elise sighed dreamily. "It's beautiful, isn't it?"

Natalie cleared her throat. "It might look pretty, but believe me, the last thing you want to do is meet the things that have started coming out at night." She limped to a drab apartment, so plain in design it almost blended into its surroundings.

A sign out front read: Oasis Gardens.

Natalie pulled out a small flashlight from her jacket and led them through the bent frames that had once been its front doors. They passed through the lobby to an emergency staircase, and took it all the way up to the eighth floor.

"Here we are. Home sweet home," she said, pointing to a closed door. She knocked.

"Who is it?" a muffled voice answered.

"Let me in, Bill. I'm tore up pretty bad."

"Natalie? Someone help me get this door open!"

Something heavy scraped across the floor on the other side, and the door cracked open. A young man squeezed through; he was tall, all skin and bones, under an unkempt mop of blue hair.

"You're alive," he said with a sigh of relief. "I didn't think you were going to make it back after night fell—hey, what happened to your face?"

"Relax, hon, I'll be fine." Natalie jerked her thumb over her shoulder. "Got some visitors, though."

Bill swept his hair aside and looked them over with beady eyes, a suspicious scowl on his face. "Who are these people?"

"Don't be such an ass, Bill. If it wasn't for them, I'd be dead right now."

Bill frowned. "Where's Charles and Anthony?" Understanding dawned in his eyes even as he spoke the question.

Natalie hung her head. "We got ambushed by a couple minotaurs."

Bill kicked the door. "Son of a bitch!" He pulled his hair

out of his face with a huff. "Get in, Natalie. We'll have the doctor check on you, and I'm sure Gil's got some questions for these outsiders."

He pushed open the door, and a low hum of conversation spilled out from inside. Candles lit a single hallway, casting a dull glow over a procession of men and women busy at work. Some cleaned out guns while others carried boxes of food and blankets around. A woman in a white coat hurried through the crowd, carrying bloody bandages in her arms and holding a syringe in her teeth. Everyone had a job to do here, it seemed.

No kids, though, Vincent noticed.

As they walked in, Bill's eyes popped open. "Wait a minute!" he barked. Before anyone could react, he drew a pistol from his hip holster and aimed down at their feet.

Vincent recoiled with the rest of his group. "What the fuck is this?"

"What is that thing? Why is it walking on its back legs and wearing clothes, and are those hands?" Bill stammered.

Vincent followed his gaze to Flea. "Oh, him? He's harmless."

"Cut it out, you fool." Natalie tried stepping between them, but Bill pushed her aside and kept his gun on Flea.

The little pug hid behind Vincent's leg, fuming. "I am getting quite tired of having weapons drawn on me by you humans! I have done nothing to deserve this persecution!"

Bill blanched. "It can talk?" His voice rose to a hysterical pitch.

"Hey! Calm the hell down!" Vincent hollered.

Bill turned the gun on Vincent. "Who are you guys? What are you doing working with those creatures?"

"Holy hell, what is this shit?" Grandma shouted.

Dante held his hands up and regarded Bill with a gentle tone. "Okay, this is getting out of hand. You need to relax and put the gun down."

A small crowd had gathered behind Bill.

Someone dropped a glass and screamed, "There's a creature inside!"

The words carried like an electric current down the hall, and suddenly, it was chaos as an angry mob formed, screaming and trembling like a beast waiting to pounce. Vincent realized the immediate danger they were in and slowly backed to the door with the others.

"Kill it! Someone kill it!"

"How'd it get inside?"

"Did it tell the minotaurs where we're hiding? Is it safe here?"

"They're working with the creatures, they're with the enemy! Kill the outsiders before they get away!"

An authoritative voice cut through the panic. "SILENCE!"

The crowd quieted down to urgent murmurs as someone charged through, parting the bodies like water. A bald, nondescript man of average height and average features emerged from the crowd with an assault rifle. Vincent couldn't quite pinpoint it, but he had seen the man's face before.

"What's going on here?" he demanded, his powerful

voice carrying across the entire floor with ease. "Did creatures get in?"

"Look!" Bill exclaimed. "These people came in with a creature. It's not a minotaur, but it can talk. Look at how it's dressed, too, like some kind of witch."

Flea growled at Bill in a very doglike manner. "I am a wizard, thank you very much."

The bald man regarded Flea curiously, then turned to Bill with a harsh glare. "Is it dangerous?"

"Of course it is," Bill said. "Just look at it, Gil!"

Gil nodded at Vincent. "Well?"

"You think we'd be traveling with Flea if he was? You idiots."

Dante nudged him in the back. "Calm down, Vincent. This isn't the time."

"Like hell I will! We just saved one of their own, but these pieces of shit are literally so scared they were about to kill us!" Vincent turned back to the crowd and felt nothing but disgust as he looked over their frightened faces. "Go to hell, each and every one of you!"

Something dangerous snuck its way onto Gil's face, and Vincent became acutely aware of how close they all were to his gun. Vincent almost regretted his words . . . *almost.*

"Boy, you really know how to make friends," Grandma mumbled.

Vincent cleared his throat, letting some of his fire dissipate. "Let's go. We aren't wanted here."

"Don't. Stay, I insist," Gil said.

Elise opened her mouth in surprise. "R-really?"

"I think we've all started off on the wrong foot here," Gil said. "Come with me."

Vincent wasn't too keen on going in any further. He looked to his brother for guidance.

"Maybe we shouldn't," said Dante. "It's obvious your people are uncomfortable enough as it is."

A low murmur of agreement went through the crowd.

Gil smirked. "It's not their decision to make."

"You sure about that?" Vincent asked.

Bill nodded vigorously. "We can't let them in, Gil. It's too dangerous."

Gil's arm moved in a blur and cracked the young man over the temple. Bill cried out in pain and dropped to the floor. Everyone gasped at the abrupt violence, even Vincent. Gil then kneeled next to Bill's sniveling form and spoke in a low whisper so only those nearest heard.

"Don't you ever question *my* decision for *my* people. This isn't the civilized world anymore. Not everyone gets a voice." He stood up and addressed the spectators. "You all have jobs to do. Get back to work!"

No one said a word of protest, and one by one they trickled away in silence. Vincent had never seen anything like it, such blind obedience.

Gil turned back to them, his hand hovering a few inches from his weapon, the threat clear. "Well, are you coming?"

Dante took the first step in. "I guess we don't have much of a say in this."

Natalie was helping Bill up when they walked by; she

watched them follow Gil down the hall, a silent apology on her face.

"Sorry you had to see that," Gil said over his shoulder. "But I have to keep these people under control for their own good."

"Did you need to hit Bill?" Elise asked. "He was just scared."

"Of course I did. You saw how much he was upsetting the others. If I didn't nip it in the bud, everyone would have panicked, and that's the last thing we need right now," Gil explained.

"And you're just the guy to make that decision, am I right?" Vincent said scathingly.

"You think these people want to fend for themselves in this new world?" Gil chuckled. "They're sheep. It's all most people are. We grow up with parents telling us how to act, then we go to school where teachers tell us what to think, and then we get a job where a boss tells us what to do. Left to their own devices, these people would die. Make no mistake."

"That's an awful way of seeing things," replied Elise.

Gil shrugged. "Does the extinction of mankind sound like a better alternative?"

"I can't say I agree with your methods, but I think I get it," Dante said.

"Smart man." Gil flashed a predatory smile.

They followed the hall around to the other side of the building and stopped at an apartment with two men guarding it. Unlike the other apartments, this one had an extra latch and combination padlock on the door.

Gil began undoing the extra security locks and said to his guards, "Make sure no one disturbs us."

Once inside, Vincent understood exactly why it had all the extra security. The apartment was a makeshift armory, overflowing with guns, ammo, grenades, and body armor. Any furniture had been stacked against the walls, leaving a single table illuminated in the center of the room, with a map of the city and several loose sheets of notes spread atop it.

A round man looked up from the map as they walked in. "I'll be damned," he said, chuckling.

"You've got to be kidding me," Vincent said.

"What are you doing here, Roach?" Dante looked around the room nervously.

Roach cracked a toothy grin. "I could ask you guys the same thing, but I guess I'm not surprised you managed to survive this long." He turned to Gil as the other man joined him at the table. "How'd you find these jokers?"

"They found us," Gil replied. He motioned to some chairs against the wall. "Bring a seat up to the table, make yourselves comfortable."

Alarms went off in Vincent's head, and fear prickled up and down his neck. His eyes flicked from one darkened corner to the next, waiting for Kojo to make his entrance or a Gate to open.

Roach's shiny lips spread over his teeth. "Who's the girl? She's pretty."

Grandma made a disgusted sound in her throat. "Keep your slimy hands away, or I'll chop your dick off."

Roach turned a blotchy red as his face twisted into an angry snarl. "Don't talk to me like that, Grandma. You need to start showing me some goddamn respect for once!"

"I might if you finally stop being such a sleazeball," Grandma snapped.

Gil cleared his throat and made a show of setting his weapon down on the table. "Let's talk to each other like adults. No need for name-calling. Okay, Roach? Okay, Grandma?" He shook his head and laughed. "I feel ridiculous calling you that. What's your actual name?"

"Everyone just calls me Grandma."

"I don't like repeating myself," Gil said. "I asked what your name is. It's a simple question."

Gil didn't explicitly say it, but his speech had slowed and the underlying threat of violence twisted his words. Vincent bristled protectively, but Grandma waved him down.

"My name's Betty Goode," she answered calmly.

"Thank you." Gil made a sweeping gesture. "Now take a fucking seat, people."

They did as he said, but as they grabbed their chairs, Vincent couldn't shake the feeling he knew Gil from somewhere. It was right on the tip of his brain.

"Why are we even here?" Grandma asked suddenly.

Gil raised an eyebrow. "What do you mean, Betty?"

"You saved us from your mob for a reason," she explained. "Like you said, we're all adults here, so let's cut the shit. Tell us what you want."

He pursed his lips, contemplating his next words carefully. "I need your help."

Grandma snorted, very unladylike. "What the hell can we do for you?"

"Have you run into one of those things eating the dead in the streets?"

"You mean the ghouls?" Grandma asked.

Gil nodded approvingly. "I'm guessing the talking dog taught you that? Did he also tell you about the Gates?"

"Sure," she replied.

"Well, I've got a problem that needs fixing. There's a Gate not even a mile from here. Ghouls have been coming out of it, and they've started to pick off some of my people. It's only a matter of time before they find our little hideout."

"You want us to help you kill the ghouls?" Dante asked. Elise shuddered.

"Don't be ridiculous," Gil said. "If we kill the ghouls, more will just come through the Gate. We have to get to the root of the problem, the Gate, and close it."

Vincent chuckled. "And we're going to do this how, exactly?"

"With Flea, specifically," he elaborated.

Flea pointed to himself. "How could I possibly help?"

"You must have come into our world through a Gate," Gil said.

"Sure, but—"

Gil continued speaking, talking over the little pug. "Then you have to know something about them, right? Like how to close it."

"I suppose I *should*." Flea bobbed his head from side to side, as if weighing two options. "I mean I do. I am the smartest wizard alive and learned directly from Sorceress Epoch, after all. Closing a Gate between two locations within Terra Mater is a trivial matter; however, a Gate between two worlds? I must be honest, I don't fully understand how it happened to begin with."

The corner of Gil's mouth twitched in displeasure. "Can you figure it out?"

"Perhaps if I was given enough time to study it, I might be able to give you a more favorable answer."

Gil hummed, his brow furrowed in deep concentration.

"What're you thinking, boss?" Roach asked.

"Shut up, Roach. I need some quiet to think," Gil hissed.

Roach closed his mouth with a sulky frown.

Vincent studied Gil's face, taking in every detail—in a flash of insight, he remembered. "You're the police chief's kid."

Gil looked up, annoyed. "How did you know that?"

"Your face was all over the news." Vincent turned to Grandma and Dante. "You guys recall that case about five years back? The one with that dead lady they found in the garbage?"

Grandma's eyes popped in shock. "This is the same Gil Garcia?"

Elise prodded Vincent. "What are you talking about? What case?"

Vincent kept a wary eye on Gil as he spoke. "A while back, the cops found a murdered prostitute in a dumpster. Not all that unusual for Oakwood, but this case in particular got a lot of attention because the main suspect happened to be the police chief's own son."

"I was never convicted," Gil growled. "They didn't have enough evidence to prove it was me."

"Not convicted isn't the same thing as not guilty," he retorted. "You got away by the skin of your teeth."

Elise shook her head. "Wait a second. That man we heard on the radio, George Garcia—he's Gil's father?"

"Yeah," answered Dante. "So why aren't you with him on Blossom Island?"

"Dad and I never saw eye to eye on things," Gil said. "We have different ideas of how things should be run now."

"Oh no, no, no," Vincent said, wagging his finger. "I bet Daddy doesn't want you there. The chief renounced the jury's decision, practically disowned you right on TV. So now you're running your own little dictatorship here. Why am I not surprised?"

Angry little veins popped out of Gil's temple, and he ground his teeth. "Suppose I did kill her. Who cares? She was a no-name whore that wasn't going to be missed."

Elise whimpered and pushed her chair back.

Roach shook his head slightly. "You should probably drop it," he murmured to Vincent.

"You're working with this sick bastard?" Vincent turned on him in disgust. "How did you go from fencing stolen goods to . . . *this?*"

Roach tugged on his face with a sigh. "Look, man, I made some mistakes, I know that, but you really have no idea what's happening here."

Vincent saw a blur in his peripheral vision and something

hard crunched against his nose. A delayed explosion of pain radiated from his face, and he fell off his chair. "Son of a bitch!" He felt his nose with a pained wince and found it covered in blood.

Gil stood over him, seething, the barrel of his gun aimed down at him. "I thought we could be respectful with each other, but you really didn't leave me a choice."

"You dirty motherfucker!" he yelled, only realizing after the fact it wasn't the smartest thing to say to a guy pointing a gun at him.

Gil's nostrils flared, but Roach jumped on him before he could do anything. "Hey, hey, let's relax. Everybody just relax," Roach said, cautiously pushing Gil's gun away. "We can use them."

Mania flashed across Gil's eyes, and for a moment Vincent thought he was going to shoot him in retaliation, but just like that—Gil stopped. He closed his eyes and breathed. When they opened, he was an average nobody again. "Technically, we only need Flea."

"Yeah, sure, or we can put them all to work for us. We can use them for our cause, whether they like it or not," Roach suggested.

A devilish grin played at the corner of Gil's lips. "I've got some ideas already." He banged on the apartment door. "Guards!"

The men out front came inside, guns ready to fire.

"Take their things and put them in our jail," Gil said.

"What're you doing?" Elise stammered. "We haven't done anything wrong. This is against the law!"

Gil laughed so hard tears formed in the corners of his eyes. "You think the government exists still, or that a cop is going to come save you? I decide what the laws are now."

They were stripped of their supplies, including Flea's potions, then herded by gunpoint to the next apartment over. The guards threw them inside, and the door slammed behind them with a deafening bang.

Chapter 9

Vincent glowered at the darkness, trying his best to ignore his throbbing nose.

"How are there no windows in here?" Elise's disembodied voice wondered. "I can't see anything."

"I'm pretty sure this apartment is in the center of the building, so it wouldn't have any windows pointing out," Dante explained.

"Why would anyone want to live in a place without any natural lighting?" she asked, appalled. "That sounds awful and extremely illegal."

"Just another one of Oakwood's charms," Dante muttered.

Grandma bumped into Vincent. "That you, Vincent?"

"Yeah, it's me. How are you holding up?"

Her cantankerous answer came back swiftly. "How the hell do you think I'm fucking doing? I'm trapped in some shit-ass building when I should be at home knitting and yelling at brats to get off my lawn, or whatever the hell old ladies like me are supposed to do nowadays."

The thought of her serenely knitting a sweater with a vapid smile was so un-Grandma-like, it made Vincent chuckle.

"How's your face feeling?" she asked.

"How do you think? It hurts like a bitch."

Grandma slapped his arm. "Don't get lippy with me, you little shit. Nobody told you to go mouthing off to that son of a bitch."

"I had to do it," Vincent replied. "The way he was talking down to us and holding us hostage like that. If I had the chance I would have thrown him out the window. He's lucky all I could do was talk some shit and hurt his feelings."

"There's a time and place to run your mouth. Was your broken nose worth it?"

He gingerly felt the crooked bridge of his swollen nose, but smiled. "Hell yeah, it was. Did you see his face? I really pissed him off good. It was great."

Vincent felt Flea brush past his leg. "You could do with some diplomatic lessons," Flea said.

"Yeah. You're lucky Roach stopped Gil from shooting you," Elise chimed.

Vincent snorted incredulously. "Oh, come on, are you guys serious? He started it. I wasn't going to just let him walk all over us like that. Dante, back me up here."

His brother took a deep breath before answering. "No, it was stupid of you."

"What?"

"What you did was stupid and childish," Dante snapped.

"We can't go around acting on our impulses like that anymore, especially now when things have gotten so dangerous!"

"Excuse me?" Vincent faced his brother's voice. "Are you serious right now? Back in the day you would have been right there with me, spitting on the guy's face."

"I grew up, Vincent. I think it's time you did, too."

"Ha! So I'm the bad guy here?" Vincent spat. "We wouldn't even be in this situation if you hadn't dragged us into chasing after Natalie."

"Should we have just left her for dead?" Dante fired back.

"Yes! I can't believe I even have to tell you this! The only asses we should be worried about are our own."

Dante stormed forward, bumping blindly into Vincent and pushing him back. "You don't mean that, Vincent."

"Don't act all high and mighty, like you're a better person than me. I'm just telling you the truth. You made a stupid call." He shook his head. "What's gotten into you? I swear, you haven't been the same since you got back, running around pretending you're some kind of hero."

"What're you so scared of?" Dante asked, disappointment heavy in his tone. "You really think you can just hide forever like a coward? That's not who we are, Vincent. We're better than that."

"Stop pretending to be something you're not. I'm not a good person, you're not a good person. You went to prison for killing Tommy. For fuck's sake, just accept that already!"

Dante's voice boomed back like a megaphone. "I know what I did!"

Neither brother spoke after that, afraid to go past the point of no return. The silence stretched on for an eternity.

Slowly, Vincent's temper subsided and his breathing relaxed. He began to regret what he had said. "Dante, I didn't mean that."

"It's okay," his brother said. "You're right."

Vincent thought he should say something else, but he couldn't put words to his feelings. It made him uncomfortable, and he felt lost.

Thankfully, a commotion from the door stopped him from having to dig too deep into his emotions. Someone was arguing with the guard out front, a woman from the sound of it. The heated argument went back and forth like two dogs barking at each other, but it eventually stopped, and the door unlocked.

Everyone jumped to attention, muscles tensed and ready for anything. Vincent clenched his hands into tight fists and crouched, his legs coiled and ready to spring at the first opening for an attack, but when Natalie appeared in the doorway he let his fists drop.

"What do you want?" he asked contemptuously.

Natalie tried smiling, but winced and grabbed at a fresh bandage on her face. "I brought you some food," she said, shaking a box of cereal. She also pulled a few candles from her pocket. "Also got you some light."

An armed man appeared behind her. "No candles," he said. "They could burn the whole place down."

Natalie made a face at him. "Oh, hell. What do you expect them to do? Eat in the dark?"

"Yes," the man replied flatly.

"They aren't going anywhere. There's no reason to be so uncivilized about this."

"But what if—"

Natalie rolled her eyes up with an exasperated sigh. "I'm just following Roach's orders. If you got a problem with it, you can take it up with him."

The guard contemplated her words a moment, then nodded. "Fine, hurry up and give them the stuff."

"Thanks so much, hon."

Elise motioned to Natalie's face as she walked in. "How's the cut doing?"

"Our resident doc gave me twelve stitches, so I should be fine. But it's like you said, it'll leave a nasty scar." Natalie winked playfully. "I guess my dreams of being Miss Texas are out the door now, huh?" She handed over the cereal, candles, and a lighter to Vincent, and then lowered her voice to a secretive whisper. "Look in the box. It's not much, but I figured you brought it for a reason."

"Hurry up, Natalie!"

She turned back to the impatient guard. "Would you relax? You're gonna give yourself a heart attack stressing out so much." Natalie looked back at Vincent, her blue eyes regretful. "I'm so sorry this happened. I had no idea Gil would lock y'all up like this."

"You better be bringing us more than just apologies after what we did for you," said Grandma.

"What's he going to do with us?" Vincent asked.

"I have no idea. He doesn't really tell people much of his

plans," Natalie said. "What the hell happened to your nose?"

"Gil happened," said Vincent.

"I swear, I'll figure out a way to help you."

"Damn it, Natalie! Don't make me come in there," the guard said.

"I'm coming, gosh!" Natalie hurried to the door and turned her nose up at the guard. "Didn't your mama ever teach you any manners?"

The apartment door slammed shut, plunging them back into darkness.

Vincent lit the candles, welcoming the warm glow, and checked inside the cereal box to see what Natalie had smuggled in. He pulled out his copy of *Gallant's Quest* with a huge smile. "I guess Natalie isn't *so* bad."

Grandma *humphed* and snatched the cereal from his hand. "Give me that. Some of us actually have our priorities straight."

Elise bent toward Vincent's face. "That looks awful. You need to reset your nose or else it's going to heal badly."

"Well, we don't exactly have a doctor handy, do we?" he retorted.

Flea padded into the candlelight and did a double take on Vincent's face. "It's almost completely sideways!" he gasped.

"I could probably put it in the right place to heal," Elise said. "But it's going to hurt."

"Have you fixed a broken nose before?" Dante asked.

"Technically no, but it's not complicated to do if the break isn't too bad."

"You really know how to instill confidence in people," Vincent said.

"Unless you've got a better plan," Elise replied. "We can't leave it alone or else it'll just heal in that shape. You want a crooked nose forever?"

Vincent beckoned for her to get closer. "All right, fine. Let's do this."

"You probably want to sit down," Elise said.

"I'll be fine. Just get it over with," he demanded.

"Okay, but don't say I didn't warn you." Elise carefully held her hands up to his nose and felt along the ridge before resting on a satisfactory spot. "You ready?"

"Sure."

"Three . . . two . . ."

"How badly is this going to hurt?"

"One."

"Fuuuuuck!"

After they ate their meager meal of dry cereal, there was nothing left to do but turn in for the night. Grandma claimed the single bedroom for herself, leaving the others to fend for themselves in the living room.

Vincent lay awake on the floor, staring up at the ceiling while listening to Flea's jowls flap with each snoring breath. He couldn't sleep. Whenever he tried to close his eyes, visions of the dead played like a macabre movie on the back of his eyelids. After a couple sleepless hours, Vincent rolled onto his side and groped in the dark until his fingers wrapped around a waxy candle; he lit it, then silently tiptoed to the kitchen to find his copy of *Gallant's Quest.*

It wasn't on the table where he remembered leaving it, though. He scoured the kitchen's empty countertops, but couldn't find it, much to his annoyance. Before he could start swearing, however, he heard a faint noise from the connecting hallway. He crept forward, and the noise became more distinct, like a faint sobbing.

Vincent turned his head in the direction of the living room. He was pretty sure he had passed by everyone else, so who the hell was crying at this hour? It didn't take him long to find the sound coming from behind a closed bathroom door. He opened it just enough to peek inside and saw Elise sitting on the edge of the bathtub, hunched over in complete darkness.

"What the hell are you doing, hiding alone in here like a creep?" Vincent whispered. "I thought you were asleep with the others in the living room. Shit, you had me freaked out for a sec. Do you know how many horror movies have the guy being lured away from the group by—"

Elise sniffed and turned her face up, eyes red and puffy with tears glistening down her cheeks.

Vincent froze. "Oh. I didn't realize you were, uh . . ." He cleared his throat and took a step back. "I'll go now."

"Where are you going?" Elise said, a hiccup breaking up her words. "Don't leave."

Vincent shifted in place uncomfortably. "You want me to stay? I don't know if that's a good idea, Elise."

She wiped her eyes and waved at him to come in, which he did reluctantly.

Vincent noticed his copy of *Gallant's Quest* tucked in her arms. "What are you doing with my book?"

Elise looked down, surprised. "Oh, this? Sorry. I was going to read it."

"Hard to do that in the dark."

She pointed to a candle by her bare feet. "That was my *intention*, but once I got in here all I could do was think about all the bodies we've seen, and the monsters that killed them."

Vincent nodded sympathetically and let her continue.

"I thought coming here, we would finally get away from that, but all we did was exchange one kind of monster for another." Her face screwed up in an effort to fight back another bout of tears. "Sorry. I don't mean to make things awkward, I-I just need someone to talk to."

Vincent took a seat next to her. "So you want to talk to me? Elise, if you're looking for someone to tell you things are going to be okay and will get better, I'm not your man."

"I don't need you to coddle me," she scolded. "I just want to talk, anything to take my mind off how screwed up everything is."

"Okay, fine. What do you want to talk about?" he said softly.

Elise lifted the book. "What about this? Have you finished it yet?"

"No, I'm not even halfway done."

"Darn. I won't spoil anything for you, then. It gets really good later on."

"You've read this before?" Vincent asked.

Elise brushed her hair behind her ear and smiled. "I finished all three books last summer. I swear I went through them in like two weeks."

Vincent wasn't buying it. "This is some serious high fantasy shit—elves, swords, and magic. You really read them all?"

"Sure I did. There's *Gallant's Quest, Lady Windamere's Legacy,* and *Draconic Absolution.*" Elise grinned impishly at his reaction. "Surprised?"

"A little. You just don't seem like the type of person to read those kinds of books," he mumbled.

"You shouldn't judge a book by its cover. People will surprise you."

Vincent scoffed. "People never surprise me. Most of them end up being selfish nobodies."

"So are you just a selfish nobody, then?" she challenged.

"Of course! The world won't give a shit about me when I finally die."

Elise's jaw dropped, but she quickly regained her composure. "Don't be ridiculous, Vincent. What about your family? Your mom, your dad?"

"My mom's dead," he said, nonchalant.

"What about your dad?"

Vincent looked down and shook his head. "He's not around either. We'll leave it at that."

"I'm so sorry, Vincent."

"I'm not. It is what it is." He gave her a sideways glance and noted with a twinge of annoyance her large, pitying eyes. "Stop that. I don't need you treating me like some kind of lost puppy."

Elise turned her head. "You really have a weird way of interpreting things."

Vincent shrugged.

"I was wondering . . . what you said about your brother earlier. Did he really kill someone?"

"Yes."

Elise's eyes probed his for more. "What happened?"

"It's none of your fucking business," Vincent said.

"O-okay. Sorry, I didn't mean to pry." Elise quirked her face into a perplexed frown. "Why do you have such a hard time talking about yourself?"

"What do you mean? I've just told you plenty of things."

"No, you don't understand. I asked you questions, and you answered—kind of. You still haven't told me anything of your own accord."

"God, you are so nosy. We barely met a couple days ago. What could you possibly want to know?"

"I don't know." Elise arched an eyebrow. "Tell me something you *want* me to know."

"Uh . . . my birthday is November tenth. Is that good enough for you?"

Elise laughed, a genuine and infectious sound. "It's a start."

***

"I'm coming to get you!"

Dante wobbled down the hall on unsteady legs, squealing with childish delight before Bo scooped him up with a playful roar.

"I'm going to eat you up!" Bo growled. He put his lips to Dante's bulging tummy and blew a raspberry. His son laughed and laughed, squirming under the attack.

Xifeng appeared from around the corner, her jaw jutting out to show her teeth. She stomped forward with a low growl. "Look out for mommy monster!"

"Uh oh!" Bo exclaimed in mock horror. He held Dante up like a shield. "Spare me. Take this little boy instead."

Dante kicked his chubby little legs and giggled as Xifeng took him in her arms. "Do you know what mommy monster does to little boys?"

"No! No!" Dante exclaimed. It was his favorite word.

"We give you kisses!" Xifeng showered Dante with wet smooches on the neck that tickled him and made him laugh even harder.

A comforting warmth radiated throughout Bo's body as he watched his little family play. It didn't matter that they were dirt poor, or that they lived in crime-ridden Oakwood. They had each other, and he couldn't ask for more.

Dante reached out to him with grasping fingers. "Daddy!" he said.

Bo took his son from Xifeng, and the little boy tugged at his lips and ears. "Daddy. Daddy face!" Dante shouted.

A burgeoning pride swelled in Bo's chest. "Look how smart he is. He's a genius."

"Don't get carried away. He's still just a child," Xifeng said, smiling.

"I can see it in his eyes, though," Bo explained, mouthing the words around Dante's fingers as they probed his mouth.

He pulled his head back, sputtering and laughing. "He's going to do great things with his life. Maybe he'll become president, or a billionaire! He might even save the world."

Xifeng chuckled. "Not that I'm doubting you, but what makes you so sure?"

"Call it a father's intuition." A disturbing thought occurred to him, and his smile faded.

Xifeng put her hand on his arm. "What's the matter?"

A cold blanket of fear wrapped itself around Bo's heart, putting out the warmth. "What if I'm like my mother?" Revolting images of him beating his innocent son filled his thoughts. Bo tried giving Dante back to Xifeng, but she refused.

"You are nothing like her," Xifeng cooed. "The past can only define you if you let it."

Bo swallowed hard. "I don't understand."

She kissed him on the forehead. "You're so afraid she taught you to be a bad man, but I think she taught you how *not* to be a bad man."

Chapter 10

Vincent sprang awake to the apartment door slamming open. He stirred, bleary-eyed and dazed, only realizing a few moments later he was alone in the bathtub. Wedged under his thigh was *Gallant's Quest*.

Vincent sat up with a drawn-out groan. "My aching back." He shuffled stiffly out the bathroom door as Gil's voice boomed through the rest of the apartment.

"Rise and shine, people! I'm putting you to work," Gil bellowed.

Vincent glowered back, detesting the other man's smug smile. Gil lifted a candle up and revealed Vincent's companions at the other end of the hall, rubbing sleep from their eyes. He then whispered something to their guard and left.

The man pointed his gun inside and said, "Gil doesn't like to be kept waiting. Move your asses."

Grandma arched her back with a loud crack and satisfied moan; she shook herself out, then gave the guard the finger.

"Show your elders some damn respect. My body's not what it used to be."

"That's not my problem," the guard said, sneering. "I got orders to shoot if you don't hurry."

"The cheeky little shit thinks he's a big man, pushing a helpless lady around." She hocked a ball of spit at him. "Screw off, punk."

Vincent grinned at her remark and gave Dante a knowing sidelong glance. "Give him some credit. Helpless is the last word I'd use to describe you."

Dante massaged his stubbly chin, pensive. "I'd think you're more bitchy than helpless."

"No, she's more like a pissy hard-ass," Vincent countered.

"Or tough and leathery."

"Maybe just a plain asshole?"

"What about a mean motherfucker?"

Grandma walked past Vincent and Dante, swatting playfully at them. "Cut it out, boys, you're making me blush with all these compliments."

Elise looked between them and Grandma, absolutely stunned by their barrage of insults. She saw the grins on Vincent and Dante's faces, and realized everything they had said was with absolute respect and reverence for the older woman.

The guard fumed quietly as they walked past, but gave them safe passage to the faux armory next door. Bill greeted them at the door and ushered them inside.

Gil looked up from the table with a curt smile, but his

demeanor was anything but jovial. "Put Flea on the table," he ordered. He spoke with the overreaching confidence of a man who felt superior to everyone else.

It reminded Vincent too much of his run-ins with the law when he was younger. He grated his teeth and struggled to bite back a snide remark.

Elise set Flea down on the table, looked at Gil for a sign of approval, but shrank away when he said nothing. Seeing her cower irked Vincent even more, but through some miracle of willpower, he kept his thoughts to himself.

Gil pointed to a red circle on his map. "This is where we are." He then dragged his finger up the map to another red circle. "And this is where the Gate is. We found it right in the center of City Hall's main lobby. We'll go there together, so that Flea can study it before it gets dark and the ghouls come out."

Flea frowned. "I must warn you, I do not think I'm capable of helping right away. Assuming I discover the machinations behind this interplanetary Gate, I would still require a staff to channel my magic and close it. My staff is currently in my lab, where it is quite useless, so I'll have to make a new one." He shrugged his small shoulders. "But, I suppose if anyone is to solve such an impossible task, it would have to be me, clearly."

"Let's pretend Flea can do something about the Gate. What makes you think we'll help? We never agreed to this," said Vincent.

Gil's lip curled back from sharp canines, and his dark eyes flicked up from the map. "How's your nose doing?"

He reached up instinctively. It was fat and swollen, painful to the touch. Vincent's face flushed.

"That's what I thought." Gil wandered around the table and took a seat on the edge. "I'll say this as plainly as I can. Flea will close the Gate for me, or I will kill you."

Vincent clenched his fist and, from the corner of his eye, saw Dante's arm flex.

Grandma pointed an accusing finger at Gil. "You're a twisted freak!"

His eyes sharpened to dangerous slits, and he said, slow and deliberate, "Don't raise your voice at me, Betty."

Vincent snorted derisively. "Her name is *Grandma*."

Gil wrinkled his nose. "*Betty*, your boy here really needs to understand the power dynamic." He drew a handgun, clicked the hammer back, and then let it sit loosely in his lap.

"There's no need for all this damn posturing," explained Grandma. "We get it."

"You don't," Gil replied. "I have people to care for, and that Gate is threatening them. I can't play games with you like we might have back in the old world. I need action, now—besides, you didn't give me a choice. I tried being nice and you spit in my face."

"That was your idea of nice?" Vincent laughed humorlessly. "You better recheck what the word actually means in the dictionary."

Gil held his hands out. "I'm giving you a chance to do some good and help the people here."

Dante crossed his arms. "Help them, or help you?"

Gil shrugged slightly. "Does it matter? The end result is the same."

"We would be helping the people here if we close the Gate. I guess that's not such a bad way of looking at things," said Elise.

"These are the same people that got so scared over a talking pug they were about to lynch us," Vincent said. "You think these shitheads need saving? Humanity's better off without them if you ask me."

Elise blinked, appalled. "Vincent! Why would you say that?"

Grandma answered for him. "Because Vincent's right. These people aren't worth risking our lives, and neither are you, Gil."

Gil chuckled. "And I'm supposed to be the bad guy here?" He motioned to Bill by the door, and the young man let the guard inside. "Take Betty back to the jail. We're moving out now."

"What are you doing with my grandmother?" Elise demanded.

Grandma placed a reassuring hand on Vincent's arm as he was about to protest, and shook her head. "Pick your fights. This isn't one of them."

Gil nodded to the guard. "Make sure to kill her if I'm not back by nightfall." He winked at the others. "A little insurance you don't try anything stupid while we're out there."

"You can't do that," Elise gasped.

The guard strode toward Grandma, and she quickly

turned to Vincent. "I'm counting on you to bring my granddaughter and Dante back alive. Make sure they don't do anything stupid."

Vincent nodded and watched the guard take her away, suddenly struck by how old and frail she looked, despite her tough demeanor.

Elise stepped forward. "At least let me say goodbye to her." But the guard forced her back at gunpoint and left the room. She whirled on Gil. "Please, she's my grandmother."

Gil retrieved his rifle from the other side of the table. "Then you better make sure I get back safe and sound," he said, offhandedly checking down the sights of the gun.

"Where are our weapons?" Dante asked.

"Do you really think we'd give weapons to creature-sympathizers like yourselves? Don't be ridiculous," Bill said, scoffing. "We're not risking you shooting us in the back."

Vincent blanched. "What are we supposed to do when we run into minotaurs and ghouls?"

Bill brushed his blue bangs aside, jeering in delight. "I hope you can run fast."

Chapter 11

A tense hour of trekking through the deserted remains of downtown Oakwood eventually led the group into a coffee shop. Across the street was City Hall, somehow tall and proud among the ruins that surrounded it. Wide steps led past a bronze statue of George Washington and into a domed building reminiscent of a miniature white house, complete with the tattered remains of an American flag fluttering in the cold wind atop it.

Flea sniffed the air. "Rain is coming."

Vincent pointed his nose up and breathed deeply. "I only smell coffee."

Flea patted his flattened nose cheerfully. "You'd be surprised what I can sniff out with this."

"Both of you shut up," Gil said calmly. He scanned their surroundings, then pointed at City Hall's steps. "If we follow those up it'll lead us to the main lobby. The Gate's in there."

Vincent took a half step out of the coffee shop and looked up and down the streets. Old blood stained the concrete, so it was obvious people had died here, but there wasn't a single body to be seen. He recalled what Flea had said about ghouls, that they eat the dead. The thought made his skin prickle uncomfortably.

"I thought you said the ghouls' nest was here," Bill said, fidgeting with a shotgun in his hands. "Why haven't we seen one yet?"

"There's still daylight, so they're sleeping somewhere," explained Gil.

"D-did you say these things have *nests*?" Elise asked in a strained whisper.

"For the most part," Flea said, tapping his chin thoughtfully. "Although some have been observed hunting and living on their own—quite fascinating, really—no one quite knows why. I'd love to study them one day."

Vincent gave Flea a disapproving frown. "You need new hobbies, Flea."

"Enough small talk. We're burning daylight." Gil led them out of the coffee shop and up City Hall's front steps.

Vincent paused by the statue of George Washington; deep marks scored the metal, erratic, like a rabid animal had attacked it. The ghoul he had seen had elongated claws in place of fingers. If one of those creatures had done that, how easily could they rip through unprotected flesh? He caught up to the others in a hurry.

Gil made them stop at the top of the steps, and as promised, they were staring directly into the lobby. Twenty yards ahead, past large Corinthian columns, and through busted rotating doors, was the Gate. It was almost twelve feet tall, its surface rippling and shimmering as it illuminated the darkened lobby with its preternatural light. It was beautiful in a way, mysterious and alluring. Vincent wondered what world awaited on the other side of the innocuous-looking thing.

"Amazing, simply amazing," Flea said, transfixed by the Gate like a moth to light. "It's . . . *perfect.* Just look at its alignment of energy. There isn't a single flaw to it! Only an extremely powerful sorceress could hope to create such a thing."

Gil nudged Flea forward with his foot. "Flea, Elise, and Dante, come with me. Vincent, you stay back here with Bill. Make sure nothing sneaks up on us."

Dante put a reassuring hand on Elise's shoulder. "I'm right behind you."

She nodded back, putting on a brave front, and they moved forward.

Flea practically ran to the Gate, his tail flapping in a blur of excitement. The pug jumped from one side to the other, babbling formulas and foreign jargon to himself—Vincent chuckled at the dog's enthusiasm.

"Ugh, disgusting. That dog's a freak of nature."

Vincent turned to Bill. "What's your problem? Flea's done nothing to you."

Bill made a face. "*Yet.* Don't you get it? It's us against them. Just you wait, that creature's going to get you when you let your guard down."

"From where I'm standing, it's you and Gil who I need to worry about."

"You're just being stupid. If you haven't figured it out yet, then I don't know what to tell you."

Vincent grinned. "I'm not stupid. I'm figuring out things just fine on my own." He wagged a finger at Bill. "No, what I can't figure out is why you thought dying your hair blue would distract people from how ugly you are."

The young man's ears turned bright red. "That's real mature of you, buddy. Why would you even say that?"

"Because *fuck you,* that's why." Vincent froze. "Did you hear that?"

Bill turned around and surveyed the empty streets. "Are you screwing with me?"

Vincent held his finger to his lips. "Shh! There, *listen!*"

Glass crunched nearby, barely discernible. Vincent searched the row of buildings across the street, but couldn't pinpoint its location. He caught a movement in his periphery and snapped his head in its direction; a loose brick tumbled off a rooftop and smashed against the sidewalk.

"What was that?" Bill held his shotgun loosely in one arm and squinted in the direction of the sound. "This damn city is falling apart."

Vincent tossed a whisper over his shoulder. "Guys? I don't think we're alone here." He turned to the Gate when no one answered. "*Guys!*" he repeated, as loud as he dared without attracting unwanted attention.

The others carried on, unperturbed. Gil, Elise, and Dante stood a safe distance away from the Gate while Flea worked. The pug sniffed the portal from various angles, then attempted to move his hand through it, but his hand hit something solid on the surface.

"Interesting . . . the Gate appears to only allow travel in one direction," Flea said.

Elise's body abruptly went rigid as if struck by lightning. The gate flickered and emitted a low, drawn-out groan that scared Flea and the rest away from it. Its watery surface bubbled violently and released jets of hissing vapor.

"What's happening? What are you doing to it?" Gil shouted.

"It's closing. The Gate is breaking apart," exclaimed Flea.

Elise grabbed at her head and swayed in place as the portal's groaning turned into a rattle. Her legs then gave out under her, and she collapsed onto her hands and knees. In the same instant, the Gate vanished in a cloud of smoke and dissipated into the air, leaving behind a small pile of pale blue crystals.

"That dog did it." A laugh bubbled up from Bill's throat. "That creature did it! It closed the Gate!"

Flea scratched his head and turned to the others with a shrug, more confused than accomplished.

"Did you do that?" asked Gil.

Flea shook his head.

Gil then focused his attention on Elise. "What's wrong with you?"

"My head feels groggy all of a sudden." Elise took Dante's hand and pulled herself onto her feet. "What happened? Did Flea close the Gate?"

In the confusion caused by the Gate's sudden closing, no one but Vincent noticed the ghoul that had appeared at the bottom of the steps.

Bill noticed the look on Vincent's face and followed his gaze. "What are you looking—" His sentence ended in a squeak.

The ghoul stared back at the two men, its great eye globes unblinking. Behind it, crawling out of the city's crevices and dark hiding places, appeared more ghouls. Their raw flesh, blackened and glistening with pus, was disgusting to behold, but Vincent couldn't turn away.

Bill whimpered something incoherent and pointed his shotgun at the nearest ghoul, his arms shaking uncontrollably.

"Stop," Vincent said through his teeth. "Don't shoot at it."

"I-I know w-what I'm doing," Bill said.

The ghoul tilted its head curiously and opened its gaping maw of a mouth with a low whisper, showing off rows of broken but jagged teeth.

Bill jabbed his gun toward it. "Stay back!"

The ghoul slunk back with a hiss.

"What's going on over there?" demanded Gil.

Vincent barely heard the question, his attention focused on the ghouls slowly closing in on them from all directions. "Just back away from them, nice and slow," he told Bill. "Don't provoke it."

"I said get back!" he shrieked at the ghouls.

He's not listening. He's too freaked out. Vincent watched the ghouls tighten their circle around them, effectively trapping them against City Hall. Vincent's body began dumping adrenaline into his blood, and he shook with anticipation. His heart beat like a primal drum, harkening his instincts back to a time when humans were just scared monkeys.

Gil appeared behind him. "Oh my god." He reached out to Bill. "Don't shoot!"

A ghoul ventured too close. Bill panicked. A single shot boomed and the ghoul flew back, clawing at its wound in agony and screaming as black blood spurted from its chest. Like a rising tide, the other ghouls joined in, their howls melding into a single terrifying sound that literally shook the air.

Vincent's voice pierced the sound with a single word. "RUUUN!"

Vincent, Gil, and Bill sprinted for City Hall. Dante took only half a second to understand the situation, and he practically dragged Elise deeper inside the building. Vincent reached down as he neared Flea and scooped him up without stopping.

Gil pulled out a flashlight when they passed a security checkpoint and plunged into a darkened hallway. His small light swept over offices and conference rooms until they hit a fork in the path.

Elise looked back, breathless, but with the color returning to her face. "Which way?"

The ghouls' screams reverberated off the walls around them, growing louder with every passing moment.

"It doesn't matter. Just keep moving!" Vincent turned right and started running. As they pounded down the hall, turning any which way, he had the horrible realization they were like rats in a maze. It would only take one wrong turn and they'd all be dead. He shook off the fear and pressed on with renewed vigor.

Vincent rounded another corner and skidded to a stop. A ghoul stood in his way, its yellow eyes glistening under Gil's flashlight. Vincent's heart jumped into his throat as the ghoul sprang forward. He had no time to react and watched in frozen terror as the monster flew through the air, spittle flying from its mouth and razor claws flexing for the kill.

At the last moment, Dante stepped into view and threw his whole body into a punch. His fist connected with the ghoul's jaw in a sickening crunch and sent it sprawling to the side in a heap. The creature twitched once, then lay motionless.

"Damn, that was close," Vincent murmured.

Dante flashed him a smile filled with bravado. "I got your back, little brother. Now come on!"

Vincent skirted around the ghoul and chased after the others. They ran through a few more lengths of hallway before stopping at the sound of ghouls coming from ahead. They turned back and heard more ghouls bringing up the rear.

"Over there!" Gil pointed out a door leading into an emergency stairwell.

They reached the second floor as a ghoul jumped out from a darkened corner, but Gil was quick on the draw and put it down in a hail of bullets. He turned his light on a door beside him and kicked it open.

The group burst into a dank hallway that reeked of death

and buzzing flies, the all-too-familiar scent of rotting meat clinging to their clothes and permeating every pore. The door closed behind them with a soft click, and it became eerily quiet.

Vincent noticed Elise leaning against the wall behind him, her eyes sunken, breathing haggard gasps. "You all right?" he asked. "I thought you said you were a runner."

She bobbed her head up and down, sending her loose curls spilling over her face. "I don't . . . know what's happening . . . so tired."

Gil moved to another door and grabbed the handle. "We have to keep moving."

As the door swung open, a wall of foul air hit Vincent square in the face, making him and everyone else gag. He covered his nose with his shirt—not that it did much—then followed Gil into a dim atrium. The floor wrapped around the edges and skylights in a high vaulted ceiling allowed a few rays of sunlight in.

Gil pointed his flashlight over the dark chasm, at a door on the other side. "There's our way out."

Vincent peered over the handrail and found the source of the horrid smell. Every inch of the floor beneath them was covered in flesh and bones. Half-eaten corpses and gnawed bones were piled high off the ground around pools of black liquid and organs; he was pretty sure he even saw some minotaurs down there.

Elise peeked and threw her face into Dante's chest with a muted squeak while Bill fell flat on his ass, babbling like an idiot.

Flea gulped audibly. "Oh dear. This has made a turn for the worse."

Vincent saw a lanky shape dart through the shadows. "What the hell is down there?"

"It makes sense now why so many ghouls attacked us," Flea said.

Vincent groaned inwardly. "What makes sense?"

"This is a ghoul nest. Every nest has a ghoulah."

He half-laughed, half-whimpered. "What's a ghoulah?"

"Every nest needs a den mother to give birth. The ghouls are defending her," Flea explained.

Something stirred among the bodies directly under them, and a slender arm stretched into view, pale and bony.

Vincent turned to the others and motioned for them to start making their way to the other door. They nodded their understanding and tiptoed forward, all the while listening to the ghoulah shuffling around. It occasionally made a horrible hacking sound, wet and phlegmy.

They made it to the other side, and he was beginning to think they were home free, when he sensed a presence behind him. His hair stood on end, and he looked back with a sinking feeling as a clawed hand gripped the handrail.

The ghoulah pulled her body up and perched on the ledge; a curtain of stringy fibers clung to her head and face, and two bulbous eyes peered at him. It resembled the other ghouls Vincent had seen, lanky and emaciated, with the exception of smooth, pearly-white skin and a distended abdomen.

"Get down!"

Vincent threw himself to the floor as Gil's assault rifle went off. Bullets shredded the ghoulah's body, sending the den mother reeling backwards with a high-pitched wail that left his ears ringing. Gil didn't let up his torrent of bullets until his gun clicked empty, and the ghoulah's smoking body fell to the first floor with a thud.

Vincent stood back up, and his body forced him to exhale a breath he had been holding. "Fuck ghouls, fuck this place, fuck everything. I never want—"

Something big flew over the handrail and landed behind him. The ghoulah's body was a messy red pulp, but she was still standing, and she was fucking pissed.

"Run, Vincent!" Dante roared.

Vincent turned on his heel and hauled ass faster than he had ever done in his life. Gil and Elise made it through the exit, but Dante waited at the door, beckoning frantically for him and Bill to move faster. Vincent glanced over his shoulder, expecting to see the ghoulah bounding after him. Instead, the ghoulah was gagging and pushing something big up through her throat. On pure instinct, Vincent threw his body to the side just as the ghoulah belched out a black glob. Bill turned at the noise and threw his arms up in surprise as a thick liquid hit him square in the chest, knocking him onto the floor with a yelp.

Vincent pressed on with a roar of defiance. He roughly tossed Flea forward through the door, then dove onto Bill's shotgun. He flipped onto his back in time to see the ghoulah flying at him. Vincent bared his teeth and pulled the trigger, catching the creature with the full force of the shot. The ghoulah flew back, screaming, and rolled into a broken pile.

Dante hoisted him up and clapped a heavy hand over his back. "You okay?"

Vincent gulped. "Y-yeah. I think so."

"Good. Give me a hand with him." Dante motioned at Bill. "Don't touch that stuff on his body."

Vincent nodded and they dragged Bill through the door, making sure to avoid the mysterious liquid splashed over his face and chest.

Vincent looked around the empty room. "Son of a bitch! Where are the others?"

"Gil must have taken them," said Dante, pointing to an open door.

"Oh god, what is this? Get it off!" Bill suddenly screamed.

Vincent looked down and saw him flailing on the ground in agony.

"Help me!" Bill pleaded. "It burns!" He clawed frantically at his face, screaming as smoke curled up from his body with a sadistic hiss. His screams quickly turned to awful gurgling.

Vincent watched in horrified silence as the ghoulah's spit burned through Bill's clothes and skin, eating a hole into his chest. The dying man swung his arms wildly as his hands melted into pulpy nubs and his jaw sagged to the side.

Something clicked in Vincent's brain and spurred him to action. He darted around the room, looking for something—anything—to wipe the acidic spit off Bill.

He heard the shotgun go off behind him.

He spun around and saw his brother standing over Bill, the shotgun pointed down. Little bits of blue and red formed concentric halos of gore around what remained of Bill's head. Vincent's mind buzzed. "What did you do?" he said, voice weak.

"There was nothing we could do," Dante said.

Vincent stormed up to him. "Bullshit! There was still a chance!"

"Was there?" His brother turned on him, eyes ablaze. "Look at him, Vincent!"

He hardly recognized Bill in the mutilated remains. He turned away from the sickly fumes bubbling up and walked away.

"Giving him a quick death was the only thing we could do," Dante said.

Vincent propped himself against the wall and shut his eyes as the room spun out of control.

"He was suffering." Dante waited for a response. "Vincent, say something damn it."

Vincent punched the wall. "This is so fucked! Fuck, fuck, fuck!" he screamed, punctuating every word with another punch until his hands were numb. He focused on the pain to try and calm himself, but his body trembled uncontrollably. "You did a good thing for him," Vincent said, his voice hoarse.

"We have to move on and find Elise and Flea."

"Okay."

They went to the only other door in the room and looked into a pitch-black hallway. Without any kind of lighting, there was no way to tell where it led.

"Can this get any fucking worse?" Vincent growled. He heard ghouls screech and howl from the atrium they came through. "Of course it can."

With no other choice, the brothers went through and shut the door, plunging themselves into an ocean of blackness. Vincent felt his brother's hand grab his shirt.

"Don't let go," he said. "Keep the wall on your right and just follow it."

"Okay," Vincent said, and they crept forward. It was a painfully slow and disorienting trip, but eventually his hand brushed against a door handle. "Let's see what's behind door number two," he muttered. He cracked it open and was delighted to find natural light on the other side.

"Vincent!" Elise yelled.

He threw the door open and saw her with Gil and Flea at the end of a wide marbled hall, basking in sunlight from a row of windows on either side.

Flea blew a sigh of relief. "Forbidden arcana, you're both alive. I feared the worst after Gil forced us to leave you behind."

The brothers jogged over to them, their shoes squeaking over the marble.

"What the hell were you thinking leaving us like that?" Vincent shouted.

Gil appeared lost in thought. "Where's Bill?" he asked.

"He's dead. You left your friend to die," Vincent spat.

"You think I would call a kid like that a friend?" Gil looked insulted.

"You son of a bitch." Anger boiled up inside Vincent and he lunged, but Dante grabbed him from behind.

"Stop!" his brother shouted.

Vincent struggled against Dante's superior strength. "I'm going to fuck this guy up! I swear to god, I'm going to break every bone in his body!"

A door banged open to their right and a ghoul spilled out. It saw them and turned too quickly, slipping, then slamming into the marble. Its clawed hands and legs lashed out wildly as it scrambled back up to attack them with a rabid fervor.

Gil stepped forward and aimed his gun, teeth gritted in an angry snarl. "These stupid animals just don't know when to stop!" He sprayed it with bullets, then turned the gun on a second ghoul as it ran through the door. The assault rifle clicked empty, and he threw it aside with a frustrated growl. "Just die already!" He whipped out a handgun and pumped out a few more bullets, finally killing it.

Vincent heard the hair-raising screams of more ghouls pour out of the open door. "How many more are there?" he moaned.

Gil checked his gun's magazine and shook his head. "Only eight more bullets left. We won't make it out of here with only eight bullets." He turned to Vincent. "We need a distraction."

Vincent's blood ran cold.

The muzzle of Gil's gun flashed twice. Vincent's right calf lit up in pain, and he fell over, crashing into the floor with a pained howl. A quick look down showed red pooling around a hole in his pants. *He shot me. The fucker actually shot me.* Vincent heard his brother bite back a scream and looked over. Dante was on his knees, his hands over his stomach, and his face contorted in pain.

"What did you do?" Elise screamed.

Vincent locked eyes with her for a split second. He yelled for her to run, but nothing came out. Gil appeared in his field of vision and grabbed a fistful of Elise's hair.

"Move, or I'll shoot you, too," Gil said.

"No!" Elise struggled to break free. "I'm not leaving without them!"

Gil blinked, speechless, but quickly regained his composure. He aimed the gun at Vincent and Dante. "Move, or I'll kill them right now."

She bit her lip and looked at Vincent, as if for help.

"Let's go!" Gil screamed. He grabbed Flea and pointed his gun at Elise. "I won't ask again!"

Elise grudgingly allowed herself to be herded to an emergency stairwell nearby.

"You can't do this," Vincent sputtered, but it was no use.

They were gone, and he and his brother were left behind as live bait.

Chapter 12

Fire burned its way up Vincent's leg, lighting up every nerve along the way in brilliant waves of agony. He ground his teeth together, shooting spittle everywhere with each stilted breath, and pushed himself up on his good leg. "Dante," he called, stumbling toward him as more ghouls howled their approach.

"He got me good," Dante replied in a shaky voice. He moved his hand away from his stomach, showing off an expanding bloodstain.

Vincent dragged his brother up onto his feet. "We got to get out of here."

Dante leaned into him. "No," he gasped. "Not until we get the others."

"We can barely walk, and you're worried about them right now?" Vincent laughed morosely with a shake of his head. "We're done. How can we make it out of here like this, let alone find Elise and Flea in this huge building?"

Dante put a hand on his shoulder. "Don't over think it.

They couldn't have gone far." He pressed his hand into his gut, hard, as if trying to stop his intestines from falling out, and then shuffled to the door Gil and Elise disappeared through.

Vincent limped after his brother, and they entered another dark stairwell and paused, wondering which way Gil had gone. A couple flights down, a ghoul entered the stairwell and began climbing up with unsettling, spiderlike movements.

"This way." Dante hunched over with a grimace and started up the stairs.

As they climbed the steps, the debilitating agony in Vincent's leg numbed to a dull throb. He quickened his pace and caught up to Dante, helping his brother the last few steps. The next floor opened into another office space, luckily with windows too.

Vincent turned at the sound of movement and saw sharp claws reach for him. "Shit!" He took a half step back and narrowly escaped getting his throat torn out.

The ghoul pounced on him with a scream and knocked him to the floor, then reached back to swipe at his face. Dante tackled the creature off and they fell into a tangled heap, wrestling for control of one another.

Vincent remembered how his brother had managed to knock out a ghoul with a single punch. He bolted upright and charged the ghoul, screaming, and swung with everything he had. His fist connected with the back of the ghoul's head, but instead of a satisfying crunch, he heard a dull thud. Vincent stumbled back, cradling his throbbing hand and cursing. It felt like he had hit a brick wall.

The ghoul turned its disgusting visage on him and charged. Through sheer luck, Vincent tripped over a chair and caused the ghoul to fly over him, missing by mere inches. He scrambled back to his feet and saw the ghoul preparing to jump again; exhausted and with no other ideas, he instinctively threw his palm up. "Stop!"

Miraculously, the ghoul paused and cocked its head.

"You got to be shitting me," Vincent murmured.

"AHH!" Dante flew forward with a wooden chair over his head and smashed it over the unsuspecting ghoul; the chair broke into pieces, leaving a sharp stake in his hand. He took one look at it, then plunged it into the dazed creature's chest with a bestial roar. Dante held it there with both hands, pinning the squirming ghoul to the floor until it stopped struggling and died.

Vincent and Dante faced each other; they were bloody, beaten, exhausted, their wits frayed, but they were still alive. Their lips twisted into crazed grins and they laughed. They laughed and laughed, partly in fear, partly in defiance—a primal response to overcoming imminent death.

Vincent turned to the stairwell and heard more ghouls clambering up. The sound sobered them up, fast. He and Dante stumbled away, navigating their way through more empty offices and conference rooms, barricading doors behind them as they passed through.

Vincent was in the middle of sliding a flagpole through the handles of a double door when his brother tapped him on the shoulder.

"Do you hear that?"

He craned his ear and heard faint pops from the floor below.

Gunshots.

"They're close by."

They took off with a renewed energy, following the signs to a staircase going down. At the bottom steps they found evidence of Gil's handiwork, dead by a window.

Vincent nudged the ghoul with his foot. "They have to be here."

They wandered the floor, passing by high-rising doors made of dark, polished wood, until they finally heard what they were searching for. Harsh whispers came from behind one of the heavy doors. Vincent nodded at Dante, and they pushed it open with strained grunts. Light from behind them poured in and illuminated an oval office with tiered seating, and standing in the center of it all, stunned, were Elise, Gil, and Flea.

Elise's face lit up. "Oh my god, you're both alive!"

"Forbidden arcana, you two are unkillable," Flea said, squirming under Gil's arm.

Gil turned his gun on them with a smirk. "I'd be lying if I said I wasn't a little bit impressed."

"We survive. It's what we do, like cockroaches," said Vincent. He motioned at Gil's gun. "How many shots do you have left? You plan on wasting them on us when you got so many ghouls running around?"

"Only if I have to." Gil waved Vincent and Dante away from the door. "Out of the way."

The two groups skirted around the room until they had swapped positions.

Gil barked a contemptuous laugh. "You really didn't think this out. What were you expecting to happen once you found us?"

Vincent glowered. Admittedly, he hadn't even considered the possibility they would find each other.

"I'm not letting you run off with them again," Dante said.

Gil's eyes opened in mock surprise. "Really? Because that's exactly what's happening."

Flea bared his canines and chomped down on Gil's hand. He yelled and dropped Flea; the pug plopped onto his stomach and scampered over to Vincent and Dante, spitting and looking mildly disgusted.

"Fucking mongrel!" Gil's eyes flew open in a rage and he made to shoot, but Elise grabbed him by the head and thrust her forehead into his nose. He howled in pain and stumbled back, clutching his face. "You bitch!"

Elise shook her head, dazed, but saw Gil had dropped his gun. She grabbed it before he could and pointed it at him. "Don't move!"

Vincent cheered inside, completely surprised by the sudden turn of events. "How's *your* nose feel, you piece of shit?"

Gil held his nose and blew out a glob of bloody mucous, and then started laughing.

"W-w-what's so funny?" Elise stammered.

"You got me pretty good there, Elise." He took a step toward her.

"Don't!" she warned, backing away.

"What're you going to do? Shoot me?"

Vincent saw her hands shaking and knew she couldn't do it—Gil knew it, too. Vincent rushed forward and grabbed the gun from her. She was only too happy to be rid of it.

Gil froze and hate seeped into his eyes. "So are you going to kill me now?"

"I should. You sacrificed Bill, and you were going to sacrifice me and my brother."

"I didn't have a choice," Gil spat.

Vincent's finger hovered over the trigger, his vision clouding over in fury.

"Do it," he goaded.

He wanted to, he really did, but he couldn't budge his finger.

Veins popped out on Gil's neck. "DO IT!"

"No!" Dante put a firm hand on Vincent's arm and pointed the gun down. "If we kill him now, Grandma will die, too."

"What are you talking about?" Vincent growled, keeping his eyes on Gil.

"You remember what he told the guard? He has orders to kill Grandma if Gil doesn't make it back alive." Dante gently pried Vincent's fingers open and took the gun.

"Smart man." Gil gave them a fake smile. "I like you, Dante. You're a forward thinker. The world needs more people like you."

Ghouls screeched in the distance, and Dante took a step back. "Get in," he ordered.

"Sorry, but I'm no one's prisoner." Without warning, Gil took off down the hall.

"Stop!" Vincent made to chase, but Dante stopped him.

"We can't. The ghouls are coming," his brother said. "Help me close the door."

"Damn it." Vincent shut the double doors, and moments later, the ghouls stampeded by.

"Will Gil die out there?" Elise whispered.

"I hope so," said Vincent.

"Whether he lives or dies, he just made this a whole lot more difficult for us." Dante cracked the door open and found the hall empty. "We have to make it back to the apartment before nightfall, for Grandma's sake." He looked back, face pale but set in a stony glare. "And pray that if Gil somehow makes it out, he doesn't beat us there."

Fate finally conspired in their favor. They navigated to the back of City Hall and found a fire escape down to the street. The sun warmed their bodies as they climbed into a thin alley, free of any ghouls. Then they ran. They ran as fast as their battered bodies allowed, unsure of where to go so long as it was away from that hellish place, and eventually stumbled upon a drugstore.

Dante motioned to a door at the back of the building, and the others followed him to it. Vincent made a pit stop behind the register and grabbed a bottle of alcohol, a pack of cigarettes, and a lighter before joining the others. Dante opened the door into a cramped office and everyone piled in; he locked it behind them, and for the first time since stepping foot into the ghouls' nest, they felt safe.

Vincent slumped to the floor, exhausted in a way he had never experienced before, like his body could switch off at any moment. He screwed the cap off his bottle and drank deeply, savoring the distinct taste of vodka.

Elise cried out in surprise and yanked it from his lips.

"What the hell? Give it back," he demanded.

"You're bleeding out. Drinking is just going to make it worse," she said.

He eyeballed her first and then his bloody leg. "Fine," he said tersely. "But I'm having a smoke, and you're not stopping me." He unwrapped the cigarettes and, after a few shaky attempts, managed to light one in his mouth. He took a deep puff, and a visible shudder went through him; he held the smoke in his lungs, then let it out slowly through his nostrils.

Dante stumbled forward and almost fell over, but Elise was there to catch him. "Sorry," he mumbled. "I'm just feeling a little lightheaded."

Elise studied his face, then lifted his shirt.

"What're you doing?" Dante asked, slurring his words.

"We need to stop this bleeding," Elise said. She gently lowered him into a chair in the corner and inspected his gunshot wound. "It passed through clean, which is good, but there's no way to tell if it hit anything serious going through. Either way, I need to get you and your brother patched up. Wait here." She hurried out for supplies.

Flea plopped down on his butt with a weary sigh. "What a day. Simply exhausting." He reached inside his robe and pulled out his pipe with a roguish wink. "Those fools didn't check *all* my pockets when they took my potions." Flea snapped his fingers, and a small flame sprouted on the tip of his thumb, which he used to stoke his pipe.

"That's a neat party trick. How come you needed my help lighting your pipe back in my bedroom?" Vincent asked.

Flea held his flaming thumb out with mild delight. "Forbidden arcana, my magic is working."

"Didn't you say you needed a staff to do magic?"

Flea puffed on his pipe and exhaled through the side of his mouth. "I do for my more powerful spells, but I am able to do the basics without it—permitted the energies aren't too chaotic."

Vincent frowned. "What 'energy' are you talking about?"

"It's all around us. I wouldn't expect you to understand since you are neither a wizard nor a sorceress." Flea hummed. "Imagine, if you can, the energy as particles floating in the air. If you wish to do magic, you must align these particles in the correct patterns and flows."

Vincent had a hard time imagining these particles without the aid of hardcore psychedelics. "So these energies were too chaotic back at my house?"

"They've been chaotic everywhere since the moment I stepped paw in this world." Flea flicked the flame on and off of his thumb like a magic lighter. "Interestingly enough, the energies are calm now."

A troubling thought occurred to him. "So what happened at the Gate?"

"I'm afraid I don't know. I certainly had nothing to do with it closing . . . it just sort of fell apart." The flame on Flea's thumb went out and he growled in frustration. "There it goes again. The magical energies have become chaotic."

Elise walked into the room with various bottles and bandages. She set her supplies down on the floor and looked Vincent over. "How are you doing?"

He got a good laugh out of that. "How am I doing? Well, let's see . . . I've had my nose broken, I've been shot, I almost died multiple times today . . . I'm doing fucking great, Elise."

"You're obviously well enough to be a smartass about it." She turned her attention to Dante, who had dozed off, and began working on him. She pulled his shirt off and wiped his torso down, being extra gentle around his oozing wound. Elise used a pair of medical forceps to pick debris out of the hole, occasionally wiping it down with disinfectant, and then began taping and bandaging his torso. When she was done, she traced her hands over his abs, perhaps a little longer than necessary.

"You mind not feeling him up right in front of me?" Vincent smirked and took a steadying puff of his cigarette.

Her face turned bright red. "I'm just making sure everything's nice and tight."

"Relax. I'm just giving you a hard time."

"You're such a fucking asshole, Vincent."

"Wow, look at you using your big girl words. Good for you," he said, giving her a patronizing slow clap.

"You're rubbing off on her," Dante croaked. He cracked

open an eye and gave him a lopsided grin.

Vincent shrugged. "What can I say? I bring out the worst in people. It's a gift."

Elise gently patted Dante on the cheek and offered him a small handful of pills. "Take these. It'll help with the pain."

He allowed her to feed him the pills in her hand. "Thanks, you're a lifesaver."

Elise blushed. "Don't mention it." She turned her focus to Vincent and began work on his leg, though noticeably rougher than she had been with Dante.

After she had patched the brothers up, they took only a moment's rest. As exhausted as they all were, they had to keep moving.

Dante walked into the street and read a nearby street sign. "I have an idea of where we are. If we go now, we can make it back to the apartment in an hour."

"What's the plan? They aren't going to just give us Grandma," Vincent said.

Dante held up the gun they had stolen from Gil. "We've got a couple shots left in this."

"Great, so we got two shots, and they have a whole armory."

Dante shrugged. "Well, then, we better get real creative, real fast."

Chapter 13

Following Dante, their group made it back to Oasis Gardens with daylight to spare.

Vincent stopped outside the front doors and regarded his brother. "You really think this is going to work?"

He shrugged. "It's the best chance we got."

"Best chance, not to be confused with a good chance," Flea mused beneath them. "There are too many things that could go wrong."

"Shut up, Flea. Leave that cynical shit to me," said Vincent. "But yeah, what he said."

Elise stepped between them. "Think positive thoughts!"

Vincent sneered at her. "This isn't a game, Elise. If you screw up, it's over."

"I won't!" she said with a huff. "I'm not helpless. Don't forget who disarmed Gil back at City Hall."

Vincent conceded that the way she had head-butted Gil was really badass, but he wasn't about to show it outright. "Let's just get this over with," he said, adjusting a small pack of supplies they had brought from the drugstore.

Their plan was simple. The first step involved finding an alternate entrance to the eighth floor. Vincent went to the emergency stairs they had first used with Natalie, but instead of climbing them, made his way to the opposite end of the building. The size of the building meant there would be more than one set of emergency stairs, and a quick search turned up another one.

The climb up was particularly hard for Vincent. The adrenaline had worn off, and his leg hurt with every step. He blinked back a wave of weariness and suddenly felt nauseous.

Elise appeared beside him and put herself under his arm to give support. "Are you going to be okay?"

Dante looked back, ashen and glistening with sweat. "We can take a quick break," he croaked.

Dante looked like absolute dog shit, but if his brother was still moving, then so could he. Vincent gently pushed Elise back. "I'm fine."

When they made it to the eighth floor, Dante tried the door. It didn't budge, but they had expected that. Most likely something barricaded it from the other side.

The second part of their plan was getting someone to open the door for them.

"You remember your lines?" Vincent asked.

Elise nodded and took her place in front of the door; Vincent and Dante pressed their backs flat against the wall on either side of the door, while Flea found a safe spot to hide.

She blew out a nervous breath, then banged against the

door. "Help! Somebody help me!" She paused, waiting for a response. "What if they don't believe me, Vincent? I've never done any kind of acting before," she whispered.

"Your motivation is Grandma will die if you don't fucking make this believable," he hissed.

Elise banged against the door harder. "Somebody please help me! I'm hurt!"

Vincent heard a commotion from the other side.

"Who's there?" a muffled voice asked.

Elise gulped. "Please open the door. Help me," she said, softer, and injecting emotion into her words—even going so far as to work up a choking sob.

A second voice said, "We aren't supposed to open this door. Use the other entrance."

"I can't move anymore. It's my leg," she wailed. "I'm so scared." Elise sounded so pathetic and vulnerable it almost tugged at Vincent's own heartstrings.

The two voices deliberated, and then something heavy slid across the floor. Elise quickly fell to the floor and grabbed her leg.

The door swung in, and a dim light washed over her.

"Who the hell are you?" a man asked.

Elise smiled graciously. "Thank you so much. Can you help me up?"

The unwitting man took a cautious step out. He was armed, but his gun was held loosely in his hands.

She reached out to him, her eyes round and doleful.

"Careful. I don't recognize her," another man said.

"Would you relax? Look at her, she's hurt." He moved

forward and grabbed Elise's outstretched hand. "Everything's going to be fine. I've got you." As he helped her up, his more cautious partner appeared through the door.

Vincent and Dante nodded at each other from the shadows, and the two moved like twin vipers, striking in unison. Dante grabbed the closest one from behind, wrapping one arm around his neck while simultaneously disarming him; the poor sap yelped in surprise, grabbing the attention of the man helping Elise, but Vincent was already on him. The brothers held their targets with vise grips, squeezing their necks tighter and tighter until they finally stopped struggling.

"Can't you be gentler?" Elise mumbled. "I feel awful enough as it is taking advantage of their kindness like this."

Vincent unceremoniously dropped his guy on the ground with a heavy sigh. "They'll be fine." He slid the pack off his shoulder and took out a bundle of zip ties and duct tape.

He and Dante restrained the men's hands and legs as they gradually regained consciousness. One of them turned to Vincent and recognition dawned on his face.

"It's you!"

"Sure is, pal. Now do me a favor and shut the hell up." Vincent slapped a piece of duct tape over his mouth.

"You've done this before, haven't you?" Elise asked, suspicious.

Vincent picked up their captives' guns and tossed one to Dante. "A couple times," he explained. "But only for things I needed."

"Why?" she demanded.

Vincent grew angry at the judgment in her voice. "It must be so easy for you to look at me from your high horse like that. Have you ever wanted for anything in your life? Do you know how much it hurts to go without food for even a week, or what it's like to sleep under an overpass in the middle of winter?"

Dante put his hand over Vincent's chest. "Stop it. She's not going to understand, and you getting angry at her about it isn't going to help her to."

"Sorry I brought it up," Elise murmured.

Dante searched through the bound men's pockets until he found a key. "Perfect."

Vincent peeked inside, checking the deserted corridor for others. The path to his right led up front, where he could hear a steady stream of activity; on his left was the makeshift jail Gil had kept them in. "The coast is clear."

Using the confiscated key, Dante quickly unlocked the door. "Grandma," he whispered, thumbing a flashlight on. "Grandma, where are you?"

There was no answer.

"Maybe she's asleep or something. Let's just go in and get her," Vincent said.

They piled inside and did a quick search of the space, but turned up nothing.

"I don't understand. Did they put her in another room?" Elise asked.

Vincent realized with crushing clarity that it was too easy—too convenient—getting to this point.

"You're all so predictable."

All eyes turned to the front door.

Gil stood in the doorway, a little bloodied and beaten up, but alive.

Vincent instinctively raised his gun, but stopped short of pulling the trigger. "You son of a bitch."

A sadistic smile spread across his face. "That's your problem. It's too easy to get leverage on you." He stepped aside and revealed Grandma, held at gunpoint by Roach.

"No . . . that's—that's not fair," Elise said around a moan.

Gil waved impatiently. "Slide the guns over."

Vincent and Dante did so reluctantly.

He looked down at the weapons, then back to them. "Don't make me say it again," he snarled. "All of your fucking weapons."

Vincent muttered under his breath and drew Gil's stolen handgun from behind his waist. "This is all we got." He crouched down and slid it over, then put his hands up as a show of peace. "Don't hurt her, please."

"That's a good boy. No one needs to get hurt here." Gil grabbed Grandma by her shirt and threw her inside.

Elise dashed forward and caught her grandmother mid-fall. The older woman looked past her at Vincent and Dante. "Jesus Christ, what happened to you two?"

"I shot them," Gil said bluntly.

Grandma whirled on him, puffed up like an angry mother hen. "You did *what* to my boys? You little shit!"

"Don't raise your voice at me," Gil said. "There's

nothing I hate more than being talked down to."

Vincent gnashed his teeth in frustration. "Why shouldn't we? You tried to kill us."

"And yet you're standing here, alive and well. What's the big deal?"

"Go to hell," said Vincent.

Something dangerous glinted in Gil's black eyes, and he stormed inside; he shoved Vincent to the floor and ground his heel into Vincent's bandaged leg with a vicious snarl. Vincent pressed his mouth shut and held his scream in his throat, valiantly denying Gil the satisfaction until he got bored and lifted his foot up.

"Don't talk to me like that, Vincent. I am the king of this domain, and you are nobody. If you ever disrespect me again, I promise I'll put a bullet in between your eyes."

Vincent fought the urge to spit in his face. "You're getting off on this, aren't you?"

Gil contemplated the question, then smiled. "I'm just doing what needs to be done to keep my people safe." He squatted down to be eye level with Vincent. "Do me a favor, Roach, and grab the box."

Roach arched an eyebrow. "You mean the one with the necklaces?"

"That's the one," Gil said.

He shrugged. "Not sure why you need them, but hey, you're the boss."

Vincent watched Roach leave, suddenly apprehensive. "What box is he getting?"

Gil completely ignored the question. "Do you even

realize what's at stake here?"

"Enlighten me," Vincent said.

"The future of the human race." Gil made a grand gesture around him. "You've seen what's happening out there. The world as we knew it is over, and if we're not careful, we'll go the same way as the dinosaurs."

Grandma snorted derisively. "You're going to save the world?"

He nodded. "It's got to be me."

Roach returned with a wooden box in his arms. "Here it is, Gil."

"Open it."

Roach set the box down and lifted the lid. A white glow poured out, washing the apartment in an eerie light. His jaw dropped. "I don't believe it. I thought we killed all of them." He reached inside and pulled out a glowing necklace.

Vincent's mind flashed back to his encounter with Kojo and immediately recognized it.

Roach stared at the glowing lump of silver in awe. "Do you know who it is?"

Gil smirked. "Of course I do."

"What'll we do? The thunderbirds won't be ready for at least a few more months," Roach said excitedly.

Vincent seethed, caught somewhere between exhausted delirium and blind fury. He had no clue what a thunderbird was, but his gut said it was something to be worried about.

Elise shielded her eyes against the light. "I don't understand. What is that thing?"

"You don't need to understand." Gil motioned at Roach.

"Put the necklaces away and meet me in the armory. We have a lot of planning to do."

Roach snapped the lid back on the box and left in a hurry.

Gil frowned at Dante. "You're not looking so good."

Dante's head dipped as if he was dozing off. "Don't know what you're talking about."

Elise held her hand to his forehead. "Oh no . . . You're burning up." She looked to Gil. "He needs help—medicine, food, water, and rest."

"We're in short supply of those. A shame. I like you, Dante. You have conviction, you're ruthless." Gil shrugged and turned to leave. "If he's as strong as I think he is, maybe he'll pull through on his own."

"Please, don't go! What do you want? I'll do whatever you ask, just help Dante," Elise implored.

Gil paused at the door. "Don't worry. I'll find a use for all of you."

"Wh-what's that supposed to mean?" she asked.

Gil chuckled and locked the door behind him.

"That fucking egomaniac," Grandma spat. "Who does he think he is?"

Elise put herself under Dante's arm. "Vincent, help me get your brother to the bed. He needs to rest, badly, and you do too."

She was right. His body was on the verge of switching off, whether he liked it or not. Vincent helped her carry Dante into the bedroom and set him down on the bed.

Dante shook his head, his eyes unfocused. "I'll be fine.

Don't worry about me."

Elise put her finger over his lips. "Don't talk. Just sleep."

Vincent's eyes drooped, and he found a spot in the corner of the room to slump into. As he slipped into unconsciousness, all he could think was how he should've killed Gil when he had the chance.

Chapter 14

Vincent awoke with a start. The nub of a candle burned valiantly on the bedside table, its flickering light making shadows dance over the walls. For a fleeting moment, he thought it had all been a dream, a prolonged nightmare he was finally waking up from, but reality quickly set in when he saw his brother fighting to breathe on the bed. Dante's shirt was soaked with sweat, and his chest shuddered with every labored breath; his eyes darted wildly under his eyelids, perhaps caught in a nightmare himself.

Grandma sat in a chair beside the bed, her head slumped into her chest. She stirred and sucked in a stuttering snore, but didn't wake. Elise was asleep also, kneeling against the bed with her head in her folded arms. They must have fallen asleep watching over Dante.

Vincent noticed Flea staring at the door, the dog's ears perked attentively. "What are you doing?" he asked.

"You don't hear that?" Flea asked. "Someone is opening the front door."

"Is it too much to ask for just one goddamn night of rest?" Vincent pushed himself off the floor with a muted sigh of pain, then shuffled to the bedroom door. His vision was blurry and his head felt fuzzy, like his senses were being smothered under a wet blanket. Vincent wanted nothing more than to pound back some painkillers and sleep forever, but he forced himself into a state of awareness. There was no telling what that crazy bastard Gil was planning, but he needed to be ready for it.

Vincent cracked open the door and confirmed his fears; someone's silhouette filled the entryway. He searched the room for some kind of weapon. His brain struggled to come up with something, and he began to contemplate throwing the dog at them, when a woman's voice interrupted his thoughts.

She said in a hushed tone, "Is that you, Vincent?"

"N-Natalie?" he said, nonplussed. "What are you doing here?"

Flea moved next to Vincent's leg and forced his head through the crack, pushing the door open. "Why, hello, Natalie! What a pleasant surprise seeing you here this evening."

"Thank the Lord, I thought you were dead," Natalie said, straining her words as she dragged in something heavy.

Vincent batted Flea back inside. "Wait here." He walked into the hall and pointed to the shape behind her. "What's that?" Natalie blew out a big breath, and he saw an extra pair of arms flail limply as she let a body thump onto the floor.

"Shit, I hope no one else heard that," she said.

Vincent approached the body and recognized their guard, alive but unconscious; someone had done a number on the back of his head. "What is this?"

Natalie crouched over the man and poked his face. "I knocked him out real good, apparently. I hope I didn't give him brain damage."

"Why would you knock him out?" Vincent wondered. He squinted around suspiciously, waiting for Gil to appear. "Why are you here?"

"Not so loud," Natalie whispered, wincing. She carefully closed the door behind her, then turned around and tossed a backpack to Vincent's feet. "This is all I could put together."

"What is this? What did you put together?"

"Supplies would be my guess," Flea said.

Vincent spun around and scowled at the pug. "I thought I told you to wait in the room."

Flea folded his arms and eyed him defiantly. "I only take orders from Sorceress Epoch. Besides, we've already determined it's our friend, Natalie, and she's come to set us free."

Vincent turned back to her. "Did you really?"

She snorted. "Boy, you sure are slow. I thought that was pretty obvious."

He shook the last cobwebs out from his head and pieced everything together—knocking out the guard, sneaking in during the middle of the night, bringing supplies—of course. "It's been a rough couple of days," Vincent murmured. "Cut me some slack."

"Best not to be lollygagging around," Natalie said seriously. "Flea, be a darling and wake the others."

Vincent turned to watch Flea jog to the bedroom, then focused back on Natalie. She looked up from the open backpack with a pistol held out for him. "You know how to use one of these?"

"I've got practice." Vincent took the gun from her.

"Good. Be careful, that's designed to take forty-cal bullets. It can shoot nine millimeters too, but you'll run a risk of it failing to eject, and you're not going to want that when you got a minotaur charging you."

He tucked the gun into his pants with a nod. "Didn't know you could mix bullets like that."

Natalie zipped up the backpack. "My daddy was a bit of a gun enthusiast. I guess I was bound to pick up some things."

Vincent heard the others waking from their slumber in the bedroom. "You're taking a big risk helping us get away. Why?"

Natalie chuckled under her breath. "You shouldn't look a gift horse in the mouth," she said.

"Not a lot of room for trust nowadays." Vincent's eyes narrowed. "If you really wanted to help, you could have done it sooner. Why now?"

She put her hands on her hips with a sigh. "Gil told us he was going to stop the ghouls with your help."

"Our help?" he said incredulously. "I don't know if you noticed, but we weren't given much of a damn choice about it. I guess that was fine, though, so long as you benefited from it."

Natalie squirmed in discomfort. "I'm sorry, Vincent. I knew it was wrong—we all knew—but we were scared. Hell, you know what it's like out there, how many of us have died."

Flea emerged from the bedroom with the others. "We're ready to leave," he said.

Natalie lowered her voice to a whisper, so only Vincent could hear. "Self-preservation is a hell of a thing, makes people crazy. What would you have done?"

What would I have done? Vincent turned away, knowing full well what the answer was.

Dante was barely standing and leaned heavily onto Elise for support. Vincent hurried over and put himself under Dante's other arm to lessen the burden. Together, they dragged him to the door.

Elise stopped to give Natalie a deep smile. "Thank you so much. Really, I can't thank you enough for this."

Dante gave Natalie a weak thumbs-up. "I guess we're even now."

"You can call us even when you all make it out of here alive." Natalie gave the backpack to Grandma, then opened the door. She made sure the hall was clear before beckoning them forward. Natalie led them through the deserted corridor to the main stairwell entrance. The barricade had been moved, and there were no guards posted.

Natalie turned to Vincent. "See? We aren't all heartless bastards." She gave a flashlight to Grandma and waved them through. "Go, quickly."

Elise stopped at the door. "Aren't you coming with us?"

Natalie shook her head. "There are some decent folks that I need to get first."

Vincent called to her as she turned to leave. "Go north until you hit the water. Follow it west and you'll find Blossom Island." He didn't wait for a response and led the way out.

They were greeted by the gentle pitter-pattering of a light drizzle outside Oasis Gardens. Ominous clouds roiled overhead, and a current of lightning coursed through the sky, momentarily lighting up the city with a thunderous boom.

Dante pulled himself away from Vincent and Elise. She tried getting under his arm, but he gently pushed her away with a shake of his head. "We won't make it far if you two have to drag my heavy ass around. I'll walk."

"You can barely stand as it is, and you have a nasty fever," Elise said.

Dante hunched over his gut and marched ahead. "We don't have a choice. When Gil realizes we're gone, he's going to come after us, you can count on that. If he catches us, my fever is going to be the least of our problems."

Elise bit her lower lip, but nodded.

Within a couple hours they had left behind the skyscrapers of downtown and swapped them for the middling homes of suburbia. The threat of Gil giving chase spurred them onward, but the weather had other ideas and turned their hasty escape into a dogged march.

The light drizzle they had started in became a full-blown

storm. Raindrops the size of gumballs pelted their faces while cold winds gusted around, forcing icy needles into their very bones. The streets transformed into gurgling streams and waterlogged their shoes, so every step made a *schloop* sound.

Vincent hugged himself for warmth, his head down against the rain and shivering miserably as he groused quietly to himself. Something heavy splashed ahead of him and interrupted his thoughts. He squinted through the torrent and saw his brother in a puddle of water.

"D-D-Dante!" Vincent cried out, his teeth chattering uncontrollably. He rushed forward and kneeled beside him, ignoring the dull pain in his leg.

Dante's eyes peeled open weakly. "I must've slipped," he whispered, his voice barely audible over the rain. "Get me up, Vincent. We have to . . . we have to get to Blossom . . ." His voice trailed off and his head lolled to the side. "I'm so tired."

Vincent looked up and saw the others soldiering ahead, oblivious. "Come back! Help!" he screamed.

Elise and Grandma took one look at the situation and hurried to his aid. Dante was practically dead, and it took their combined efforts to carry him into a nearby house. Vincent kicked the door open to a deserted living room, and they set him down on the couch.

"Why didn't you say anything?" Vincent felt Dante's face, boiling hot to the touch. "You idiot, you're going to run yourself into the ground."

Dante regained consciousness, and his eyes fluttered open. "Where am I?" He groaned and tried moving, but grabbed his stomach with a pained howl.

Seeing his brother semiconscious, delirious, and in so much pain wrapped a tight coil of fear around Vincent's heart. He didn't have to be a doctor to know his brother was in serious trouble. "Is he going to be okay?" he asked no one in particular.

Elise put on a brave face, but Vincent noticed she couldn't meet his eye. "He just needs some rest. Hopefully he'll be better by morning."

Flea wrung his small hands nervously. "If only I had access to the lab. I could brew up a potion to help," he lamented. "This is infuriating. I feel so useless!"

Grandma looked up from the backpack, empty-handed. "Nothing in here but food and water." She kneeled beside Dante and wiped the water from his face. "You're a damned fool, boy. You should have known your body couldn't keep up," she said softly.

A sudden shiver went through Dante's body, and he curled up into a ball, groaning.

Grandma tossed Vincent her flashlight. "You go find some blankets. Elise, you go find dry clothes for all of us before we freeze to death."

"What about me?" Flea asked. "I must help, too."

Grandma gave a rare smile. "Find me a pot I can boil some water in."

The group hunkered down for the night, feasting on a dinner of canned beans while dressed in strangers' clothes. After their meal, Vincent started a fire in a large cooking pot and set it down between them as a makeshift campfire. No one felt much like talking. Flea had passed out in a recliner with bean sauce all over his face, and Elise opted to skip dinner and sleep on the floor beside Dante.

Vincent watched his brother through the fire in silent contemplation; Dante looked like he was burning—a Viking on a funeral pyre. It was a ridiculous thought. Dante couldn't die. Ever since they were kids, he could count on his older brother. He was a constant, like gravity. It didn't matter how bad things got because Dante would always be there to pull him out.

Always.

Or so it always felt.

"Doesn't feel real, does it?"

Vincent turned to Grandma. "What?"

The flames danced in her glasses as she stared into the fire. "You never really think about it. Everyone dies eventually, we know that, but it doesn't feel real until it's knocking at your fucking front door." She shrugged. "Isn't that just the most fucked-up thing? You don't realize what you have until it's too goddamn late."

Vincent clenched his jaw, disappointed by his own ignorance. He walked to the couch and stood over Dante. Tonight was a grim reminder that his brother wasn't invincible.

"You shouldn't beat yourself up over it," Grandma said.

Vincent remained motionless. "I was watching him the whole time. I knew. I should have made us stop sooner."

"Don't you worry, Vincent. He'll pull through. The kid's

tough. How else could you have both survived in Oakwood?"

He gave a tired sigh. "You helped us out."

"A bit here and there," Grandma said. "But your brother did the bulk of it. He had to raise himself and you in this shithole city. That's a burden I wouldn't wish on any kid."

Vincent sensed movement and looked down at his brother.

Dante shook his head, eyes squeezed tight. "No," he mumbled. "No, no." He began thrashing on the couch, repeating the same word with increasing intensity.

Vincent grabbed him by the shoulders and tried to hold him still. "Relax, Dante, relax," he cooed. "I got you."

Dante's bloodshot eyes flew open, and he grabbed Vincent's arm. His eyes were unfocused, like he saw through Vincent to someone else. "I never meant to kill you, Tommy. It was an accident. I shouldn't have started that fight, but you got to believe me. It was an accident."

"I know—we all know. You were drunk, he was drunk— it was just a stupid mistake."

Dante blinked, and his eyes came into focus. He did a double take as if seeing him for the first time, then dropped his head back down with a sigh. "I'm not a murderer. I'm not."

Vincent hummed his understanding. "No one's saying you are."

Dante's eyes grew heavy, and his grip loosened. "I don't want to be a bad person, Vincent. I don't want to . . . I can't . . . won't . . ." He drifted into a restless slumber.

***

"Here it is!" Bo exclaimed, gesturing grandly.

Xifeng stepped out of the car, her eyes transfixed on their new home.

It was a tiny place, not even one thousand square feet. A yard of dead grass and weeds lay on either side of the pathway up the middle, split by age. Its seafoam-green walls were scored with black marks and peeling in places, and someone had taken the liberty of writing "Fuck pigs!" on the side in neon-red spray paint.

Bo's initial excitement quickly turned to apprehension when his wife didn't say anything. "I know it's not much to look at now, but I'm going to fix it up!" Her continued silence made him more anxious, and he began to babble. "I got a really good deal on it. With all the money we saved, I can put it toward renovating the house. There's even a backyard—well, it's more like a deck, but I could tear that out and make space for you to garden. I know how much you like gardening."

He followed Xifeng to the front door and let her in. Before going inside himself, he looked out at the street and chewed on his lip nervously. What was he thinking, buying a home in Oakwood? He watched a couple men with shifty eyes walk by.

Bo gulped, already regretting his hasty purchase. The realtor had made it seem like such a good deal at the time. He closed the front door behind him and went up to Xifeng. The carpet in the living room was a grimy shade of black except in spots where furniture had been. Bo walked into the corner and pulled up the carpet, showing her the scuffed wood underneath. "I was thinking we could just get rid of the carpet entirely and have wood floors, what do you think? Wouldn't it look nice? Xifeng?"

She wandered into the connecting kitchen.

Bo wasn't sure if her silence meant stunned amazement or utter disappointment, but he noticed her eyes lingering on the kitchen cabinets. "Look at this," he said, pulling out a crumpled piece of paper. He opened it up on the counter; it was a page from a home improvement magazine. "I saw you looking through this the other day," he explained, pointing at the designer kitchen displayed. "I might not be very smart, but I can make these cabinets for you. It'll look beautiful, almost like the real thing." He furrowed his brow, agitated. "Xifeng, say something!"

She turned, her cheeks warm and rosy—practically glowing—and smiled. "It's perfect."

"Really?"

"I can already see our son growing up here." She threw her arms around his neck and kissed him on the lips.

"Son?" Bo kissed her on the forehead, relieved. He motioned at the small bump under her shirt. "What makes you so sure?"

Xifeng smiled impishly. "Call it a woman's intuition."

Bo made a thoughtful sound in his throat. "I came across something the other day while reading in the library."

Her eyes went up in surprise. "You were reading?"

His face flushed red, embarrassed. "They're just middle school books, but you know how hard it is for me."

Xifeng pressed her finger to his lips. "Stop it," she said

sternly. "Why are you always so defensive? You don't have to be with me."

He pressed his face into the crook of her neck and breathed deeply. Her scent was light, soothing, washing away his fears.

She whispered into his ear, "What is it you wanted to tell me?"

Bo pulled his head back. "I saw a name in one of the books . . . Dante. I looked it up, and it means 'to endure.'"

Xifeng cradled her stomach and smiled. "Our son, Dante."

Chapter 15

Vincent stood over his brother like an ever-vigilant sentinel. Dante squirmed under a blanket, sweating profusely and breathing in harsh, shallow gasps, his eyes pressed shut in pain. They had tried moving him to a bed earlier, but picking him up caused him to scream out in agony—in fact, any movement sent him into howling fits.

It frightened him to see Dante so weak, so vulnerable.

Elise gently moved Vincent off to the side. "I need to change his bandages." She carefully pulled Dante's blanket down and lifted his shirt. The white wrapping on his torso was soaked through with dried blood and yellow pus. It was even worse underneath. Elise took a wet rag and brushed a foul-smelling ooze from the bullet's entry wound. "Vincent, help me turn him over."

He shook his head. "We can't. It'll hurt him too much."

"I have to see his back," she said seriously. "If I don't clean it out, it'll only get worse." Elise pointed to Vincent's leg. "I'll have to check you next."

A deep ache went through his leg, but he didn't show it. He wanted Elise's full attention on his brother.

They rolled Dante onto his side; he ground his teeth and stifled an agonized breath in his throat. A wide stain of red and yellow soaked the couch cushion beneath him.

"It'll be over soon," Elise reassured him. She peeled a sopping wet bandage off Dante's back and cleaned out a gaping hole the size of a quarter. As she promised, it was over within minutes, and they lowered Dante's body back down over a clean shirt.

"C-c-can we not do that anymore?" Dante whispered, his blue lips turning up in a weak smile.

"Don't talk. Just focus on your rest," Grandma whispered. She tilted his head up and held a bottle of water to his lips. "Drink up, baby. You need it."

Elise pulled Vincent aside and sat him down in the kitchen. She kneeled before him and started to roll his pant leg up to get to the bullet wound in his calf.

Vincent absentmindedly watched her work and noticed she didn't smell completely awful. He lifted his arm and sniffed, and then pulled his face away in mild disgust; the last time anyone had taken a shower was more than five days ago. "Sorry if I reek," he muttered.

"I once went a whole month without a real shower. Trust me, you're fine."

Vincent's lip pricked in disgust. "Not a fan of hygiene?"

Elise snickered, but proceeded to unwrap his bandage. "I spent half a year in East Africa, mainly helping build schools. It just so happened that a nasty drought hit the area during my last two months there. It was really bad, Vincent—food shortages, disease. Wasting precious water on frequent baths would have been stupid."

He answered with a noncommittal grunt. "Why put yourself in that situation?"

"What do you mean?"

Vincent shrugged. "I just don't see the point. You do all that work, but you don't get anything out of it. Why?"

A humorless laugh escaped her breath, and she shook her head in disbelief. "Because it makes a difference and helps people's lives. If all it takes is a bit of sweat and time, I'm all for it. Besides, I love that feeling you get when doing something good—the warm, fuzzy feeling in your stomach, and that feathery, light sensation in your chest." Elise smiled. "It's the best thing in the world."

Vincent rolled his eyes. "Fucking hell, Elise. What are you going to tell me next, that you puke rainbows?"

Elise showed him his leg, puffy and purple, then poked it hard.

"Hey! What was that for?"

She shot daggers back. "I know being mean is kind of your thing, but would it kill you to be a little nicer to the person fixing you up?"

He bit back a rude remark and nodded grudgingly.

"Gee, Elise, do you puke up rainbows?" she asked, clearly mocking him. She let out a frustrated breath and added, "You can be such a dick sometimes, Vincent."

She's hanging around me too much.

Elise finished cleaning him up, and as she wrapped his

leg in a new bandage, Flea entered the kitchen behind her.

"Grandma wants both of you," the pug said.

They walked into the living room as Grandma pulled a thermometer from Dante's mouth. "Look at this," she said, handing it to them.

Elise looked at the reading, worry etched in her face. "His temperature is at one hundred and five. The fever is getting worse because he's fighting a bad infection," she explained. "That, plus all the blood he's lost . . . it's not good."

Vincent gulped. "Not good? How bad is not good?"

"Dante needs medicine," Grandma said gravely, leaving no doubt it wasn't opinion, but fact.

A question wormed its way into Vincent's head, and he dreaded having to ask it. "Will he die?"

Their silence was all the response he needed.

Vincent hobbled to a window. Everything was covered in a damp sheen and most of the street was now one giant puddle, but the rain had stopped. The clouds glided overhead, plump and gray, teasing at more rain to come. "Where can I find the medicine he needs? I'll go get it."

"A pharmacy would carry it," Elise suggested. "But you can't go alone, it's too dangerous. I'll go with you."

"That's a good idea. You'll know what to look for anyways." He waved for her to follow and went to open the front door, but a frail hand stopped him.

"Be real careful out there," Grandma said.

"I will," he replied, impatient. He tried pulling away, but Grandma held her grip.

"I'm serious, Vincent. You're not going to do your

brother any good if you die out there. Don't take any unnecessary risks. I swear to Christ I'll kill you if you get yourself hurt doing some heroics."

"Just keep Dante safe, Grandma." Vincent turned to Flea. "The same goes for you."

Flea scoffed. "I don't know what you expect from me. I'm powerless without my staff." He motioned at his chubby little body. "And if you have not noticed, I only weigh eighteen pounds." He relented with a subtle grin. "But I suppose I can always bite things, however much I may loathe such brutish tactics."

Grandma pressed her lips in a grim line and pulled Vincent and Elise into a tight group hug. "Get going before I realize what a fucking terrible idea this is."

The door locked behind them as they stepped out in the unwelcoming and gloomy neighborhood.

"Which way should we go?" Elise asked, her breath foggy in the cold. She shivered and pulled her jacket tight around her body.

"Back downtown," Vincent said stonily.

"But that's back in the direction of Gil. He might be out looking for us."

Vincent wasn't too keen on the idea either, but waved to the single-family houses surrounding them. "You think we'll find anything here?"

Elise looked unhappy about it, but nodded her understanding. "Lead the way."

They made a beeline into downtown Oakwood, but with Vincent's bad leg and their general exhaustion, it was a slow trip that burned more daylight than he would have liked. The clouds darkened overhead at an alarming rate, and the air became thick with the humidity of an imminent rain.

"Is the weather like this normally?" Elise asked.

"No, I'm usually sweating my ass off in my living room this time of year," Vincent replied, breathing heavily around his words.

"I wonder why the weather's acting up."

Vincent stopped at a pile of rubble to sit and rest his leg. "Because it's the End of Days! The Apocalypse!"

"Don't call it that."

Vincent gestured at the empty city around them. "Open your eyes, Elise. The evidence is all around you." He massaged his leg with a low groan. "What I would give for a glass of whiskey, a cigarette, and one of Grandma's cookies right about now."

Elise blew a breath into her cupped hands and rubbed them together vigorously. "You could try being a little more optimistic, you know? If everyone pulls together I just know we can get through this—this—whatever this is."

"Do you even listen to yourself? It's like watching a Saturday-morning cartoon." Vincent stood up and continued down the sidewalk.

"It all has to start somewhere. If you believe things can get better, then you'll be willing to do the work to make it happen. When you think negative thoughts, then you won't even try, and if you don't try you're guaranteed to fail. So which would you rather do?" Elise threw up her hands. "You know what? Don't answer that."

Vincent was more than happy to oblige and continue their search in silence, but it only lasted a few blocks before Elise opened her mouth again.

"How do you and Grandma know each other?" she asked innocently.

"I met her when I was a kid," he replied.

Elise quickened her pace until they were walking side by side. "You know what I mean. There's more to it than that."

Vincent swatted her question away like an annoying gnat. "Why are you so nosy?"

She stuck her chin stuck out defiantly. "Maybe if you'd talk a little more I wouldn't have to ask so many questions."

"We aren't out here to talk. Also, have you considered that these things are none of your business?"

"It's not business. It's called getting to know someone."

"Well, I don't want to get to know you, how about that?"

"Fine, but I still want to know more about you."

Vincent came to an abrupt stop and threw his arms up in frustration. "What do I have to do to make you shut up?"

"Just answer the question! How do you know Grandma?"

He shushed her angrily. "Not so loud! You trying to attract everyone's attention in a mile radius?"

"Don't change the subject," Elise hissed. She planted her hands on her hips with a sassy tilt of the head. "Well?"

An irritated growl bubbled in Vincent's throat. "Fine!" he snapped. "But that's the *only* question I'm answering."

Elise fell in step with him, beaming toothily like a kid about to get her birthday present.

"I was seven and Dante was nine when we met her for the first time. Her liquor store just popped up in the neighborhood one day. We'd go in there to buy candy and soda all the time. At first, she was kind of scary, but she must have warmed up to us. She'd let us hang out with her in the store after school." Vincent caught himself smiling nostalgically. "Sometimes *during* school, too. It was nice. I'd just sit in the corner and read, and on Sundays she'd bake a whole pan of cookies just for us."

Elise smiled at the last part. "Grandma would make cookies for me too whenever she babysat me. Were they the cinnamon ones?"

"Of course." Vincent reminisced about those days. It felt like an eternity ago. "Grandma did a lot for us. When Dante and I were left to fend for ourselves, she figured it out pretty quick. She gave us envelopes of money every month to help with the bills. Dante tried giving them back at first, but she'd get all pissy and start yelling."

"Fend for yourselves? What do you mean by that?"

Vincent squared his shoulders with huff. "I said I'd only answer the *one* question."

Elise sulked. "Fine. Go on, then."

He held up his empty hands. "That's it. There's nothing else to the story."

"What?" Elise seemed disappointed. "Come on, there's more to it than that."

He hummed thoughtfully and made a big show of trying to dig deeper. "She taught me my impressive vocabulary of swear words, if that's what you're asking." Vincent began listing them off on his hand.

"Okay, I get it. You don't want to talk about it anymore." Elise's face scrunched up cutely, and she eyed him with a mischievous giggle. "I bet you feel better now, huh, thinking about all those good memories."

"I don't know what you're talking about." The black clouds above *might* have looked a little less gloomy.

"You can't lie to me. I see it in your eyes." Elise grinned and patted him on the chest. "Don't you worry, Vincent, I'm going to fix your cold and stony heart."

"Give me a break, Elise . . ." His thoughts trailed off as they came upon a pile of bodies. A single spear stuck up from the top like a triumphant marker. "Minotaurs," he murmured.

Elise nodded, but pointed past the bodies. "Look, a vet's office."

Vincent followed her finger to a darkened waiting room, underneath a sign with a picture of a dog and cat playing. "So what?"

"Vincent, there's going to be medicine in there." She jogged ahead, excited. "Finally, our luck's turning around!"

"But isn't that medicine only going to be for dogs and cats?"

"Humans and animals can actually share a decent amount of medication."

"We can? Nifty." Vincent pulled his shirt over his nose and chased after her.

The walls inside were covered with pictures of puppies and kittens frolicking in fields of flowers, and the air carried a pungent odor of animals. Elise scurried behind the front desk and into a back office, leaving Vincent to himself.

He wandered to a display shelf of various pet products and picked up the closest bottle; it was a specialized oatmeal shampoo specifically designed for dogs. He nearly choked when he saw the price tag on it. "Unbe-fucking-lievable."

What kind of rich asshole has that kind of money? He envisioned a woman with gaudy jewelry, toting around a yapping Chihuahua in her bag. *If it costs this much to give a dog a bath, how much is it to take care of a kid? They're walking shit factories.* He shuddered at the thought of raising a child.

Elise hollered from the next room and came out a moment later with two orange bottles of pills. "I've got morphine and cephalexin!" she exclaimed triumphantly.

"Morphine I know. What the hell is cephalexin?"

Elise popped open one of the bottles and counted out a couple pills. "Take some of the cephalexin right now, it'll help your leg."

He eyed them suspiciously. "What're they going to do to me?"

"Relax, it's just an antibiotic."

Vincent dry-swallowed the pills, then pointed to the morphine. "Let me get some of that, too. My leg is killing me right now."

"Not until we get back to the house," Elise said flatly. "It might make you a little loopy and we need our wits about us."

"Good thinking," Vincent said. He reached for the door, but his hand froze on the handle.

"What's wrong, Vincent?"

"Quiet!" He gave Elise a serious look that silenced any protest, then motioned to his ears.

They heard voices nearby, low and urgent. Someone, *or something*, was shouting. Vincent stumbled away from the door and dragged Elise with him behind the front desk, out of sight.

"Keep moving! They are gaining on our position!" a powerful voice thundered.

Vincent's heart skipped a beat as an ear-piercing scream followed. Ghouls. It was joined by others in a hair-raising chorus. Vincent dared a peek around the desk to try and see what was happening outside. The distinctive clanging of metal on metal grew louder and closer, and before long he saw several minotaurs stomp by the windows in full battle regalia, their bronze armor plastered in dark blood.

The minotaur leading the charge stopped and spun around. "Hold your positions!" he roared. His voice rang true and clear, and five other minotaurs fell into a tight formation around him.

They held their shields out, side by side, creating a wall of metal, and then pointed their spears out in a bristling porcupine effect. Ghouls jumped into view and leapt to their deaths on the minotaurs' defensive formation, impaling themselves on the spears amid raging cries of frustration. The minotaurs held their formation valiantly, but more ghouls kept appearing and piling their dead bodies on, bogging them down until they finally broke ranks.

The minotaurs scattered and drew their swords, and then

charged into the fray of ghouls. Vincent watched in morbid fascination as minotaur and ghoul pitted their savagery against each other. One by one, the ghouls were cut down with martial skill and brute strength.

A ghoul got under the shield of one minotaur and slashed the bull's ankle, bringing him to his knees with a bellowing roar of pain. The minotaur punched the ghoul's head clean off before trying to regain his footing, but a second ghoul jumped onto his side. He lost his balance and staggered into the veterinary office, smashing through the glass door in a brilliant shower of clinking glass.

The minotaur slid to a stop next to Vincent, too distracted by the ghoul on his chest to notice the two human onlookers. He tried throwing the ghoul off, but it slipped one of its claws under the minotaur's helmet; the minotaur made a gurgling death cry as its throat was torn out.

For a few terrifying moments, the ghoul was too focused on feasting on the fresh kill to notice Vincent and Elise. It chewed with gnashing teeth and rent flesh and tendons away in bloody strips.

Elise gagged, and the ghoul's face snapped to them in the same moment.

Vincent's heart leapt into his throat. "Fuck!"

The ghoul opened its mouth, but a spear pierced its head and pinned it to the far wall. Vincent spun around and clamped his hand tightly over Elise's mouth as heavy footsteps crunched over glass. He dared a peek over his shoulder and saw a minotaur's muscled arm pull the spear out of the dead ghoul's head.

"Damned ghouls," the minotaur said.

A second minotaur replied, "I have never seen them like this."

The minotaur closest to them turned to regard the other, both oblivious to Vincent and Elise's presence. Vincent forced his breathing to slow down and gave Elise an intense stare he hoped would convey his message to shut the hell up. She trembled in his arms, but did a terrific job of remaining quiet.

"Something has rattled the ghouls," the minotaur beside them said. "I have only ever seen them in full force like this when a ghoulah was killed."

The other minotaur rumbled his understanding. "This was a dirty fight. No glory to be had."

The first minotaur nudged his dead comrade with a heavy hoof. "What do we do with him?"

"Nothing. He was Nameless, and by dying to a lowly ghoul, will forever remain Nameless."

"He had the Rot. Do you think he would ever have attained a name?"

"There is no room for weakness, even in those with Rot. Do not forget why King Minos sent us here. We must purge this plague from our race . . . come, Granitefist, our orders are to march south with the others." He left, his tone final.

The remaining minotaur rumbled a sigh over his deceased ally. "In life you were trapped by the Labyrinth, so in death you are free." He thumped his fist against his breastplate. "Find peace, brother." Then he left.

Vincent and Elise waited until the shifting and clinking

of the minotaurs' armor faded into the distance.

"Oh my god," Elise gasped, patting her heart. "That was close."

Vincent swallowed some spit down his dry throat and nodded. So much adrenaline pumped through his body, he didn't even need the morphine anymore. "Let's get the hell out of this place."

Elise helped him up and they hurried outside. The clouds cast long shadows over the bloody aftermath of the battle, which could only mean night was coming soon. They wasted no time and took off running.

Chapter 16

Night overtook them well before they made it back to the house, and with it came a deafening silence. Something chewed at the fringes of Vincent's thoughts, a nagging worry that something was wrong. The minotaurs had said the ghouls were agitated because their ghoulah had been killed.

I was the one who poked that hornet's nest. Vincent wondered if ghouls understood the concept of revenge.

As they turned into a side street, their destination in sight, Elise quipped excitedly, "Finally back, and we made good time."

"Yeah," he said absently. From far away, the house looked less like a home and more like an architectural relic of a long-dead civilization. Like something that could be unearthed thousands of years later and erected in a museum. What would the plaque read?

This is Oakwood. It was a really shitty place to live. Good riddance.

They paused at the house's walkway, and Vincent's eyes

followed it to the front door.

"No," Elise whispered.

The door wasn't where it should have been. It had been ripped from the hinges and thrown aside. What remained was a gaping doorway. In Vincent's mind, it looked like a yawning mouth waiting to swallow him whole.

He saw Elise dart up the path, and his mind snapped back to reality. "Damn it, wait!"

"Grandma? Grandma! Dante!" Elise screamed.

Vincent opened his mouth to tell her to shut up, but when he went through the front door, he noticed the couch was empty. A dark blot permeated the cushion where he had left his brother, and a blood trail led from it to a broken window.

Elise paced the room with her hands in her hair, firing off questions in a panicked stream. "Where are they? Where did they go? What's going on? Vincent, they're gone! Say something!"

"Stop it! I just need to think for a second."

The wooden coffee table was snapped down the middle as if something heavy had landed on it. White stuffing fell out from deep gouges in the couch. Upon closer inspection, Vincent saw the marks were made in groups of three to four with a kind of symmetry that reminded him of claws. He strode to the broken window and looked out into a narrow walkway on the side of the house. Droplets of something dark and sticky shone under him, making a vague trail into the backyard.

He heard a sound from behind and spun around. Elise

met his gaze, her face white with terror. "Was that you?" he whispered.

Elise shook her head.

Vincent nodded his understanding and tiptoed toward the noise. It sounded like it had come from the next room over. He passed through the kitchen and grabbed a knife off the countertop before making his way to a door that had been left ajar. He barely touched it, and it swung open, its hinges cackling like an old man.

It was an ordinary bedroom with nothing amiss, but upon closer inspection, he picked up a faint sound from under the bed. It reminded him of a snoring pig. "Is that you, Flea?"

Flea's head poked out from beneath the bedskirt. "Forbidden arcana, I thought I smelled you."

"Where are the others?" Vincent demanded.

Flea's buggy eyes fell to the floor.

"I saw blood in the front room. What happened?" But Vincent already knew the answer.

The pug turned his sad eyes up to him. "Ghouls found us."

"Son of a bitch!" Vincent pounded the heel of his hand against the wall. "How long ago?"

Flea flinched at his outburst. "They showed up maybe an hour ago. If I had to guess, they caught Dante's scent. When the first ghoul came through the door, Grandma told me to hide." Flea held out his hands in a pleading gesture. "I wanted to fight, truly I did. However, without my staff, I am defenseless. I could only hide, and for that I am sorry."

Elise's hands dug into Vincent's arm. "What do we do?" she asked.

He yanked free and rushed to the front door.

"Where are you going?" Elise called after him.

Vincent barely heard the question. One thought played through his head with increasing intensity. *Find them.*

He limped out the door and found the broken window at the side of the house. The blood trail led him to the backyard, where something had been dragged through the tall weeds and through a hole in the fence. He vaguely registered Elise's voice, but ignored her and darted ahead.

Vincent crawled into a connecting yard and easily picked up the trail from there. The blood glowed like beacons under the moonlight, and he followed it around another house and into the street. Fear knotted his insides when he realized the splatters had gotten bigger.

A cold breeze picked up as he tracked the blood through the neighborhood; it nipped at his nose and burned his throat with every sharp breath, but he didn't slow down. The pain was a grim reminder this was no dream, and it drove him harder.

"Dante! Grandma!" Vincent shouted. His voice carried down the street and echoed back, taunting him. He tried again, louder, until his voice grew hoarse. All thoughts of his own safety flew out the door. It didn't matter what else heard him—ghouls, minotaurs, sadistic men with guns—so long as Dante and Grandma did, too.

He came upon an overturned truck in the middle of an intersection, a bony, naked leg poking out from behind it.

Vincent circled the vehicle, giving it a wide berth as he tried to make out what he was seeing. On the other side was a ghoul, facedown in a puddle of blood, its skeletal body and disgusting skin unmistakable.

Past the dead ghoul was another figure, sitting up against the truck with her head bowed.

"Grandma!" Vincent fell at her feet as his leg finally gave out, unable to take any more abuse. The old woman stirred at his voice, and his heart jumped in joy at seeing her alive. He felt a resurgence of hope that he would find his brother hiding nearby. "Wake up, Grandma," he said, patting life into her cold cheeks. "Come on, come on," he muttered anxiously, all the while scanning his surroundings for Dante's cocky, self-assured grin.

"Vincent?" Grandma said weakly.

"It's okay, Grandma. Everything's going to be all right now. I'm here." She shivered in the frigid night, so he pulled off his own sweater and began to wrap it around her. He glanced at the dead ghoul beside her and grinned. "You really did a number on that fucker."

Grandma straightened her glasses with a shaky hand and tried sitting up, but fell back with a pained grunt. "Son of a bitch."

"Stop moving," Vincent said sternly.

"Vincent," she whispered.

"Wait here. I'm going to get Elise."

"Vincent," she said again, more forcefully.

"Do you know where Dante is? I didn't see him on the way here and—"

"Vincent!" Grandma took a shuddering breath, winded from the effort of getting his attention. "You've always been a knucklehead, but just listen to me this one time, damn it."

Something in her tone stopped his heart. "What's wrong?"

Grandma spat at the dead ghoul. "That goddamn, piece of shit, fucking ghoul . . ." She licked her dry lips before continuing. "I fucked up badly, Vincent. I was careless. This one got me from behind real good." She leaned forward and motioned at what was left of her back.

A chunk the size of a soccer ball had been torn out of her side, leaving behind a pulverized mash of muscle and protruding bone. Dark bits and organs dangled out from the wound, and fresh blood flowed with every pulse of her heart. The fact she was even conscious and talking was a testament to what a tough old bitch she was.

But being tough could only carry a person so far.

"Oh my god. No, no, no, no. This isn't happening." Vincent reached down instinctively with the adolescent idea of putting everything back inside her, like doing so would just magically fix it.

"Don't touch me," she snapped, swatting his hand away. "It hurts like hell as it is."

"But we have to do something, or else . . ." Vincent didn't want to finish the thought.

Grandma leaned back into the truck and brushed a few tears off her face. "I'm not coming back from this, boy."

"Don't you fucking say that! You're not finished yet."

"Please . . . don't," Grandma pleaded. She struggled to

control her emotions as more tears rolled down her cheeks.

A lump formed in Vincent's throat, and something hot stung the back of his eyes.

"Don't fucking say a word," Grandma insisted. "Listen to me." She swallowed down a pained grunt before continuing. "Your brother's gone. He was unconscious when the ghouls showed up, so they just carried him off. I tried getting him back, I really did." Grandma pursed her lips to stop them from trembling. "I'm sorry, Vincent. I let you down. I let your brother down."

"You didn't let anyone down, Grandma. You don't know Dante's gone. There's still a chance."

Grandma's eyes turned steely, and her wispy hair blew in the wind as she shook her head. "Don't lie to yourself, Vincent. We both know what those ghouls are capable of. Look at yourself. You can barely move. Do you think you can track them down, let alone fight them off?" Grandma clamped her hand around his wrist. "Listen to me: don't you dare go chasing after him. You'll only get yourself killed, too, and I know your brother wouldn't want that. I don't want that."

Vincent shook his head. He wanted to dig her words out of his brain, but they lodged in there like a tumor. "You're asking me to just abandon him?"

Grandma didn't say anything.

Vincent's arms dropped to his sides and his eyes glazed over. "That's not fair, Grandma. That's not fair."

She chuckled hollowly. "Have you ever known life to be fair? I'd say it's a downright bitch." Grandma held her hand to Vincent's cheek. They felt like little icicles against his skin. "Be strong, Vincent. Keep moving forward."

Vincent refocused his attention on Grandma. "I don't want to."

"I fucking taught you better than this!" she yelled, suddenly furious.

"But I—"

"It's not about what you want." Grandma scoffed. "This is never going to be about what you *want*. That's how a child thinks. You've got a goddamn responsibility to survive this shit, so you better do what needs to be done no matter how fucking awful it is." Her eyes softened around the edges. "Sit down with me a bit, Vincent. Keep an old woman company just a little longer."

Vincent's body moved on its own accord and sat beside her. Together, they watched the sky.

"I've never told you about my husband," Grandma said softly.

"I didn't even know you had a family until a few days ago," he croaked.

"His name was Randall. We married straight out of high school—it seems crazy now, but we were young and in love." Grandma paused, almost reluctant to continue, but Vincent's silence spurred her on. "He was a God-fearing man and went to church almost every day of the week." She chuckled. "Of course I never went with him. Could you imagine that, Vincent? Me singing and praising Jesus like those spineless idiots, too afraid to walk through life on their own two feet. Because that's all it is, wishful thinking that some big guy in the sky is looking out for you." Grandma's tone became bitter. "Fucking idiots."

"What happened to him?" Vincent asked.

"He was handing out food to the homeless on Thanksgiving and someone shot him." Grandma made her hand into a gun and mimed pulling the trigger. "Pow, right in the chest. He died with a case of green beans in his arms, and do you know what the fucking murderer took from him? Twenty bucks. Twenty fucking dollars was what my husband's life came out to be worth."

Vincent turned his head to Grandma. She stared ahead, her eyes flat.

"The police—fucking useless—never caught the guy." Grandma choked back a sob. "Randall was a good man. Better than anyone I've ever met. He always helped those who needed it. Money, clothes, blood and sweat—it didn't matter to him. He'd just give and give. It drove me mad. And for all the good Randall's praying and deeds did him, he still ended up murdered. *Short twenty bucks and in a grave of green beans!* What's that supposed to mean, Vincent?"

He thought for a moment, then shook his head.

"Nothing. It means nothing." Grandma shook her head. "My son, Philip, is just like his father, so you can probably guess where Elise got all her charitable bullshit from."

Vincent had a realization. "You left them all behind after Randall died, didn't you?"

"I did." Grandma faltered. "I think . . . that was a mistake."

Silence took over the conversation and Vincent looked

down at his hands, soaking in her words. "Why are you telling me all this?" he asked.

Grandma didn't answer.

Vincent wasn't sure how long he stayed there, but eventually Elise and Flea found him, sitting in the exact same spot.

Elise dropped to her knees, sobbing. She tried asking him what happened, but he couldn't speak. Strangely, he felt nothing inside. It was as if he burned through all the emotions he had left, leaving behind an empty vessel.

Elise took her grandmother's head in her arms and screamed. When she couldn't scream anymore, she buried her face in Grandma's shoulder with a low moan and rocked back and forth.

Flea's ears drooped, and he put a hand on her trembling shoulder. He didn't say anything because he knew words were meaningless.

***

Bo glared through his dirty car window at the liquor store across the street. His sons bounded out the front doors and ran off with sodas in their hands, laughing and oblivious to his presence. He tried to recall the last time he'd seen them. They were so much taller and lankier now, all knees and elbows.

Bo got out of his car and zipped up his jacket, despite it being in the middle of summer, then walked into the liquor store. Grandma sat behind the register with a cigarette in her mouth and an open paper before her; it was strange to finally see the cantankerous old woman his own children had known for years. He wondered what about her appealed to his boys so much.

He walked through the aisles, pretending to browse the snacks. From the corner of his eye, he could tell Grandma was nonchalantly studying him too. Bo made his way to the fridges at the back of the store and grabbed a tall can of beer.

"That'll be two fifty," Grandma said, when he set it down on the counter.

Bo dug through his pockets and tossed a crumpled-up bill on the counter. "I'll need smokes too," he said. His voice was hoarse from disuse.

"What kind?" she asked.

"Doesn't matter."

This earned him an intrigued look from her. Grandma studied his face while reaching for the cigarettes under the counter. Bo saw a flicker of recognition.

Grandma's eyes turned to daggers. "What're you doing here?" she asked, her tone accusatory.

Bo paused, impressed she made the connection under the weeks of dirty facial hair he had grown out. "Just coming in for some smokes and booze," he replied. "I don't know what you're talking about."

"Bullshit." Grandma put his cigarettes on the countertop. "I can see it in your damn face. They're spitting images of you—a goddamn shame, considering what a piece of shit you are."

"Give me my change," Bo replied calmly.

She wrinkled her nose and dropped his money into his

outstretched palm. "Why are you here, Bo?"

"Maybe I just wanted to see them one more time?"

Grandma gave a humorless laugh. "There's a special place in Hell for men like you."

As Bo dropped the smokes into his pocket, his knuckles brushed against the cool metal of a gun. "I'm counting on it."

"It's not too late, you know. They'll never love you, but you can still do right by them."

Bo laughed out loud, exercising parts of his throat he hadn't touched in years. Still chuckling, he wiped a tear from his eye and said, "I've got a request."

"Eh?"

"Make sure they forget about me."

Grandma's nostrils flared. "So you're running away like a coward?"

"Big talk for a hypocrite," he replied. He took Grandma's silence as an invitation to explain himself. "I've asked around. Locals told me you bought this place up five years ago with pure cash. You don't have family here, you don't have friends. You don't belong. You're just a stranger in a strange land, which makes me wonder what you're running from yourself." He gave her a toothy smile. "We're more alike than you realize."

Grandma's voice trembled when she spoke. "You and I are nothing alike. Get out of my store and don't ever come back. They aren't your boys anymore."

Chapter 17

Vincent roared and threw his empty can against the wall. It bounced off with a hollow clang, and the force of the throw sent him spiraling to the floor. His shoulder thumped dully against tile. He sprawled out on the floor, vaguely aware he should be hurting from the fall, but the alcohol coursing through his veins had burned off all feeling.

Flea appeared in his field of vision, swaying as if on a tiny ship caught in a storm. "Forbidden arcana, you must stop this."

"Stop moving so much, you're making me sick," Vincent said around a burp. He flipped onto his stomach and pulled himself onto the kitchen counter, where a warm can of beer awaited.

"Vincent, don't," Flea pleaded.

Vincent popped the tab and turned to hurl a cussword at Flea, but he failed miserably and fell, hitting his side against the counter on the way down. He slid to the floor and spilled beer all over himself in a cry of pain. "Fuck, that kind of hurt," he slurred. He took a long drink; it was tasteless and tingled his throat on the way down to his stomach.

A pair of bare feet appeared in his peripheral. "Is he still at it?"

He squinted up at Elise, her eyes red and puffy and her hair matted against her face. "What the hell do you want?" he spat.

Elise glowered at him. "What's wrong with you?"

Vincent laughed hysterically.

"It's been almost two days. Do you plan on drinking yourself to death?" she asked.

Vincent lifted his eyebrows and pondered the beer in his hand. "You make it sound like a bad thing."

"You're pathetic."

He eyed her dangerously. "I'm pathetic? All you've been doing is crying in the fucking bedroom this whole time."

Flea put a hand on his shoulder. "Vincent, don't."

He shrugged the dog off. "You think *I'm* pathetic? Look in a mirror!" He pointed angrily at Elise. "You're the one moping around feeling sorry for yourself. They're gone, just get over it already."

She shut her eyes tight and swallowed back the beginnings of another round of tears. "That's rich coming from you," she stammered.

"They've moved on and left us behind on this fucking shitty Earth. There's nothing left for us—for me—here. Sooner or later, we're going to die too. We might as well enjoy ourselves before we get killed by a creature . . . If I was braver, I'd do it myself."

"Stop it!" She shouted so shrilly it surprised even herself. "S-so you're just going to give up? We've been through so much already, and you just want to *give up?* You're telling me to get over it, but you haven't gotten over anything either. You're just pretending it never happened by drinking until you can't think straight anymore." She stabbed a finger toward him. "You're just too scared to admit it."

"Don't pretend like you know what I'm thinking. You and I, we're too different. You'll never understand."

Elise folded her arms. "Oh, p-p-please. Don't act like you have it so much worse than I do. This isn't a competition."

Vincent felt a vileness surge up from within. He threw the can at her feet, forcing her to jump back. "Don't you dare talk to me! This is all your fault. If we had just minded our own business, we would never have found Gil."

"Vincent," Flea said, his tone warning him to stop.

Vincent saw the cogs turning in Elise's head, so he continued with a vicious sneer. "You get it now, don't you? You just had to be a goody two-shoes, right? Save Natalie from the fucking minotaurs. Look what it got us. Dante's dead, Grandma's dead, and it's all your fault. I have nothing left to live for!" he screamed, pounding his chest. "It should be you in the backyard! Not Grandma!"

Flea pounced on his stomach and slapped him across the face. "That is enough!"

Elise hugged herself and turned away. "I feel sorry for you, Vincent."

Vincent's blind fury lifted like a thick fog, and he could suddenly see clearly again. He watched her storm off and heard a door slam on the other end of the house.

"Are you proud of yourself?" Flea asked, disappointed.

He turned away. "Just go. Leave me alone."

"She's all you've got left now," Flea said bluntly. "Even I can see that." He started to leave, but paused. "Do not push her away. I think you will regret it."

Vincent wandered to the living room and fell on the couch. He used to enjoy all his time alone. Solitude was comforting, peaceful, uncomplicated. Only with Dante and Grandma gone did he realize he had never been *truly* alone. If he died tomorrow, who would mourn him? No one. He might as well not exist as far as the rest of the world was concerned. Vincent was invisible. It was a terrifying and sobering thought.

Vincent awoke later that day to his stomach knocking at the gates of his mouth. He scrambled to the kitchen and vomited into the sink; his stomach clenched painfully until it had expunged all its contents into a disgusting mess. He wiped the back of his hand across his mouth, then fell to his knees. He stayed there for a long while, before mustering the strength to stand and make his way into the backyard.

A fresh mound of dirt rested in a clearing among the weeds, unmarked. Digging it up had been difficult. The earth was hard and compacted, and when he and Elise had finished, blisters covered their palms.

The whole thing was demeaning. Grandma deserved better. Vincent wondered for a moment if she would have preferred to be cremated and spread somewhere nice. Maybe the ocean?

"I really don't give a shit. I'm dead already. Do what you need to help cope."

Her words rang so clearly in his ears. It made Vincent smirk. She was a plain woman with plain views, who never felt the need to romanticize things.

Vincent turned Flea's words over in his head, and he cringed at the things he had said in his drunken stupor. *Elise probably didn't deserve that kind of treatment,* he thought.

"That's right, you shithead! You better sack up, boy, and apologize to my granddaughter. Christ, you can be such a knucklehead sometimes."

Even as a figment of his imagination, Grandma still berated him for the stupid things he did. Vincent felt a laugh come up and let it fly, unrestrained. He threw his head back and laughed as loud as his lungs would allow. The sound echoed through the neighborhood and found its way back, as if the city itself wanted in on the fun.

Vincent's laugh slowly died out to a muffled cry behind his hand. He looked down and wept.

The next morning, after he had sobered up, Vincent went to the bedroom Elise had locked herself in. He knocked, but didn't receive an answer. "Elise, I know you're in there." He tried again, louder.

"Go away," came her muffled reply.

Vincent leaned his head into the door. "I just want to talk."

No response.

"Come on, Elise."

She was ignoring him.

"I'm coming in, whether you like it or not." The door opened to her hiding under the bedcovers with her back to him. Flea lifted his head from the foot of the bed, but Vincent waved him down. "I'm not here to cause any more problems."

Flea narrowed his eyes. "I might not be able to do magic anymore, but I still have teeth and will bite your ankle fiercely if you get out of hand again." He bared his fangs, which came off as more adorable than intimidating.

Vincent chuckled at the empty threat, but admired Flea's courage.

"If you're looking for more beer, there isn't any in here," Elise said.

He leaned against the door, trying to frame his next words carefully. He hadn't really planned this out. "I'm done drinking now."

Elise laughed once, the sound devoid of emotion.

Vincent dug his toe into the carpet and made a small hole in it as he worked up the courage to say what needed to be said. He took a deep breath. "I apologize." Elise made no motion to respond, so he kept talking to fill the silence. "I got a little crazy back there. I shouldn't have said it was your fault . . . that wasn't fair, I know that."

Elise turned over and peeked out from under the blanket. "Is that it?"

He sat on the edge of the bed and shrugged. "I don't know what else to say. I'm not really good at these kinds of things."

Elise glared at his response. "Is that all you're apologizing for? Because *everything* you said was wrong, not just the part about it being my fault."

"What?" he said, nonplussed by her response.

Elise took his hand in hers and looked deep into his eyes. "I want you to understand that you're not the only one who's lost everything."

"What are you talking about?"

"Hasn't it occurred to you that we've all lost things because of this? I don't have a big family, Vincent. It's just my mom and dad back in Oregon. My friends are all back there, too, and that's the problem: they're in Oregon and I'm here." Her voice faltered, but she pushed on. "I tried to be optimistic about this, but after everything we've been through—I have to wonder if anyone's even alive at this point."

The thought never even occurred to him. It seemed so obvious once she spelled it out for him. He wondered how long these thoughts had resided in her head, a parasite eating away at her insides.

"Even if through some miracle some of them are alive, how am I supposed to find them? All our communications are gone, we've all been scattered. We might as well be on different planets." Elise sat herself up with the blanket wrapped around her like a protective cocoon. "Tell me honestly: do you think I'll ever see them again?"

"There's always a chance, I guess."

"Vincent," she pressed. "Tell me the truth. I want to hear someone else say it."

"I . . . No, I don't think you will." Vincent knew the answer was true, but the voice saying it sounded like a real asshole to his ears.

Elise gave a short laugh that quickly turned to fresh tears. "That's what I thought." She took a few moments before she dried her eyes and put on a brave smile. "Just because they're gone, doesn't mean I'm not here." Elise placed her hands on his shoulders. "Just because Grandma and Dante are gone, doesn't mean *we* aren't here."

"So what now?" he asked.

Elise's eyes creased in a weak smile. "We keep moving."

"To Blossom Island?"

"To Blossom Island," she confirmed.

Her words did something to him. He felt like the unraveled ends of his brain came back together to form coherent thoughts beyond drowning himself in alcohol. Vincent looked around in disgust, suddenly repulsed by the house.

"There's still daylight. Let's go now," Vincent said.

"Are you sure?" Elise asked. "Shouldn't we gather up supplies?"

He shook his head. "I know Oakwood like the back of my hand. I can get us there before it gets dark."

While truthful, he really just wanted—*needed*—to go. Everything about the house was wrong and it felt like a magnetic force was trying to propel him away.

Vincent got up and offered Elise his hand. "Let's go, please."

Chapter 18

Blossom Island was located in Oakwood Bay, a short distance off the mainland. The small plot of land offered a decent view of Oakwood and its neighboring cities, but otherwise had nothing of note. It was the perfect place for the elderly to retire and be forgotten.

True to Vincent's word, he got them there in one piece, just as night began wrapping its suffocating hands around them. They stood before a single bridge connecting Blossom Island to the rest of Oakwood. Vincent immediately recognized the strategic genius of it. With only one way onto the island, any creatures would have to funnel over the bridge, creating a defensible position.

A cold breeze whistled over the water, singing a haunting tune with the water lapping gently at the rocks below them.

"Look over there." Elise pointed to a row of torches leading across the bridge. Their flames danced wildly in the wind's breath, a delicate tango to avoid being blown out.

"This is indicative of life. Shall we go in?" Flea suggested.

Vincent shook his head, uneasy. This place felt primitive, tribal, like hunters were waiting in ambush. He squinted past the torches and saw nothing; if they crossed the bridge they would be sitting ducks under the light, easy prey for whoever might be watching from the other side. "I don't like this."

"I don't either, but we can't stay out here in the open." Elise took the first step forward. "Come on, Vincent, I just want this to be over."

Vincent nodded his agreement, and then pointed at Flea. "What about him?"

"What about me?" Flea asked suspiciously.

"We can't just go in with a magic dog. You want a repeat of what happened with Gil's people at the apartment?"

Elise nodded her understanding. "They might freak out."

"He has to hide," Vincent explained.

"What, do you expect me to whip up an Invisibility Elixir on the spot?" Flea groused.

Vincent snorted. "At the end of the day, you're still a dog. It wouldn't be hard for you to hide in plain sight."

Flea opened his mouth, stricken by the suggestion. "*Me?* A mere *dog?* Are you mad? I am one of the most highly intelligent wizards you will ever meet in your life. How dare you!"

"Quit stroking your ego for a second and hear me out," Vincent said. "All you have to do is walk around on all fours and say things like: 'woof' and 'bow wow.' Also sniff some poop—lick it, maybe—presto, no one's the wiser."

Flea gasped and recoiled in horror.

Vincent shrugged. "I'm just saying: that's what dogs do."

Flea crossed his arms and turned his nose up at him. "I refuse to be debased in such a manner."

"You wouldn't have to do it all the time," Elise said. "Just if others are around."

"Is that supposed to make me feel better?"

"Suck it up," Vincent said brusquely. "Now, give it a try. Show me your best impression of an actual dog."

Flea got down on all fours, muttering under his breath. He then looked up with the displeased frown of a child forced to eat his veggies. "Woof, woof. Are you happy now?"

Vincent frowned. "Don't literally say 'woof.' You have to bark."

Flea tried again, growling out a "bow wow."

Vincent pressed the bridge of his nose with a sigh. "Forget it. Just don't say anything. Give me your robe too. Dogs don't wear clothes."

"I will not parade myself around *naked* with my privates flopping about," Flea shrilled.

Elise prodded Vincent. "We don't have to take his robe. People dress their dogs up all the time. This wouldn't be any different."

Vincent gave it a moment's thought, then relented. "I guess we're good to go, then." He sucked in a nervous breath and strode forward. "Here goes nothing."

"Wait." Elise bit her lower lip. "What if George turns out to be another Gil? You said they were father and son, right?"

Vincent had already considered the possibility. For all they knew, Gil might have learned his behavior from the

Police Chief. On the other hand, could someone rise to that rank if they were really like that? *I wouldn't doubt it.*

Elise gave a nervous laugh. "I guess I'm learning it's better to be careful nowadays."

"Good . . . Stay on your toes."

Elise nodded, and together, they walked across the bridge, apprehension taut between them. A long cargo trailer materialized from the gloom of dusk, like the kind pulled by eighteen-wheelers on a highway. It had been flipped onto its side and completely blocked the way in.

A woman called out from behind it. "Who's there?"

"We heard a radio transmission saying there's a refuge out here," Vincent replied.

Footsteps moved across the metal container, and a woman appeared over the edge, a long bandage on the side of her face.

"Natalie?" Vincent said in disbelief. "You made it!"

She beamed down at them. "I was wondering when you'd show up. Wait there, fellas, I'll get the ladder."

A second later, a metal ladder slid down the side of the cargo trailer. Elise pushed past him and scrambled up. He made to follow her, but stopped at the sound of someone clearing their throat by his feet. Flea looked up expectantly.

"Right, you're a normal dog." Vincent scooped him up under his arm and climbed the ladder. At the top of the container, he found Elise giving Natalie a tight hug in front of a small group of strangers. They were all armed, he noted, but had a much more relaxed stance than the people at Oasis Gardens.

Natalie eventually pried herself away, pushing Elise back like you would a needy child. She gave Vincent a curt nod, then looked over his shoulders, curious.

"We're the only ones," Vincent explained.

Natalie visibly deflated. "What happened?"

"Ghouls." Vincent didn't elaborate.

"I'm sorry to hear that."

"Yeah," he replied. "So am I."

One of the gunmen stepped forward from the group. He was short and had a doughy face, but under the chubbiness Vincent could see broad shoulders and strong arms. "You know these people?" he asked gruffly.

Natalie looked grateful for the change of topic. "Sure do. They saved my life and even told me about this place. They're good people."

Vincent expected the man to look at him with a mix of suspicion and animosity. What he got was smiles from him and the people behind him. "Come on in! Welcome to Sanctuary," he said jovially, waving them past.

"That's what they're calling this place: Sanctuary." Natalie shrugged. "I guess it fits."

"Pardon my French, but you look like shit." The man, all smiles and laughs, clapped Vincent on the back and knocked the breath out of him. "My name's Conrad."

"Vincent," he replied with a cough.

Conrad dipped his head to Elise. "And the pretty lady over there?"

Elise gave her name with a blush.

"And who's the little guy?" Conrad asked, looking at

Flea. He reached down and ruffled his ears, but Flea snapped back. "Yikes! Mean little bastard, isn't he?"

Vincent chuckled nervously and gave Flea a hard squeeze. "Flea's just a little anxious with everything that's happened. He misses home."

Conrad rumbled his understanding. "Poor pup. Tell you what, I can swing by tomorrow and drop off some canned dog food I found. I was going to save it in case our food stores ran out, but what the hell—we got plenty here as it is."

"Thanks a bunch. I'm sure he'd love that." Vincent caught Natalie's questioning eye. "Yep, Flea's just a regular dog. Lounges around all day and plays fetch."

She got the not-so-subtle hint and didn't bring up the fact Flea also talked and had enough ego to fill a football stadium. Natalie waved them over to her. "Come on, guys, I'll get you settled in."

They climbed down a ladder on the other side of the cargo trailer and onto a quiet road that led into the island. They walked in silence until the amiable banter of the men and women from the bridge disappeared.

"So are you trying to keep Flea a secret?" Natalie asked.

Flea flapped his jowls. "Vincent believes I should pretend to be a stupid dog so I don't scare the primitive and ignorant locals."

"I just don't want him making anyone panic," Vincent said. "He's harmless, but you know how people are around creatures. I want to avoid all that drama."

"Harmless only by my grace!" Flea squirmed in Vincent's

arm, but gave up with a sigh. "Just wait until I make a new staff, then you'll finally show me some respect."

"You're adorable when you pout like that," Vincent said.

"I am not a cute puppy for you to gawk and coo at," Flea protested. "Will you at least put me down? I can walk on my own."

Vincent purposefully patted Flea on the head before doing so. "You mind keeping this little secret between us?"

Natalie nodded. "Don't worry. No one here but me even knows Flea exists."

Vincent raised an eyebrow. "Did no one else from the apartments come with you?"

"No," she said bitterly. "I was so sure some would, but most didn't want to risk the guaranteed security Gil gave them for the slim chance of another refuge here. He's a bastard, but at least he protects them."

"Only until they stop being useful to him," Vincent added.

Natalie's demeanor darkened. "Yeah, it made me wonder if they were afraid of finding nothing here, or of making Gil angry." In the uneasy silence that followed, she put a smile back on. "Let's keep going. No point in brooding over that shit in the past. It's completely different here, you'll see."

Blossom Island was comprised of single-lane streets, giving the place a tight-knit and neighborly feel. No two houses looked alike either, custom-built with unique architectural designs on large plots of gardened land. Elise and Natalie made small conversation as they walked, and Vincent caught bits and pieces of it; he learned there was a cafeteria, an armory, daily gun-handling lessons, and a clinic here—almost like a real community. He had to admit, it felt secure and put some of his worries at ease.

They eventually passed through a small shopping center that consisted solely of specialty shops selling overpriced antiques, jewelry, golf equipment—even an entire store dedicated solely to grand pianos. Vincent supposed those were the kinds of things rich people in retirement considered most important. Everyone needs a good grand piano, after all.

"Over there," Natalie said, pointing out a small bank. It was the only building with any light coming from it. She led them through the front door and into an empty lobby. "Hello, anybody here? We've got new visitors." She frowned when no one answered. "He must be in the back."

They walked past a long candlelit counter where the tellers would have sat, and into an office space in the rear. As they rounded the corner, Vincent saw a large man come out of the bank's vault and shut it tight, spinning the combination lock before turning to greet them.

He was a towering man, balding, with peppered hair and a neat mustache. Vincent immediately recognized Oakwood PD's dark uniform. George Garcia.

"Newcomers, Natalie?" George asked.

"They escaped with me from that Gil fella I was telling you about," Natalie replied.

George looked them over with probing eyes. "Join me in my office," he said, leading them into a cramped room. He squeezed around a small desk and forced himself into a tiny chair, then motioned at some seats across from him. George was a big guy, not necessarily fat, but large with strength akin to a lumbering bear. It afforded him an aura that demanded respect.

Vincent and Elise sat down while Natalie posted up against the wall. Flea waited by the door, looking grumpy.

"So what are your names?" George asked, at a volume bordering on uncomfortably loud.

Elise shifted in her chair. "My name is Elise, uh, sir."

George's eyes moved to Vincent, and he met the Police Chief's intimidating gaze with one of his own. "Vincent," he said.

The big man rose from his seat abruptly, causing Vincent to rise instinctively for a fight, but George offered his hand instead. "Welcome to Sanctuary."

Vincent, embarrassed by his reaction, tried taking George's hand in a firm grip, but could barely fit his fingers around the big man's mitt. Their handshake left him feeling woefully inadequate.

"So you're the leader here?" Vincent asked.

George's mustache quirked up over his smile. "I guess I'm the de facto leader. People felt it was appropriate since I'm the Police Chief of Oakwood." He paused thoughtfully. "I suppose it would be more accurate to say I *used* to be the Police Chief. Organized government seems to have collapsed everywhere, so titles like that are meaningless. Now I'm just a survivor like anybody else."

"I'm sure you are," Vincent said, sneering.

"I'm sensing some hostility," George replied.

Vincent looked between the others. "Are we just going to ignore the elephant in the room?"

"What are you getting so worked up about?" Natalie asked.

Without taking his eyes off George, Vincent said, "He didn't tell you? Gil's his son."

Natalie blanched and turned her attention to George, horrified. "You didn't think to mention this to me earlier?"

George breathed a deep sigh, but nodded. "It's not something I like advertising, Natalie. I'm sure you understand why. I haven't spoken with him in years, though—didn't even know he was in the city until you showed up."

"So are you going to do something about him?" Vincent asked hotly. "Your kid's out there terrorizing people!"

George remained decidedly calm. "I already tried."

That tidbit of information caught him by surprise. "What do you mean?"

George's chair creaked as he leaned back. "After Natalie told me where Gil was, I took some of my people to investigate. I know what kind of man he is, and I knew the type of trouble he would cause in this state of lawlessness. I couldn't find him, though. Oasis Gardens was empty."

"Empty? Where did all the people go?" Elise stammered.

"That's the million-dollar question. A lot of food and clothes were left behind, but the place was a ghost town. Something must have scared them because they cleared out in a hurry."

Vincent boiled. "No, you're lying. He just happens to vanish when you go searching for him? That's bullshit and we all know it! You're covering up for your son."

"He has my name, but he's no son of mine. Not since he . . . murdered that poor woman in cold blood." George rubbed his eyes wearily. "He always had a violent streak, ever since he was a child."

Vincent saw the resemblance between George and Gil, and for a moment, all he could see was Gil's face staring back. His fingers clenched into white fists, and his body grew hot; hurting George was the only thing that made sense.

George must have sensed the murderous intent because he said, "Don't confuse me and Gil for the same person."

Elise took Vincent's fist in her hand; her skin felt soft and cool. "Stop this, Vincent. George didn't do anything wrong."

And just like that, it felt like a pressure valve had been opened, and all his steam blew off in an instant, leaving him winded and tired.

George rumbled his approval. "I can only imagine the kinds of things Gil put you all through, and I completely understand if you want to blame me for it all. It's your right to be angry at me. I accept that." He then shook his head, and his tone became cool, straightforward without a hint of malice. "But if you want to stay here, you need to come to terms with that anger you're feeling. Right here, right now. Otherwise, you're out."

Vincent sat up, terrified by the sudden prospect of being turned away after fighting so long and hard to get here.

"You'd just kick me out?"

He nodded. "You strike me as the kind of man who can hold a grudge, but there's too much at stake for me to let that go unchecked. Anger makes people do stupid things. I won't risk the lives of everyone here because you can't control your emotions."

Harsh, but fair. George's offer sounded like something Grandma herself would have said. The thought comforted Vincent.

George held out his hands. "What will it be?"

Elise chewed on her lip, her eyes shifting anxiously between the two men as the tension grew tighter by the second.

Finally, Vincent nodded. "I want to stay."

A tangible wave of relief washed over everyone in the room.

"I'm glad. I really am," George said. "Turning good people away is the last thing I want to do right now." He stood up, signifying the end of the conversation. "I've got work to attend to. Natalie, can you find them a home to stay in? I think there's an empty one next to yours."

"Sure thing," she said. "You two are probably exhausted."

"That doesn't even begin to describe it," Elise replied.

When they were back outside, Natalie regarded them hopefully. "That was . . . intense, but how do you like the place otherwise?"

"I like it," Elise said amiably. "It feels like we've got a second chance here."

"How many people are there?" Vincent wondered.

"I was told about two hundred. Not bad, huh?" Natalie replied.

"You're kidding, right?" Vincent chuckled. "My high school graduating class was bigger than that."

"Don't be so negative. It's better than nothing," Elise said.

"Not by much."

Natalie wrinkled her nose playfully at them. "Look at you two, bickering like an old married couple. Maybe I can even come over in the evenings to play bingo."

"Bite me," Vincent spat.

She winked and headed off toward a cluster of homes nearby, eventually leading them to a two-story, Spanish-styled home, with white plaster walls and a roof of red clay tiles. A brick path took them through a tidy garden and to an overarching entryway.

Natalie fished a key out from under the doormat and unlocked the house for them with a grand gesture. "Your new home awaits."

Elise's eyes popped. "This whole place is for us?"

Vincent let out a low whistle. "What happened to the previous owners?"

"Most of the folks living here ran off within the first couple days," Natalie said. "Sanctuary is mostly abandoned right now." She backed off their porch. "Get a good night's sleep, you two. George is probably going to assign you jobs first thing in the morning—that's what he did with me." She pointed to the house next door. "I won't be home until my shift at the bridge is up in a couple hours, but if you need anything just knock. Don't be strangers, you hear?"

They said their goodbyes before Vincent ushered Elise inside and locked the door. He clicked on his flashlight and pointed it around a high-ceilinged foyer, grunting his approval. "Nice place. We can pretend everything isn't utter shit outside by playing house in here."

Elise pushed her finger into his lips with a stern hush. "Don't."

"Don't what?" he mumbled around her finger.

"Don't ruin this for me, okay?"

Vincent brushed her hand aside with an understanding nod.

"Thank you." Elise lit a candle sitting on an accent table by the door, and climbed a set of stairs that overlooked the foyer.

"You can be yourself now," Vincent told Flea.

The pug pushed himself up with a yawning stretch. "Forbidden arcana! Walking around like that hurts my back! How do dogs do this?"

Elise appeared by the second-floor banister. "It looks like there are three bedrooms. I called dibs on the master bedroom already."

"When the hell did you do that?" Vincent asked incredulously.

Elise looked up in mock thought. "Uh . . . dibs." She smiled childishly. "I guess I just did."

"Hey!" he called out, but she was already gone. "At least we each get our own room then," Vincent muttered. "Come on, Flea."

They went upstairs to a sparsely decorated hallway, save for a single photo of an elderly couple. *The previous owners.* Vincent took it down and flipped it around, so he wouldn't have to see their smiling faces whenever he passed through. He entered the first bedroom on the left; it didn't look like it had ever seen use. There was a four-poster bed in the corner with frilly sheets that smelled faintly of dust, and oil paintings of angels and winged cherubs covered the walls.

Vincent grimaced at a chubby boy pondering the gravity of life in the painting next to the door. "You can take this room. I'll get the other one."

"At last, a proper bed." Flea climbed onto it with some difficulty and plopped down on his back with a satisfied sigh.

Vincent left Flea to sleep and continued down the hall. A dim glow came from an open door at the end of the hall— Elise's master bedroom—and before that was the door to what would be his bedroom. Thankfully, his room was nothing like Flea's. Someone had smacked sense into the last owners, and they had opted for a more modern look, one free of creepy angels.

Vincent made his way to the bed and started knocking the extra throw pillows to the floor, but a muffled cry grabbed his attention. He pressed his ear to the wall by his bed and heard Elise attempt to choke back muffled sobs from the other side. For a good minute, he considered going over, but when he realized he didn't know what he would say, he decided against it.

Instead, Vincent slid to the floor and let her cries lull him into an uneasy sleep filled with bitter memories.

***

Bo's hands shook as he tried unlocking the front door. "God damn it," he muttered. Hundreds of scratches marked up the lock. He blew a heavy breath and tried again, finally getting the key in. As he went through the door, he tripped over himself and crashed onto the wood floor, where he stayed for a couple minutes to wait out the horrible, spinning sensation. He tried focusing on the cool wood against his face, but heard faint whispering from the kitchen.

"He's home! What do I do?"

"Don't worry. I'll tell him what happened."

"He's going to get mad again. You heard him, he's drunk."

"Stop worrying. I'm right here with you. I'll protect you."

"Vincent!" Bo hollered. "You little bastard, what did you do this time?" he continued, slurring his words together. He pushed himself up with some effort and staggered into the kitchen.

Dante kneeled beside Vincent, their foreheads pressed together as he attempted to console his hysterical younger brother. They both turned to Bo as he came in; Vincent's red eyes went wide with fright, but Dante glared, rebellious.

"D-D-Dad," Vincent sputtered. "I was getting a cup from the cabinet, but I started to fall, so I had to grab the door!" He broke off, crying and unable to finish his thought.

"What're you talking about?" It took Bo's drunken brain a few moments to see the broken cabinet door on the counter, ripped clean from its hinges. "What did you do?" he gasped. "What did you do to your mother's cabinet? *You stupid boy!*"

Dante stepped between him and Vincent. "It was an accident, Dad. He didn't mean it."

"You little piece of shit," Bo growled. His own voice sounded strange to him, more animal than human.

"Dad, don't!"

Bo charged forward and swatted Dante aside, then bowled a closed fist across Vincent's face. The boy's head jerked back, and he fell onto the ground with a gasp. Before Vincent recovered, Bo picked him up by his neck. "You little fucking monster," he said, squeezing his hands tight. "Look what you did. Why, Vincent, why? You ruin everything!"

Vincent opened his mouth to speak, but only managed gagging sounds; his small fingers pulled weakly at Bo's hands.

Bo could barely look at him. His son was disgusting, like some kind of hideous deformity. It made Bo want to vomit. "I swear to god, I'll kill you," he said, seething and tightening his grip. "I'll end it right here."

A sharp pain across the back of his head forced him to drop Vincent. He staggered against the counter, momentarily stunned. When he looked back, he saw Dante with a junior league baseball bat in his hands.

Dante pulled his brother away and pushed him out of the kitchen. "Go to Grandma!" he yelled.

"What about you?" Vincent rasped, massaging his throat.

Dante's eyes hardened, filled with nothing but hate. "Don't worry about me. I'll meet up with you later. Just go!"

For a split second, Bo saw his younger self standing there with the bat. His drunken thoughts bounced between confusion and anger, a pinball of craziness. It finally settled on anger. "Get out!" he hollered. The veins in his neck popped from the effort. "You ungrateful shits. I hate you, I hate you, I hate you!"

Chapter 19

A gentle knock came from Vincent's door. "Wake up, sleeping beauty. We're due for scavenging duty in an hour."

He rolled over with a croak of disapproval and pulled the covers over his head. "I'll be out in a few minutes."

The door burst open with an exuberant "Rise and shine!" Natalie marched to his window and threw the blinds back, letting in the dull morning light.

Vincent didn't stir.

"That isn't exactly the effect I was hoping for," Natalie murmured. "Seriously, Vincent, wake your lazy ass up. Elise made us breakfast. It's your favorite. Cold beans from a can."

Vincent's stomach rumbled in protest. He cracked a bloodshot eye open and checked the clock on his bed stand. "Fucking hell, it's not even six yet. We've got a whole hour before we have to be there."

"The early bird gets the worm." Natalie prodded his body.

"Then the worm should sleep in," he mumbled, drifting

back to sleep. Footsteps marched to the foot of his bed, and suddenly cold air bit at his exposed body. His eyes flew open, and he hugged himself in a desperate move to keep his fleeting body heat. "Fuck you, Natalie!"

A self-described *morning person*, she had made waking Vincent part of her daily routine. Natalie winked back mischievously, a pink line of scar tissue running down her cheek. "If you want to do that, you'll have to get your ass up, cowboy."

Vincent gave her the one-finger salute, and she turned to leave.

"See you downstairs," she said, tossing his blanket on the floor.

He sulked on his bed for another minute before sitting up with a low groan. He had to massage the morning ache out of his leg first and pressed his thumbs around a dark red spot on his calf. Once it was at a tolerable level, he dressed himself and headed downstairs.

Vincent stopped at Flea's bedroom and peeked inside. Flea had converted his room into a miniature laboratory/library. Stacks of texts Vincent had gathered for him were piled knee-high, littering the floor and forcing him to navigate the room like a maze. He passed over varying academic subjects that read like an overachieving college student; there were books on botany, biology, history, advanced calculus, economics—too many to list them all.

Vincent remembered with mild annoyance that he never got the chance to finish *Gallant's Quest*, which had been forgotten at Oasis Gardens. He hated not finishing a book he started.

Vincent found Flea hidden in a cove of opened books, stirring a cooking pot of brown goop over a portable gas stove. Next to him was a long shelf of various plants, jars of preserved critter parts, bottles of vinegar and club soda, and all other manner of odd knickknacks such as marbles and breath mints.

Vincent pointed into the cooking pot. "What the hell is that supposed to be?"

Flea closed his eyes in concentration and muttered a word over his concoction. It belched out a small poof of smoke and turned a deep shade of magenta. "Regenerative Potion," Flea explained. "If it turns out the way I think it should, you'll be able to heal from severe wounds in seconds." He scooped some up in his ladle and took a taste test, smacking his lips and reflecting on it like a chef would a complex sauce. "It's missing something," he mused. "Would you like to try?"

Vincent rejected the offer with mild disgust. "No, I'm good."

Flea shrugged nonchalantly and added a clove of garlic to his potion.

"How's the staff coming along?" Vincent wondered.

Flea's little ears perked up. "I'm glad you asked." He scurried under his bed and came back out with a length of wood a yard long. It had been stripped clean of its bark, and foreign symbols—runes, Flea called them—had been carved all along the length of it. "Despite this accursed planet's chaotic energies, I've managed to create a primitive channeling staff." He tapped the tip against the floor. "I finished up the final touches last night, and I'm letting it rest for a few more hours before I test it out."

"So you'll finally be able to do magic?"

"Yes," Flea said. "You will finally cease your skepticism and cower before my true power."

Vincent raised an eyebrow. "If I didn't know you better, I'd peg you for some kind of evil sorcerer. The things you say make me think you want to conquer the world or something."

"I am not a sorcerer," Flea corrected. "I've gone over this with you multiple times already."

"Oh great, here we go."

Flea ignored Vincent's comment and continued like a professor lecturing a particularly dense student. "Firstly, there are no sorcerers, only sorceresses. Secondly, a sorceress is one who can *create* the energies required to perform magic. They are born with this ability. I, however, am a wizard. I do not create the energy, but simply rearrange what is already there. Sorceresses produce power, and wizards utilize what's there. To compare the power wielded by the two would be to compare a lowly ant to me or you."

"Thank you so much for imparting such wisdom to me, oh wise one," Vincent replied.

Flea completely missed the sarcasm and nodded curtly. "Do not fret. You will learn eventually. Perhaps we should move on to quizzes to ensure you do?"

Vincent hastily changed the subject before the idea could take root. "Is there anything you want me to keep an eye out for today?"

Flea sorted through his various bottles. "Everything seems to be stocked. If you could get me some vampire's blood, that would be wonderful. I would be able to take this potion to new heights."

"Vampires?" He mimed fangs with his fingers. "Like sharp teeth, drinks blood, vampires?"

"Of course. What other vampires are there?"

Thinking back to all the popular depictions of vampires being human murder machines, Vincent said, "Aren't vampires *dangerous*?"

Flea had already shifted his attention back to his potion. "Just be cautious," he said flippantly.

Vincent wasn't sure which was more ludicrous, entertaining the idea vampires actually existed, or the prospect of getting close enough to one to extract its blood. "Yeah . . . I'll be sure to keep an eye out for them," he drawled. He left the bedroom and headed down to the kitchen, where he found Elise and Natalie sitting down to breakfast.

"Good morning," Elise said cheerily to him.

He grunted something back and took the empty seat next to her. He looked down at his bowl of mushy refried beans; one of the scavenging parties found a whole truck of the stuff last week, so it had become Sanctuary's stock meal.

Vincent poked at his beans miserably. "What areas are we searching today?"

Natalie pulled out a piece of paper from her back pocket and unfolded it on the table between them. It was a gridded map of Oakwood, one of many hand-copied maps the scavengers got. She circled a spot in downtown with her finger. "This is what's planned for today."

Vincent forced a wad of beans down his throat. "That's going to be a three-day job at the very least with all the skyscrapers in the area. What a pain in the ass."

"How do you always know where George plans on sending us?" Elise asked.

"I made friends with some of the coordinators," Natalie replied.

"Well, can you tell them to coordinate us somewhere useful? All we're going to find in downtown are computers and office stationery." Vincent pushed his half-finished bowl away. "There's got to be some farms close by, right?"

Natalie poked a spoon at his face. "Fat chance. The nearest farm is probably a hundred miles from here."

"*Pfft*. I'd walk two hundred miles for a good steak."

Elise moaned dreamily. "Or some fresh fruit. What I'd give to have an apple. I'd even take a Red Delicious at this point. I don't care how mealy they are."

Natalie made a face. "Cut it out, guys. My poor stomach can't take this kind of taunting."

Months of preserved foods really made a person appreciate the comforts of fresh food. The three of them sat in silence, caught up in their own food daydreams until they couldn't bear it anymore. They finished breakfast and gathered up their supplies from the foyer.

Vincent double-checked he had his rain poncho in his backpack. The weather had only gotten colder and rainier in the winter months, and getting caught in it while scavenging supplies was an experience he didn't want to go through again. He then grabbed his holster off a coatrack, gave the gun in it a quick check, and buckled it around his waist. He watched Elise pluck a baseball bat out from the umbrella holder by the front door. "When are you getting your own gun?" he asked.

"I don't know. The wait list at the armory was pretty long last time I checked." She shrugged flippantly. "Besides, I haven't gone through the firearms course, so they won't consider me until I do."

"You haven't done that yet?" he asked with a hint of annoyance.

"So what?"

Vincent eyed her incredulously. "So what? Elise, you need a gun to defend yourself."

"I have you two to protect me," Elise said, pointing between him and Natalie.

"And what if we're not around?" Vincent asked.

Natalie rolled her eyes. "When is she ever going to be alone? The only time we'll ever need a gun is when we're outside Sanctuary, and we always go out there as a group." She covered one side of her mouth and spoke to Elise in a stage whisper: "I think he's overreacting."

"Overreacting?" he shouted. "This is serious life-or-death shit we're talking about. Elise needs to know how to take care of herself."

Natalie threw her arms up. "Whoa, it was just a joke. Calm down before you start getting that weird anger vein thing in your forehead—never mind, too late."

"I'll get around to it soon," Elise said. She turned quickly and went out the door before Vincent could continue his rant.

Natalie patted him on the shoulder. "You're always wound up so tight. You should learn to relax a bit. Do some yoga, meditate. Hell, get laid. Elise might be down for that."

He choked his surprise. "Say that again?"

She walked off with a cheerful smile. "It's just a friendly suggestion, hon."

Vincent gathered his things and followed them out, glowering darkly. They hiked up to the bridge, where a crowd of a couple hundred had gathered behind the cargo trailer. The three found a spot in the middle of the pack to wait, amid a constant buzz of conversation punctuated with the occasional laugh.

At exactly seven, George appeared atop the trailer with a megaphone in hand. He held it to his mouth. "Morning everyone," his voice boomed.

The crowd quieted down almost instantaneously.

"You all know I'm not one for grand speeches, so I'll make this quick. Before you all get your assignments today, I just wanted to make you aware that today marks the three-month anniversary of Sanctuary's founding."

Vincent covered his ears to muffle the crowd's raucous cheering and clapping; Elise whooped and hollered along with the rest of them.

George waited for the elated cheering to quiet just enough for him to say, "And our little town has grown from two hundred to almost two thousand. At this rate, we'll have to start sharing homes."

Vincent literally felt his body vibrate from the crowd's response, and George had to wait several more minutes before the people settled down. When he spoke again, his voice was heavy and somber. "While our town may be flourishing now, let's not forget the Catastrophe of July fifteenth. The day creatures invaded our world and took too much from us. Never forget the people we've lost . . . Please, bow your heads with me in a moment of remembrance."

A suffocating quiet fell over the crowd as Vincent put his arm around Elise's shoulder. She shuddered under his touch. When their eyes met, she took his hand in hers and squeezed, and they lowered their heads together in solidarity.

Vincent could hardly believe so much time had passed already. His memories felt so fresh, as if he had talked to Dante and Grandma only the day before. His thoughts wandered to the ghouls' nest in City Hall, and he suddenly wanted to cry out, knowing his brother was probably just a pile of bones there. It was a cruel fate he didn't deserve.

George cleared his throat and pulled the crowd from their somber thoughts. "Be careful out there. Never drop your guard, and don't take needless risks. Your life is the most important thing in Sanctuary—don't forget that." On that final note, he stepped down and disappeared into the crowd.

The scavenging party gradually came back to life and began to move forward. Small groups split themselves up among four tables at the base of the cargo trailer. Vincent and the others went up to one being managed by a wrinkled old man.

"Names?" asked the old man. He scribbled down their full names, then thumbed through a stack of folders with clerical efficiency. "You'll be searching H-12 today." He reached into a bin by his feet and counted out six granola bars and three bottles of water. "Here are your supplies. *Next!*"

The trio packed up their food and entered a line to use one of the ladders leading over the bridge blockade. A crude sign proudly proclaimed: 9 DAYS SINCE LAST ACCIDENT. They joined a trickle of people on the other side and followed them across the bridge.

Chapter 20

Vincent, Elise, and Natalie traveled with a small pack of fellow scavengers into Oakwood. It had been weeks since the last minotaur sighting, and the ghouls kept to themselves at night now, but the journey was far from uneventful. There were always bodies, bones and dried cadavers of the unfortunate ones. For Vincent, it had become a morbid game to try and piece together the puzzle of their deaths.

He came upon numerous skeletons in loose rags, chained together by manacles that had since fallen off without the flesh to hold them in place.

Minotaurs, obviously.

He then came upon the undeniable remains of a child missing half its bones.

The short sword next to the body says minotaur, but the missing bones tell me a ghoul got to the body sometime after the kid died.

It was impressive how much the Catastrophe had numbed his brain to such things.

The Catastrophe. That was what everyone called it, the day the Earth became host to both humans and creatures. He didn't know how that name came to be, or how it became universally accepted that anything nonhuman would be called a creature. It just sort of did. It made sense, though, so it stuck. New lingo for the new world.

Sometime around noon, they reached their destination. The other scavengers wandered off to begin searching for supplies to take back.

Natalie whistled and pointed out the destroyed remnants of Oakwood's police department a couple blocks away. "Is this part of our scavenging zone?"

Vincent double-checked with their map and nodded. "It's right on the outskirts. Probably worth checking it out. They might have guns in there at least."

The building looked like it had weathered an assault of epic proportions. Rubble had been strewn about the streets, and large chunks of the wall were missing, like bombs had been lobbed at the building. He noticed a crushed police cruiser nearby that begged investigation.

"What do you think happened here?" Elise asked.

Vincent climbed onto the hood of the car and studied the vehicle's indented rooftop; something had fallen on top of it. It took him a moment to realize there was a shape to the indentation. When he stepped back, he saw a giant footprint. "Holy shit." He looked up and saw a car lodged through a window on the third floor. "Did a goddamn giant pass through here or something?"

"A giant?" Elise walked over to him, looked at the police cruiser, and then at the car on the third floor. "You mean like the one killed at the end of *Gallant's Quest?*"

"Damn it, Elise, I didn't finish the book yet!"

Elise covered a gasp with her hand, realizing she had committed a cardinal sin: she spoiled part of the story for him. "Sorry, I forgot."

Vincent hopped down, muttering obscenities under his breath. "Remind me to ask Flea if giants are a thing—and no more spoilers!"

"Giants, huh? Well, that's just peachy," Natalie grumbled. "Another type of creature to keep an eye out for."

"No one from Sanctuary reported anything like it yet. Even if there really was a giant here, maybe it's gone like the minotaurs?" Elise suggested.

"Or maybe no one has survived an encounter with one to warn us about it," Vincent said.

"You are just a shining beacon of hope," Natalie said, making her way toward a hole leading into the police station.

Chunks of concrete and bent steel beams spilled out from it like the guts of a dead animal, and a large silver shield with "OPD" engraved into it hung precariously over the hole. The interior was similarly ruined, which provided them few paths to explore. They went where the building and destruction allowed them to go. After a bit of careful maneuvering around debris, through holes in walls, and shimmying along the occasional collapsed hall, they found themselves in an office on the fourth floor. It was an expansive space, untouched for months and covered in a thick layer of dust.

Vincent ran his finger across a desk and watched a small cloud of dust particles release into the air, reflecting the sunlight coming through the windows along the walls.

"You guys know the drill. Let's split up and grab what we can," Natalie said.

They scattered to separate corners and began their search. Vincent worked his way through each desk's drawers, but they all contained office supplies and useless piles of paperwork. Sanctuary had plenty of paper and pens, so it would be a wasted effort to bring back any of it.

Vincent wandered into a side hall and found a connecting break room. A chair lay in a bed of broken glass under a vending machine. He scurried over, hopeful for scraps, but a quick look meted out only disappointment.

"Anything in there?" Elise said from the entryway.

He glumly flicked one of the vending machine springs and watched it vibrate, decidedly empty. "Has a scavenging party been through here already?"

Natalie stepped beside him with a sigh. "Afraid not, pal. The coordinators have been careful about not double-dipping in areas that have been cleaned out." She jabbed her thumb over her shoulder. "Come on, there's a whole other side to look through."

They followed the hall around to the other end of the building, a mirror reflection of the office they had just passed through.

Elise and Natalie fanned out along the edges of the room while Vincent took a straight path down the center. A frosted-glass door in the far back caught his attention. As he neared it, he saw gold lettering spell out "Chief of Police." He cupped his face against the glass, but couldn't see anything inside.

"What'd you find?" Natalie asked.

"This must have been George's office," Vincent said. He jiggled the handle. "It might be worth checking out."

Elise stepped between him and the office door, frowning. "We can't just go barging into his office. It'd be an invasion of his privacy."

Vincent sauntered to a nearby desk and rummaged through its drawers for something heavy. "How is this any different from us sleeping in other people's homes, or taking the food from abandoned stores?"

"Well, for one, we didn't know them personally," Natalie said.

Vincent found a stapler and tested its weight in his hand. "Which makes it better somehow?"

Natalie shrugged at Elise. "He's got a point."

Vincent beckoned Elise over. "Come here for a sec, would you?"

She approached with an air of caution. "What do you want?"

When she was clear of the door, he threw the stapler through the glass.

Elise's jaw dropped. "Vincent!"

He went to the door, shaking his head. "Calm down, Elise. No one has to know."

"I'll know," she said, pouting.

"Good for you." Vincent snaked his hand through the

broken glass and unlocked the door from the other side.

George's office was a pristine relic of order. A heavy mahogany desk dominated the center of the room with matching bookshelves behind it. Several framed documents and medals adorned the walls, each lined up perfectly and evenly spaced apart with an anal retentive attention to detail. Of course, there was also the obligatory American flag in the corner.

Vincent went around the desk and plopped down in the former Police Chief's chair, kicking his feet up over the table. All the papers and stationery had been carefully organized on the desk, not even a single loose sheet out of place. It made his skin crawl to see everything so tidy and clean. He grabbed a thick envelope and threw it aside haphazardly to bring a drop of disorder to the whole setup.

Natalie turned away from one of the bookshelves with two photo frames in hand. "Look what I found."

One was of a younger George shaking an important-looking woman's hand while receiving a plaque; the other was of him with a smiling little boy, a fish on a line between them.

"Is that supposed to be George and Gil?" he asked, taking the fishing photo from Natalie. He leaned back into his seat and studied the picture. It was hard to believe the grinning, bucktoothed kid was the same man he had met at Oasis Gardens. It was actually kind of awful. It looked like he had a perfectly good childhood, fishing with Dad and having a blast. So how hell did he grow up into—

"Stop it."

Vincent blinked as a hand swept the picture away from him, interrupting his thoughts. He watched Elise put the photo back in its original place. "What's that all about?"

"I know that look," she said.

"What look?" he shot back defensively.

Natalie sounded her understanding. "You mean *that* look."

"What the hell are you two talking about? I don't get any looks!"

Elise planted her hands on her hips. "Trust me, you do. First you get really quiet, and then you get this deep scowl on your face. Not long after that you're usually yelling about something." She pointed a triumphant finger at his face. "There! See? You're doing it right now."

"Am not!" Vincent paused and forcibly unfurrowed his brow with his fingers. "This is just how I normally look."

Natalie snorted. "Like you're concentrating on crushing a walnut in your asshole?"

"Oh, so you're a fucking comedian now?"

Elise smothered a giggle. "That was pretty funny, Vincent."

He waved her comment away with a dismissive hand and started going through George's desk. He pulled the drawers out one by one, digging through blank forms and folders of no real relevance, but stopped at the bottom drawer— locked. He grabbed two paper clips from a dispenser on the desk, twisting the end of one into a narrow U shape and extending the other into a point.

Elise gave him an exasperated look. "Are you serious?"

Vincent sneered, and not even ten seconds later, he had

the lock picked and the drawer open. Inside was a stack of fishing magazines and a chocolate bar. "You've got to be kidding me," he said, unable to hide his disappointment. "Who locks this kind of crap up, anyway?"

"What were you expecting?" Elise asked.

"I don't know. Drugs, maybe?"

"Why would the Police Chief have drugs in his desk?" Elise asked.

Vincent waggled a finger at her. "People like George are never as squeaky clean as they make themselves out to be, especially if they're in a position of power. The higher up they are, the more skeletons they got in their closet, I guarantee it."

"How do you even get through the day being this paranoid?" Elise asked.

Natalie looked up from a pile of letters by the office's mail slot. "I think he's right," she whispered. "Vincent's on to something."

Vincent leaned over the desk eagerly. "What is it? What did you find?" Natalie dropped a stack of unopened envelopes onto the table, and he snatched them up. He frowned as he sifted through them. "I don't get it. What am I supposed to be seeing here?"

"Look at the dates on them," Natalie said.

The last piece of mail was postmarked July fifteenth, not surprising since that was the date of the Catastrophe, and the rest varied between that and July fifth.

Vincent scratched his head. *Ten days of unanswered mail?* "I don't get it."

"Don't you see?" Natalie's eyes widened, wild. "He doesn't answer his mail right away, which can only mean one thing." She paused for dramatic effect. "He must be a dirty cop! *Dun, dun, dun!*"

Vincent threw the letters in her face, annoyed. "Fuck off."

Natalie gave Elise a playful wink.

Vincent ruffled his hair with an irritated growl. "Ahh, this is bullshit! You're always giving me this crap! *'Why don't you lighten up, Vincent?'* Because neither of you are going to take this shit seriously! I'm stressing out every day over these things, getting gray hairs, so that you don't have to. And what do I get in return? Nothing but half-assed jokes at my expense! And let's get something clear: that shit wasn't even funny!"

Elise and Natalie exchanged stunned looks, then burst into abrupt laughter. Elise dropped to her knees, clutching her stomach in gleeful agony, unable to stop.

Natalie wiped a tear from her face, laughing without any reservation. "Vincent—y-you—and then you—I can't even!" Her broken sentence bubbled into incoherent chuckles, which only made Elise laugh harder in turn.

Vincent looked between the two women in absolute confusion. "I don't get what's so funny." The beginnings of a chuckle tickled the back of his throat, and before long, he joined them on the floor in a fit of crazy laughter.

This went on until the three of them were rolling on the ground, gasping for breath. Vincent managed to pull himself back onto the chair, his stomach aching. He suddenly craved something sweet and remembered the candy bar in George's desk.

"You can't do that," Elise sputtered, still trying to quell the last fires of her laughter. "We're s-supposed to bring all f-f-food back."

Vincent fought back a chuckle and unwrapped the candy bar anyway. He offered it to Natalie, who took it without complaint.

Elise regained control long enough to reproach her. "Really, Natalie?"

The other woman gave a goofy, chocolate-smeared grin.

Vincent took the candy bar back from her and took a big bite, leaving a bit for a third person to finish. He waved it under Elise's nose.

"But the rule is we have to bring all food back," she whined.

Vincent smirked. "Lighten up, Elise. Just enjoy the moment with us."

She licked her lips and reached up tentatively. "You don't think George will find out?"

"Christ, Elise. How is he going to know unless one of us tells him? And you think I'm paranoid?" Vincent shook the chocolate bar one last time. "Come on, take it."

She snatched it from his hand and stuffed the rest down her mouth in one bite. Elise let out a low moan of satisfaction. "That's really good," she said, smacking her lips around the chocolate.

"Now you're an accomplice," Vincent said.

"No," Elise wailed. "Don't say that!"

The rain started on their way back to Sanctuary. Big droplets of water came down in sheets and lightning thundered overhead. It was the kind of storm that managed to get under their ponchos and soak their clothes through. As they neared home, other groups of scavengers emerged from the city's woodwork like rats fleeing a sinking ship.

Vincent found the wrinkled old man who had seen them off, sitting grumpy and miserable in the same spot as before. A tent whipped uselessly over his head at the wind's mercy.

They dumped the miscellaneous junk in their backpacks onto the table, and after cataloguing the items, the old man ordered a young boy to box it up and carry it into town. He then shooed them away as another group of scavengers came up from behind.

Vincent, anxious to get out of the rain, led the charge home; he was exhausted from the day's hike and wanted to be under a warm blanket.

Natalie splintered off at her house and waved goodnight. "Breakfast at my place tomorrow," she yelled over the wind.

He and Elise nodded, and then continued up the sidewalk, splashed through their waterlogged walkway, and hopped onto their porch. Vincent's hand shivered from the cold, and it took a few frustrated attempts to get the door open. They hustled inside and slammed the door shut with a breath of relief while the wind and rain howled and beat incessantly to get in.

Vincent took a few, squishy steps into the house. "Ugh, I hate soggy socks."

Elise sounded her agreement and began putting away her

things, as did Vincent. They hung their wet ponchos and backpacks on the coatrack to dry, then trudged upstairs.

As they passed by Flea's room, he poked his head out and asked, "Did you manage to find any vampire's blood?"

Vincent shuddered. "No, thank god." He met Elise's curious look and added, "Apparently those exist, so don't be surprised if we run into vampires one day."

She cocked her head at Flea. "What about giants? Vincent found something that looked like a footprint, but it was huge."

"Of course giants exist," Flea said, shaking his head at such a silly and obvious question. "That's like questioning whether dragons exist."

"They . . . don't?" Elise said optimistically.

Flea tilted his head, a skeptical look on his face. "You don't honestly believe that, do you?"

Elise clamped her hands over her cheeks and tugged on her face with a groan. "Vampires, giants, *and* dragons? Why?" she bemoaned.

"Dragons are magnificent creatures. Beautiful and graceful. Deadly as well, but that's to be expected," he said nonchalantly.

Vincent patted her on the back. "Don't worry about it too much."

Elise turned toward her bedroom. "I'm going to bed before Flea says anything else to give me nightmares about."

Vincent chuckled and headed into his room. He reached down to undo his gun holster, but stopped when he recalled the conversation he had with Elise that morning. A thought occurred to him, and he turned on his heel and walked back into the hallway. Vincent unholstered his gun and knocked on Elise's door.

She answered, already dressed in her pajamas. "What's up?" She glanced at the gun in his hand and raised an eyebrow. "What are you doing?"

"I wanted to ask you a question," he said. "Can I come in?"

She hesitated, then took a step back and opened the door for him. As he walked in she asked, "Is something wrong?"

"As a matter of fact, yes." Vincent ejected the magazine from the gun and racked the slide a few times to ensure the chamber was empty. "You see this gun is empty, right?"

Elise nodded, uncertain where the conversation was going.

Vincent offered her the gun. "Here, take it."

She stepped back, aghast. "What are you doing?"

"Hold the gun, Elise."

"N-no. I don't even have training. I really shouldn't."

Vincent eyed her slyly, finally understanding why she hadn't taken the firearms course yet. "Are you too afraid to even hold a gun?"

"That's not what I said," she stammered.

"Then take it," Vincent demanded. "Look, it's empty." He dry-fired into the ceiling a few times, and Elise yelped each time the firing pin clicked.

"Stop doing that!"

He tried forcing the weapon into her hand, but she clenched her hands and shook her head.

"What's going on, Elise? You know you have to take the course."

Elise pressed her lips into a tight line. "I wouldn't expect you to understand."

"Try me."

"Those things are literally designed to kill. Killing something, or *someone,* that's a big choice. I don't like the idea of holding a weapon that can boil the decision down to the pull of a trigger."

Vincent barely stopped himself from smacking his forehead in disbelief. "Elise, you are so goddamn—"

"What?" she snapped. "I'm so *what?*"

He breathed through his nose and forced a smile. "Elise, you need to learn how to use a gun. There's no choice in the matter."

Elise folded her arms. "No I don't, and there's nothing you can say to change my mind, so please leave."

"Hang on a second," Vincent said. "Just hear me out. You're always talking about how you want to help others. How do you expect to do anything if a creature attacks?"

Elise hesitated. "I can get you or Natalie to do something."

"What if we're not around? What if we're the ones that need help?" Vincent pressed. "Come on, you're not stupid. You won't always have the option to get help. It takes only a split second for someone to die, and sometimes you'll be the only one who can stop it."

"That's so easy for you to say," Elise protested. "We're different. You can pick up a gun and shoot like it's nothing.

I can't do that, though. I don't ever want to be like you." She looked surprised by her own words and uttered a quick apology. "That didn't come out right."

Vincent took a deep breath. "You need to understand this: the only person who will always be there for you one hundred percent of the time, no questions asked, is yourself. There *will* be times when Natalie isn't there. There *will* be times when I'm not there. When that time comes, you better know how to protect yourself. Do you understand what I'm saying?"

She laughed in response, the gesture empty. "Where'd you get that from?"

"Grandma told me that." Vincent moved closer, and Elise allowed him to slide the gun into her hand. "See? It's not so bad."

She focused on the gun, reluctant, but tightened her fingers around it. "Who taught you how to shoot?"

Vincent guided her arms up and put a slight bend in her elbows. "Grandma taught me everything I know."

"Was she good at it?"

Vincent used gentle hands to guide her body into a proper shooting stance as he spoke. "Grandma was the best goddamn shot. Whenever we went to the shooting range, she'd kick my ass at target practice."

Elise shuddered. "Did she like it? Shooting guns, I mean."

"No, I don't think so. She treated it more as a chore. Like it was just something she had to do." Vincent moved Elise's finger over the trigger. "Do it."

Elise's body tightened, and the gun clicked anticlimactically.

Vincent gave her a sideways glance. "Was that really so bad?"

"I guess not."

Vincent took the gun from her and nodded. "I'm not saying you have to like it, but you need to learn. Promise me you'll go sign up for the firearms course first thing tomorrow? I don't ever want anything happening to you."

A little smile played at Elise's lips. "You act tough, but you're really just a big softy."

He gave her a lopsided grin and backed out the door. "Shut up, Elise. Goodnight."

Chapter 21

When Elise came knocking at his door the next morning, Vincent rolled out of bed feeling more rested than usual. He met her in the hallway, and they headed out for Natalie's together.

Flea called to them as they passed his bedroom door. "Do you have a moment?"

Vincent poked his head inside. "What do you want?"

Flea looked up from a small table, his staff proudly displayed on it. "It is time."

Elise leaned against Vincent and rested her chin over his shoulder. "Time for what?" she asked cheerfully.

Flea took his staff in both hands and carefully lifted it up. "The magical inscriptions have fully matured, and the staff is ready . . . Prepare your primitive minds to be amazed." He pointed the head of the staff at a candle and hesitated. "Actually, give me one moment to set the mood." Flea ran to his window and climbed a step stool up to the blinds. He closed them, blocking out the morning light, then ran back to his staff. "Okay. *Now* I am ready." He whipped his robe over the lower half of his face in a grandiose display, and said in a pseudo-mysterious whisper, "It is time for you to understand the gravity of my magical powers!"

Vincent put his palm to his face. "Oh brother."

Flea waved his staff over the candle. "Now observe this—" He paused and looked at the candle, confused. He waved his staff over it again, but nothing happened. "That's strange."

"Are you going to show me anything?" Vincent asked. "We got places to be."

Elise nudged him in the ribs with a disapproving tut-tut. "Don't be mean, Vincent."

"It seems to be more difficult than I had anticipated," Flea said with a nervous chuckle. He pointed the staff directly at the candle and concentrated. Deep lines formed in his already loose and creased face.

A faint glow formed on the wick, growing progressively brighter the harder Flea concentrated. Finally, he let out an explosive sigh; the runes on the staff flashed a bright white, and a flame magically sparked to life on the candle.

Elise applauded giddily. "That was amazing, Flea!"

Vincent frowned, unimpressed. "He hasn't even done anything yet. I can use a lighter if I have to set things on fire."

"A minor setback!" Flea shouted, looking a little wounded by Vincent's comment. "Observe, you simpleton."

"Why you little—"

Elise squeezed Vincent's shoulder. "Just let him finish.

You know how he gets when talking about his magic," she whispered.

Vincent grumbled his misgivings, but allowed the pug his insult.

Flea rolled up his sleeves and placed a jar of water on the table. He waved his staff over it with a whisper, and with some obvious effort, the water floated out of the jar. This elicited a genuine gasp from both Elise and Vincent. The water twisted into a roiling sphere and hovered in place, Flea's eyes locked onto it with a strained focus of will. He bit down on his lip and wiggled his staff as spittle flew out between his teeth.

The sphere started to freeze solid before their eyes, but then it began to bubble simultaneously.

Vincent took a hesitant step back. "Uh, Flea, you got this thing under control?"

The pug's body shook and he sucked in wild breaths of air through his nose. His face contorted in concentration, and he grunted from some unseen exertion of effort. The staff's runes flickered like a dying light, and then the half-boiling, half-frozen ball of water exploded outward.

Vincent cried out as globules of boiling water and sharp shards of ice pelted the whole room, his body included. He stayed with his arms over his face a few seconds before lowering them. "Is everyone okay?"

Elise, cowering behind him for cover, stood tentatively. "I think so."

Flea peeped over the table and looked warily from side to side. His big eyes centered on a sliver of ice embedded in the wood in front of his nose. "Oh my."

Vincent felt a small trickle of blood on his forehead. "What the fuck was that all about?" he hollered. "You could have killed us!"

"I'm not sure. My control must have slipped," Flea said sheepishly.

"Freaking hell," Vincent muttered. "This is what happens when you can't control your magic?" He turned to Elise. "How bad is it?"

She studied his face and wiped at a spot over his eye. "It's just a small cut."

Vincent whirled on Flea. "You ass, you could've blinded me!"

Flea didn't hear a word, lost in his own little world of thought. He gave his staff a couple shakes and muttered to himself like a mad little scientist. "Did I miscalculate the augmentation runes? No . . . perhaps the wood is inferior . . ." Flea tapped the staff against the floor and the runes glowed, only to sputter out weakly. His ears perked up, and he ran his nose along the staff, sniffing vigorously.

"Flea, are you listening to me?" Vincent asked.

"Huh, what did you say?" he replied irritably.

Vincent waved dismissively. "Let's get out of here before he blows us all up, Elise."

"Wait!" Flea went around the table and ran up to his feet. "Let me try one more thing that's sure to impress you."

"I'll pass."

"Please. Just one more," Flea pleaded.

Elise gave Vincent a slight shrug that said, "What could it hurt?"

Flea's eyes lit up, and he took a couple steps back; he set his legs apart in a wide stance and planted his staff down before him. "Hit me."

Vincent scoffed. "*What?*"

Flea beckoned at his body. "Kick me as hard as you can."

Vincent sounded his uncertainty and gave Elise a look.

"Do not fret, you won't be able to hurt me," Flea explained.

"Oh, I think I could fuck you up pretty bad," he said.

Flea shut his eyes, his face in a calm, meditative state. "You will not. Even as we speak I am projecting a protective shield around me."

"Oh yeah?" Vincent squatted down and reached out with a tentative hand. He stopped short of Flea's stomach. "You got your shield up *right now?*"

The little pug nodded.

Vincent poked his fingers into Flea's stomach, and the dog fell back with a sharp exhalation.

Flea opened his eyes, perplexed. "How did you do that? My shield was supposed to be up."

"Obviously it isn't." Vincent shook his head, underwhelmed by the display. "So this is the great magic you're always bragging about?"

"No," Flea wailed. "I assure you, it must be some kind of fluke." He stamped his foot irritably. "It's the accursed energy on this planet! It's always so confused, so chaotic! I had thought with a staff channeling my powers I would overcome this."

Vincent snorted. "Really? That's your excuse?"

Flea scowled cutely. "It's hardly an excuse. It is the only explanation for my inability to perform magic. I *am* the greatest wizard," he proclaimed, with such conviction that Vincent wondered who he was trying to convince.

"Maybe you just need a little more practice?" Elise suggested sweetly.

"Or a lot more," Vincent muttered.

Elise showed her disapproval by pinching his side, and then went into the room and kneeled beside Flea. She rubbed his back and said, "Chin up. You'll get your magic back."

"I'm not so sure I will," Flea replied, ears drooping. "The chaotic energy is a ubiquitous property of this world. My magic may be broken forever."

With all the talk of magic and energy, an idea occurred to Vincent. "If the energy is so chaotic here, then how can a Gate even exist?"

Flea looked up, somber. "What do you mean?"

"I'm just reaching here, but a Gate is made with magic, right?"

Flea nodded slowly.

"Well, if it's made of magic, shouldn't the chaotic energy break them apart?" Vincent shrugged. "Seems to me that *some* magic can exist on Earth."

Flea's ears perked up. "Forbidden arcana, you might be on to something."

Vincent nodded. "I have my moments."

"Sometimes it takes a remedial intellect to point out something so obvious!" Flea hurried to a whiteboard pinned to the wall and began scribbling complex equations and strange symbols onto it.

Vincent cocked his head at Elise, one finger pointed to Flea. "Did he just—?"

Elise jumped to her feet and ushered Vincent away before he fully processed the backhanded compliment. "Let's give Flea his space to work. We have to go meet up with Natalie now anyway."

"He just called me stupid again, didn't he?" Vincent asked as they walked outside.

Elise smiled sweetly, but didn't answer the question.

Chapter 22

Vincent stood by his bedroom window, a cold wind nipping at his nose as he smoked. He flicked the tip over an overflowing graveyard of cigarette butts buried in ash, while absently observing the clouds above. They drifted lazily across the sky, fat and bloated, ready to rain at any moment. And it was quiet. Vincent liked that about the new world. As much as the Catastrophe fucked things up, that was one thing it did right.

Fewer people, less noise.

His bedroom door slammed open. "Vincent, guess what day it is!"

He ignored the intrusion and hoped it would go away on its own, but he could already feel his peaceful repose slipping away.

"Vincent!"

Going, going . . .

"Vincent, are you listening to me?"

And gone.

Vincent put out his cigarette and turned to find Natalie and Elise at the door. "Why does no one ever fucking knock around here?"

Natalie fanned a few tendrils of lingering smoke out of her face. "You got something to hide?"

He rubbed his temples and put on a tight smile. "Just tell me what the hell you're doing in here."

"Don't you know what today is?" Elise asked, bubbling over with excitement.

Vincent smirked. "Can you tone it down a bit? People don't smile that much, and it's creeping me out."

Elise opened her mouth in a big O, looking very offended. "It's November tenth, you dummy."

Vincent put a cigarette between his lips and patted down his pockets for a lighter. "Yeah, so what?" he said.

Natalie snorted. "You have got to be kidding me."

Elise set her head at a sassy tilt. "It's your *birthday*."

His brow went up in mild surprise. "It is?" He thought about it for a moment. "It is."

Elise pulled out a brightly wrapped box from behind her and held it out to him. "Happy birthday."

Vincent looked at it, dumbfounded, then back to Elise. "What is it?"

"It's a gift. For you." She forced it into his hands and he read the label.

To a dear friend: Happy Birthday.

"Don't open it yet," she said giddily. "You have to see everything else first!" Elise took him by the hand and raced downstairs.

Vincent stopped in their living room entrance and marveled at colorful decorations that had been set up. Rainbow-colored balloons bounced against each other, tethered to the furniture; paper tassels hung from corner to corner; and letters dangled on the far wall, spelling out Vincent's name in bright colors. Flea waved from the couch, a tiny party hat strapped to his fat head at a jaunty tilt.

Elise walked to the middle of the room, then turned around with her arms spread out. "So? What do you think?"

Vincent joined her, astounded that Elise had done so much for him. He couldn't remember the last time he had a real party. Most times, his birthday was just an excuse to get shitfaced at a bar. "How did you even know it was my birthday?"

"You told me, remember?"

Vincent ran his thumb over his present, confirming it wasn't just a figment of his imagination. "And you actually remembered."

"Well, duh," she said. "It's an important day, why wouldn't I remember it?" Elise waved offhandedly. "Anyway, open your present! I know you're usually supposed to save that for last, but I can't wait to see your reaction."

Natalie punched him playfully on the shoulder. "Go on, open it already. She hasn't been able to shut up about it for the last month. Shoot, if you make her wait any longer she might explode from the anticipation, literally."

Vincent carefully undid the wrapping paper and found three dog-eared books in his hands. He read each title aloud, unable to hide the awe in his voice. "*Gallant's Quest, Lady Windamere's Legacy,* and *Draconic Absolution.* You got the whole trilogy here."

"He loves it!" Elise squealed.

"A resounding success," Flea cheered.

"How did you even find these?" Vincent asked.

"It wasn't easy," she said with a playful wink. "I looked for them for almost two whole months. Whenever we went scavenging I was also keeping an eye out for them."

Vincent nodded, impressed. "Without me noticing?"

"You're not the only one who can be sneaky," Elise said.

He grinned, still caught in a mild daze. "I don't know what to say. Thank you?"

Natalie laughed warmly, the sound deep and hearty. "You act like you've never had a birthday before."

He smiled sheepishly. "I was never big on them even as a kid, and when it was just me and Grandma, she'd usually make—"

"Cookies!" Elise interrupted. "Hang on one sec." She hurried into the kitchen, and then reappeared with an overflowing plate of cookies. "It's not a cake, but I figured it's something you could appreciate."

His eyes blew up to the size of silver dollars. "Are those what I think they are?"

Elise wiggled her eyebrows enticingly. "I don't know. Are they?"

Vincent was practically salivating as he picked one out. It was still warm and had a slight give under his fingers. The first bite was exactly how he remembered Grandma's cookies. Chewy, cinnamon-infused, melt-in-your-mouth goodness.

Perfection.

Natalie watched the look on his face, intrigued. "All right, I need to see what the fuss is all about." She popped a whole cookie into her mouth and immediately moaned. Her eyes rolled up in a euphoric high.

Elise, grinning ear to ear from their reactions, kneeled down so Flea could take one. The pug took a tentative lick of the cookie, then abruptly stuffed the whole thing into his mouth, swallowing it amid snorts and smacking lips. When he was done, he blinked as if waking from a dream. "Oh my—that was embarrassing."

Elise took a dainty bite of her own creation. "What's the verdict, guys?"

"Mmmf," Vincent replied, too busy chewing to formulate any real words. Elise's cookies were good—nearly identical to Grandma's, and possibly better. That, combined with the awful rations of cold beans and dry cereal in the last month, meant he could kill for more. He greedily grabbed a cookie in each hand and set to work eating them.

That was all the answer Elise needed. She did a little happy dance on the spot, all smiles and giggles.

They played out the rest of the day enjoying each other's company. They talked and joked for hours; it was the kind of conversation that flowed naturally from longtime friends, and Vincent learned a little more about everyone.

Elise had planned on going to med school to become an

immunologist or a surgeon—she had never quite made up her mind before the Catastrophe hit.

Flea, in predictable Flea fashion, talked about his magical achievements. Apparently he was credited with creating the Armoring Potion and Truesight Tincture, both of which could be found in the most prestigious alchemical encyclopedia on Terra Mater, *The Potionologist's Companion.*

Natalie was also quite the interesting lady. She was an avid big game hunter and had made several excursions with her father to Africa. She claimed to be proficient in bow and spear hunting as well, but Vincent suspected she might have been exaggerating her skills in that regard.

At some point the conversation veered into stories of past sexual exploits. Natalie put Vincent to shame with the amount of freaky shit she had gotten into, some of which had happened in the months since coming to Sanctuary.

"Don't make that face at me, guys. If you knew how big Conrad's—"

"Stop! Stop! For the love of god, stop talking."

When Elise's turn came to spill the beans, she blushed profusely and changed the subject, bringing out a deck of cards to play with. They played poker, blackjack, and Texas Hold 'em. Of course some playful gambling was involved with cookies in lieu of chips. Unfortunately for Vincent, Elise and Natalie were natural card players. Even Flea, who had to pick up the games on the spot, fared better than Vincent, who lost way more cookies than he was willing to part with.

"This is bullshit! You can't do this to me on my birthday!"

As day progressed to night, Vincent popped out a bottle of whiskey he had squirreled away for a rainy day. Despite Elise's initial misgivings, he got everyone to drink with him, and they finished out the celebration by getting drunk off their asses. It was a different kind of drunk from his previous birthdays though; it wasn't to forget.

Elise stood up on wobbly legs with a heavy hiccup, her cheeks rosy. "Guys, I think I'm—I'm a little drunk. M-maybe it's time to go to bed?"

"What are you talking about?" Vincent shot back. "I'm not even buzzed. What'd you have, like eight shots of whiskey? That's nothing!" He poured himself another drink and threw it back in one gulp.

Natalie belched from the couch, sprawled out over it with her head hanging over the armrest. "No, Vincent. Eight shots is only nothing if you're an alcoholic." She pointed to a lump of fur on the floor. "The wittle guy's all tuckered out."

Flea had passed out on his back, snoring so loudly it made his lips flap. He mumbled something incoherent, then scratched his stomach and rolled onto his side, kicking an empty shot glass away from him.

Vincent scowled. "You guys are such lightweights. Come on, just a little more."

Natalie checked the time on her watch, then shook her head. "It's already nine, and my head feels just fine where it's at, thank you very much. Any more and I'll be throwing up in your bathroom." She hoisted herself up with a slight grunt. "Good night, folks. It's been a lovely evening."

Elise waved a napkin at her and put on a fake Southern belle accent. "Bye bye! Y'all come back soon, you hear?"

Natalie eyeballed her. "Cheeky bitch. Are you making fun of me?"

Elise hiccupped into a giggle. "Never," she said gravely, and then fell over laughing.

"I rest my case, judge. The girl is *done*. I'm *done*, and Flea is *done*. Get your girl's ass up to bed. I'll carry Flea."

Vincent crawled over to Elise, now snoozing on the hard floor, and picked her up. She wiggled limply in his arms, so it took him a few tries to finally get her weight over his shoulder. He carried her upstairs to her bedroom while Natalie tucked Flea into his bed.

Vincent carefully laid Elise out on her bed, then lit a candle on her nightstand. She mumbled a protest, but let him pull the blanket over her. He noticed an unloaded pistol resting beside the candle, and it brought a smile to his lips. She had kept her promise and gotten herself a gun from the armory.

Natalie called to him from the front door. "See you tomorrow, Vincent!"

He walked to the banister and said, "Don't pass out on my lawn!"

She waved farewell, then slammed the door behind her and wandered toward her house, laughing over a joke only she knew.

He went back to Elise's bedside and stooped to blow out the candle, but paused when he was eye level with her. He brushed her dark hair out of her face and tucked it behind her ear. Despite being piss drunk and snoring like a motor, Elise still had an alluring quality about her he hadn't noticed before—put bluntly, she was pretty.

Vincent caught himself staring at her while she slept and looked away, acutely aware of how awkward and creepy that was. He blew out the candle and turned to walk away when he felt a warm hand grab his wrist.

Elise breathed a heavy sigh. "I've been thinking, Vincent, and something doesn't make sense to me."

He had heard that kind of slurred speech thousands of times before. He gently shook her hand off and said, "Go to bed Elise. You're drunk."

"No! Listen to me," she demanded.

Vincent rolled his eyes. "All right, fine," he said, prepared for a drunken monologue.

Elise composed herself before speaking the very important matter on her mind. "You're always telling me we need to look out for ourselves. Did Grandma think that way too?"

"Sure she did."

"That just doesn't make sense to me, though. If she was *really* so self-centered, then why did she help you and Dante?"

"What are you—she was—that's different."

"Is it?" Elise prodded. "You aren't her family. If she really believed helping others was a waste of time, then why did she take care of you? Isn't it . . . a little fishy?"

"Elise, you're not thinking straight. Go to bed already."

Elise shook her head furiously under the blanket. "I think that deep down, under all that swearing and smoking, she really cared . . . for two little boys who needed help. It didn't matter who you were because her heart told her it was the right thing to do. Do you understand me?"

"Elise . . ."

"Do you understand me?" she asked again with more force.

He took a few seconds to reply, but said in a soft whisper, "Yeah, I think I do."

A dreamy smile crept over her face. "You're a good guy, Vincent. I want you to know that I think you're swell." Her eyes began to close when she suddenly shot up like a jolt of electricity. "Oh no!"

Vincent jumped in his shoes, startled by her outburst. "What, what? Something wrong?"

"I forgot to take the extra cookies to George," she moaned. She kicked the covers off and tried getting out of bed, but Vincent gently pushed her back down.

"What are you talking about?" he asked.

"I have to give him the extra cookies," Elise explained. "It's not too late, I bet he's awake still."

"Hey, would you cut it out?" Vincent said, holding down a squirming Elise. "What cookies do you have to take to him, and why?"

"He helped with the cookies—I mean, he got the ingredients," Elise stammered. "I have to repay him."

Vincent nodded his understanding. "I'll go take the damn cookies to him myself. You can barely walk right now."

"You'd do that for me?" Elise asked in awe. "Oh, Vincent, you're the best."

To hide the heat in his cheeks, he hastily asked, "Where are these extra cookies I'm supposed to be taking him?"

Elise's eyelids began to droop as she spoke. "They're in the . . . blue container . . . kitchen . . ." Her voice trailed off into a deep and contented snore.

Vincent found the container of cookies she described in the kitchen and hurried to the bank, spurred on by the cold wind blowing through the empty streets. The front door was locked, so he banged on it a few times, eager to get back home and under the warmth of his own blanket.

A dark shadow stirred inside, and a moment later George appeared behind the glass door, looking mildly surprised by his presence.

"What're you doing out here so late?" George asked as he opened the door.

Vincent opened his mouth to answer, but a wall of cologne wafted out and wrapped around his face and nose, making him choke. He backpedaled, sputtering and fighting for breath. "Jesus Christ, George. Maybe you should ease up on the perfume!" He coughed a few more times. "Shit, man!"

"Sorry about that," George said. He looked down at a blue bottle in his massive hand and grimaced. "I got a terrible nose for this kind of stuff, so I can never tell how much I've put on."

Vincent nodded, a safe distance away. "No kidding. Why are you even using the stuff? You got a lady you trying to impress in bed—or suffocate?"

A laugh rolled up from a deep cave inside George's lungs, booming across the parking lot. "No, it's much simpler than that." He motioned at his thick body. "Look at me, Vincent. I'm a big, hairy man, and I sweat a lot. I'm locked up inside all day figuring out the logistics of running Sanctuary, so I start to smell something awful. I'd use deodorant, but we're short on supply, so I thought cologne could work for now."

"Maybe for everyone else's sake, you should make an exception and just use whatever deodorant we got left." Vincent pinched his nose and strode forward to give George the cookies. "These are from Elise."

He took them with a grateful smile. "Very nice. I'm guessing your birthday went well?"

Vincent stepped back into the safety of the parking lot for the sake of his nose. "You know what? It really did. I enjoyed it a lot."

"I'm happy to hear that. It's still hard to find things to smile about these days."

Vincent stuffed his hands in his pockets and frowned. "What did Elise have to do to get the stuff for the cookies?" he asked, suspicious.

George held up his share of them.

"That's it?" Vincent raised an eyebrow in question.

George chuckled at the skepticism. "I was just doing

something nice for her, for you."

"There's no such thing as a free meal."

George returned the skeptical look. "Are you telling me I made a mistake?"

"I'm just trying to wrap my head around your reasoning. We catalogue all our food and carefully ration it out. Why let Elise waste precious ingredients on something as stupid as a birthday?"

"It's not rocket science, boy," George began. "This isn't a dictatorship. None of you are military personnel trained to survive grueling hardships. We're all just . . . people, forced into a bad situation. Do you know what people need during these dark times?"

Vincent shook his head.

"Hope. Nothing binds us together tighter, nothing makes us fight harder, than a healthy dose of hope." George bobbed his mountainous shoulders. "What are we fighting for here, Vincent? Do we just want to survive like animals, or do we want to *live*?" He pointed a thick finger at him. "Think about that." He then took a step back and began to shut the door. "Have a good night, Vincent."

Vincent stood in the parking lot alone, mulling over what Elise and George had said. Their words ran counter to everything he had ever learned from growing up in Oakwood, but he supposed it made sense . . . in a weird sort of way. He smiled and started back for the house. He had some much overdue reading to do.

***

"You stupid boy!"

The switch whistled through the air and struck Bo over the head; he bowed in excruciating pain and did his best not to show it. Showing pain made her hit harder.

"Again!" The switch snapped against the table at the command.

He refused to look at the school assignment.

"I said again!" the woman shrieked.

The sound cut into him like shards of glass and sent a shiver down his thin frame. Bo, trembling, glanced at his mother and wondered if she enjoyed tormenting him. She knew it was an exercise in futility, like banging his head against a brick wall, expecting it to give.

There was an idea: he could smash his head against a brick wall until he died. At least then he wouldn't have to endure this never-ending punishment.

"Don't make me ask you again, Bo."

He looked up at his mother, to his nine-year-old eyes a looming giant of a woman at five feet tall, and then turned his attention to the book on the table. He recited the passage for what was probably the hundredth time, but as he read further down, the symbols and lines blurred together and rearranged themselves in ways that didn't make sense.

He misread the next word.

A white hot line of pain formed across his cheek. He winced and felt the heat of a swelling bruise under his skin.

"How?" Bo's mother moaned. "How can you be so stupid?" She threw the switch down in a fit of frustration and slapped him on the side of the head.

Bo fell onto the ground, ears ringing, and quickly curled up into a tight ball in preparation for what came next.

"Get up! I said get up!" She kicked him hard in the thigh. "Why can't you be like your sisters and do well in school? I'm killing myself at the factory so you can have a better life, and this is how you repay me?"

"I'm trying, I promise! I just don't understand it!" he wailed.

She twisted her face into something hideous. "I just don't understand it," she mimed. "You're lazy! Stupid! Useless!" She devolved into harsh, indiscernible ravings like a mad dog, frothing at the mouth.

Bo endured the ensuing beating like he did all the others. It lasted until she exhausted herself and left the room to get dinner.

He dragged himself to his feet and limped to the corner, where he curled into a sniffling ball of self-pity and anger. He had been reduced to nothing more than an animal, wounded and humiliated.

It wouldn't be until years later, when Bo was an adult, that he would learn he was dyslexic. At the time, he wondered if it would have saved him from any of the beatings.

Probably not.

Chapter 23

Over the next few days, Vincent blew through the books Elise had gotten him with the voracity of a man starved of food for weeks. He rolled over on his bed with *Lady Windamere's Legacy* open, already halfway through it, when his stomach grumbled angrily at him.

Vincent sat up abruptly, surprised by the intensity of it. A quick look at the clock on his nightstand told him why. It was creeping toward two in the morning, and he hadn't eaten since dinner. He grabbed his nub of a reading candle and headed for the kitchen.

When he passed by Flea's open bedroom, he saw the pug passed out face-first in the pages of a large textbook. A pot simmered happily over a low flame next to him, some new potion of a brilliant shade of yellow.

Vincent turned off the stove and put Flea to bed; the little pug snorted and licked his nose, but remained fast asleep.

Vincent's stomach reminded him why he was up in the first place, and he made a hasty exit downstairs into the kitchen. Vincent searched through the cabinets, frowning at their predictable selection of food: energy bars, canned goods, cereal, some bags of nuts, and spaghetti noodles.

He popped the lid off a can of creamed corn and went to eat his late snack by the kitchen sink window. He slurped up his food messily, intent on getting back to his book, and was so preoccupied with Gallant's fate in the story that he almost missed it.

Movement came from Natalie's front door, something so imperceptible he dismissed it as a trick of the eyes. There was another slight movement, and that time he realized something was there. He set the can down with a belch and strained his eyes against the darkness.

A shadowy figure made a hasty retreat from Natalie's house; there was a brief break in the clouds, and they passed under a strip of light from the moon. Vincent saw a person dressed entirely in black, head obscured beneath a hood.

"What the hell?" His senses sharpened, interest piqued.

Why was someone sneaking around her house like a thief? The mysterious intruder stopped in the street, made sure no one else was around, and then darted down the road. Without thought, Vincent sprang into action, grabbing his jacket off the coatrack on his way out the front door.

Vincent pulled his collar tight around his neck and ran after the person, sticking to the sidewalk and darting between shadows for protection. The neighborhood lit up in a brilliant flash of white, rumbling light, and Vincent slunk into a bush like a frightened animal caught in the open. He watched a streak of lightning course through the clouds overhead, then disappear. A second later, a droplet of water hit his cheek. "That's just great," he murmured, and it began to rain.

Vincent left the bush and quickened his pace, eventually coming to a three-way intersection, deserted. If he followed the road right it would take him into the center of Sanctuary; if he took the road left it would lead him to a rocky bluff at the edge of the island. He squinted in either direction, searching for any signs of his mystery man, and found his target headed down the left road. Vincent pressed himself low to the ground, years of skulking in the dark telling him to minimize his presence. Keeping a safe distance, he followed the person to a dead end sign.

The person climbed the rotted fence at the end of the road and made his way toward the sound of crashing waves and storming weather, Vincent secretly on his heels. They eventually stopped at a cliff that overlooked a painful death of sharp rocks and rushing waves, reaching as high as a house. Across the raging waters loomed the dark silhouette of Oakwood's coast.

Vincent planted himself behind the cover of a weathered tree and watched what happened next with increasing suspicion and fear.

The person took out a giant flashlight, the kind you have to hold with a handle, and held it overhead in Oakwood's direction. The bulb flicked on, then off, then on and off again. It went on like this for a full minute at varying intervals before finally stopping. Several minutes passed, during which the weather only grew worse. The bay's water crashed against the bluff, lapping over the edge and spraying water everywhere.

A pinpoint dot of light appeared across the bay, blinking on and off sporadically. It didn't take Vincent long to realize it was some kind of code, possibly Morse code. He couldn't believe it. Someone was sending messages off the island, and even more amazing, someone was answering!

But who, and why?

Lightning struck, illuminating the sky and cliff below it; Natalie's determined face appeared briefly in the night before being swallowed up by it. Vincent clamped his hand over his mouth, barely stifling his gasp at the revelation.

He kept out of sight while Natalie finished. She then tucked her flashlight under her arm and darted past him, unaware of his presence. Vincent emerged from his hiding spot and watched her disappear into Sanctuary, wondering what the hell he had witnessed.

Whatever it was, he had to tell the others.

"Elise, Flea, wake up!" Vincent pounded up the stairs and knocked on their respective bedroom doors. "Wake up!"

Elise cracked open her door, sleepy-eyed, hair sticking out in sporadic tufts. "What are you doing?" she mumbled.

Flea appeared behind him, looking similarly disgruntled. "I have half a mind to turn you into a frog, you rude fool."

Vincent shushed him with an irritated scowl. "I just saw Natalie talking to someone off the island."

Elise's eyes opened a smidgen. "What are you talking about?"

Flea plopped down on the floor. "Yes, please elaborate. You are making very little sense, and I am so very tired."

Vincent took a moment to collect his jumbled thoughts. "I was downstairs getting a snack when I saw Natalie sneaking away from her house."

"Sneaking about in the middle of the night? That sounds a little dangerous." Flea snorted. "Naturally, you followed."

"Not my best idea, I know."

"You don't seem to have many of those," Flea said.

Vincent ground his teeth. "Anyways," he growled. "I followed her to the edge of the island and saw her signaling with a flashlight toward Oakwood. When she finished, someone signaled back. I think it might have been Morse code."

"Are you sure that's what you saw?" Elise asked dubiously.

He motioned at his damp clothes. "I did not dream this shit up. I was definitely out there, and I know what I saw."

"So what did this message say?" Flea asked.

Vincent shook his head. "I don't know Morse code."

"Well, why not?" Flea asked.

"Because I never bothered learning it," he snapped.

Flea sniffed haughtily. "How disappointing. It only took me ten minutes to memorize it from one of the books you found me."

Vincent smacked Flea gently over the head. "I know you're a smart little shit, but can we please focus on what's important here?"

Flea pouted, his pride more wounded than his head.

"Fine, you brute. Did you bother asking Natalie what she was doing there?"

"No."

Elise shook her head, confused. "Why not? I'm sure there's a perfectly good explanation."

Vincent smacked his forehead, exasperated. "There isn't going to be any kind of *good* explanation for what I saw. You don't think this is shady as all hell?"

"It's a little fishy, but Natalie's our friend," she said.

Vincent snorted at the suggestion. Grandma had always taught him to err on the side of caution; suspicion and wariness were your best friends when confronted with the unknown. "Natalie's up to something, and it isn't good."

"You're reading too much into this," Elise said.

"She's sending messages to someone off the island!" Vincent shouted. "Until now, the only survivors we knew about were on Sanctuary. Whoever is out there obviously knows about the island, so why are they choosing to stay out there, instead of here where it's safe? Something is not right, Elise!"

She wilted away from his yelling. "You don't have to be a jerk about it."

Vincent kneaded the bridge of his nose. "Sorry. I'm just a little freaked out."

"It's okay." She gave him a reassuring smile. "So what're we going to do?"

"If this is truly as grave a situation as you believe, shouldn't we tell someone? George, perhaps?" Flea said.

Vincent swatted his suggestion back. "No, no, we can't

tell anyone else about this. We have to handle this ourselves."

Flea scratched his head. "I don't understand. Why?"

Vincent chose his next words carefully. "People can do some fucked-up things when they're scared. We've seen it before with Gil's group, and it would be the same thing here. I know it doesn't seem likely right now, but that's only because George has created a safe haven. If people start feeling threatened, you'll see their true faces, and it'll get ugly. They'd string Natalie up, I guarantee it." He shook his head. "And who do you think they'll turn to after that?"

"We would be guilty by association." Elise hugged herself, contemplative. When she spoke again, she refused to meet his eyes. "We'll do it your way. I don't like it, but . . . I think you're right."

Flea made a flustered sound and rubbed his temples. "Argh, you humans make everything so complicated. Mixing potions makes more sense than this."

"How do you want to handle it, then?" Elise asked.

"First, I'm going to figure out who she's talking to," Vincent said.

Chapter 24

When Natalie showed up at the front door for breakfast, Vincent greeted her like nothing was wrong.

"Look at you, Mr. Early Bird," Natalie said. She tapped him playfully on the arm. "What's the special occasion, cowboy? Wait, don't tell me. Did you and Elise finally do the deed?" She elbowed him jocularly as a crease formed in his brow. "Relax, I'm just teasing."

He made a noncommittal sound. "Just come in."

They headed into the kitchen together, and he set the table for breakfast. As he rifled through their cabinets, he said in a conversational tone, "Did you notice that thunderstorm last night? It was a real nasty one."

Natalie took a seat at the kitchen table and picked her teeth. "Can't say that I did, but what's new, right? The weather's been awful ever since the Catastrophe."

Vincent didn't react to the lie.

She pulled her finger from her mouth and flicked something away without a second glance. "You grew up around here, has the weather always been so bad?”

“Never. We have dry winters here.”

She nodded sagely. “Seems strange, then, doesn’t it?”

“It’s not any stranger than minotaurs and ghouls.”

“Speaking of minotaurs, when was the last time we’ve even seen one?” Natalie asked.

Vincent had to think about it. “It’s been at least a month.”

“Now *that* is weird. I wonder where they all went?”

He chuckled. “What was it you told me before? Don’t look a gift horse in the mouth?”

“Yeah, I suppose,” she drawled. “But it just doesn’t make sense. Why conquer a whole city just to abandon it?”

Natalie brought up a good point.

“Maybe it was for sport?” Vincent suggested.

Her face darkened. “I know what hunting for sport is. What they did was more like an extermination.”

“Morning, guys,” Elise said, coming into the kitchen. She paused and studied their faces. “Did I miss something?”

“No, don’t worry about it,” Natalie said. “Now how about some grub? I’m starving!”

They ate a cold breakfast of dry cereal and water, then left for scavenging duty. The day went by without incident, but Vincent couldn’t help but feel on edge the entire time. Whatever concept of safety and comfort he had developed over the last few months had been ripped from him the moment he realized other survivors were hiding out in the city. Now he felt naked and exposed, wandering through

Oakwood. Every empty window, suspicious alley, and open door gave him pause. Vincent put up a good front, though, and kept his suspicions under wraps. Natalie couldn't know that something was wrong.

After saying his good nights to Elise and Flea that evening, Vincent went to the kitchen window, where he could get a good view of Natalie's home, and waited.

At around two in the morning, same as the previous night, she snuck out of her house; Natalie led him to the exact same spot at the edge of Sanctuary, and she relayed another message with her flashlight. And again, someone messaged back—Vincent mentally recorded the spot, then went home.

The next morning, an hour before the trio's usual meeting time, he snuck back to the cliff. He made sure no one saw, especially Natalie. He squinted over the water to the spot he had memorized, noting a baby-blue house nestled in a neighborhood overlooking the waterfront. He was back home before anyone could figure out he was missing.

This routine went on for a whole week, like clockwork. Vincent would follow Natalie out to the spot at night, and the following morning would check where the responding message had come from. It was the baby-blue house every time. That house was where he would get answers.

When Vincent got back to the house that morning, he gathered Elise and Flea together in his room.

"Tonight's the night," he said.

"Was it the same spot as before?" Elise asked.

Vincent nodded. "Have your things ready to go, but pack light."

"Should I bring my gun?" Elise asked, already grimacing at the answer she knew was coming.

"Yeah. There's no telling what we'll find out there." Vincent motioned to Flea. "You'll need to bring some potions, too. They might come in handy."

"You don't mean to say I'm going with you two?" Flea asked.

"Of course you are," Vincent replied.

Flea wrung his hands nervously. "Are you sure? This may be dangerous, and I would only be a burden to you."

"I need your brain," Vincent said. "If a creature is hiding out there, we'll need you to fill us in on how to deal with it."

Flea looked entirely unconvinced. "But I cannot do magic, remember? I haven't figured out a way around the problematic energies here. My knowledge can only help so much without magic to back it up."

"Come on, you're always bragging about how great you are. You're going to let a minor setback scare you away?" Vincent crossed his arms. "Unless, you know, you're full of shit and aren't actually all that great."

Flea eyeballed him. "You dare doubt me? I *am* great; however, we're all full of fecal waste. I don't understand how that pertains to anything."

Vincent realized, chuckling, that Flea had interpreted what he said literally; Elise joined in, hiding a girlish giggle behind her hand.

"What's so funny?" Flea demanded.

Vincent stopped laughing and became somber again. "You don't have to come, but we might not make it back without your help."

Flea stiffened at the thought, then nodded with a knowing sigh. "You are right. You would both be lost without me." He threw his hands up in a fit of frustration. "You're always getting me into troublesome situations, Vincent! Ever since I came to this accursed world of yours, it has been danger, danger, and more danger—hardly fitting for a wizard of my caliber." He wandered out of the room, mumbling angrily under his breath. "I should be doing research, not dangerous reconnaissance missions."

Elise smiled, the gesture halfhearted. "I hope this all turns out to be one big misunderstanding."

Vincent went around his room that evening and gathered up his poncho, flashlight, and gun. After checking his magazine, he changed into dark clothes and pulled a black beanie over his head. He then unfolded a map onto his bed and checked the directions one last time. He had already outlined the path he would take with a red pen, and if everything went according to plan, the walk there would only be about an hour and a half. Plenty of time to get into position. He folded the map back into his pocket.

Everything was ready.

Vincent went to Flea's room and knocked. "It's time to go." He opened the door and found him waiting inside, a small satchel hanging from his shoulder. "What the hell is that for?"

Flea patted the bag, and glass clinked noisily. "These are all the potions and elixirs I have brewed."

"You can't bring all that. People are going to hear you from a mile away."

The pug clutched his satchel with both arms. "But I want to be prepared for anything."

Vincent furrowed his brow. "We're trying to be sneaky. Bring only a couple."

"Only a couple?" he shot back. "How am I to choose? I can't predict what situations we'll find ourselves in."

The lines in Vincent's forehead creased deeper. "Figure it out," he growled. "We're burning precious time."

Flea set his satchel down and began rummaging through its contents. "Do you think we'll need a Gill Potion?" He lifted a crystalline vial of clear liquid. "It will allow us to breathe underwater."

"What? No."

Flea set it aside with a muted grumble, then pulled out a few more bottles. "What about a Poison Nullifier, or Dragon's Breath? One will cure any poison, the other will allow the imbiber to breathe fire." He then lifted a vial of brown sludge. "Surely my signature Armoring Potion would be useful—although, it's not quite the same. I had to improvise some parts of the recipe."

"Christ, we don't have time for this," Vincent griped. "Just bring the Dragon's Breath and Armoring Potion."

Flea dropped the Dragon's Breath into his pocket, then handed the Armoring Potion to Vincent. "One for each of us." He then pulled his hood over his head and hurried out the door. "Come along, Vincent. You're wasting time just standing around."

His fingers involuntarily clenched into tight claws. He shut his eyes and took a calming breath. "Let it go, Vincent. Just let it go. We've got more important things to think about tonight."

Elise waited at the bottom of the stairs, glum but ready, dressed in similarly dark colors. The three of them nodded to one another, then slipped out the front door.

Natalie's house loomed ominously before them as they slunk past. Vincent wondered what she was up to in there, hidden behind those walls. What was she plotting?

He shook his head and turned his focus back to the task at hand, leading the others to the island's bridge. Vincent stopped them behind a tree and looked up the road to the blockade. Shadows flickered in a warm glow above the cargo trailer, and the distinct sound of muffled conversation filled the air.

"How are we going to get across without them noticing?" Elise asked.

"With a distraction," Vincent explained. "Wait here." He moved to the other side of the street and gathered a small bundle of twigs and grass from around him, and then placed it all under a lone bush.

Everything was still damp from the previous day's rain, but it wasn't anything some lighter fluid couldn't fix. He produced a small can of it, doused his kindling, and then set it aflame with his lighter. Vincent gave it a few coaxing breaths to really get it going, and then darted back to Elise and Flea.

"Vincent, what are you doing?" Elise hissed.

"Calm down. I just need something big enough to get their attention. It won't cause any real harm." *I hope,* Vincent thought.

It took a few minutes for the bush fire to really get going, but when it did—

"Holy shit! Do you see that?"

"Get water! Someone go into Sanctuary and get help!"

Vincent and the others shrunk back as Conrad led a handful of men and women down from the cargo trailer and to the fire. While the bridge's guards were preoccupied, Vincent—holding Flea like a fat football—followed Elise over the blockade in silence. Once on the other side, they took off at a dead sprint.

He didn't stop until they had cleared the bridge and were well out of sight of the island. Vincent clicked on his flashlight and checked the nearest street sign to make sure he was on the right path.

"Oh no," Elise groaned.

Vincent turned to her, and she looked back, wide-eyed. "You okay?" he asked.

She swallowed hard and nodded. "Y-yeah, I'm fine. It's just . . . all this sneaking around in the dark . . . my heart's pounding, Vincent." Elise paused. "But it's kind of exciting, and I think I like it. Look what you've done to me."

He grinned. "It's not like we're the new Bonnie and Clyde." He drew his weapon and began walking.

They turned onto the street with the baby-blue house sometime after midnight. Vincent wasn't sure what to expect. For all he knew, every single house on the street was occupied, and he was walking into a death trap.

"Here goes nothing." Vincent threw caution to the wind and crouched low, practically slithering his way to the house.

They came upon it not even a few minutes later, standing out in sharp contrast to the duller-colored homes around it. Vincent grabbed Elise's hand and they dove into a cluster of bushes on the side of the road. He peeked through the bush's almost-bare branches and studied the house's darkened windows, carefully searching for any signs of movement. After ten minutes of nothing, he decided it was empty.

Vincent turned around and gazed out over the bay to Sanctuary. He had never seen it in the dead of night, and it looked like a black fortress in the water, both unwelcoming and mysterious.

He tilted his face up as a light drizzle started. "Now we wait," he murmured.

Flea noticed the strangers first. The small dog yanked on Vincent's sleeve, frantically pointing off to the side. Vincent peered through their bush hideout and saw a few shapes walking in their direction. The hairs on his neck rose, and he clutched his gun close to his chest, already planning how he would use it and which path he would take to flee. But as they drew closer, it became apparent Vincent's group was undetected.

Vincent picked out a muted conversation and felt a

modicum of relief when he saw two men and a woman walk past, into the house. They were humans at least, and not some diabolical new creature to worry about.

Vincent checked his watch. It was 1:45, only fifteen minutes until showtime.

The three newcomers walked onto the balcony on the second floor a few moments later. One of them had a heavy-looking flashlight, similar to Natalie's. Vincent turned back to Sanctuary, and when two o' clock came, he saw blinking lights across the water.

After Natalie relayed her message, the people in the house whispered amongst themselves. Vincent tried to make out what they said, but it was futile. They came to an agreement, and the one with the flashlight sent a message back to Natalie. Afterwards, they retreated into the house.

Vincent checked with Flea. "You said you know Morse code, right? What'd they say?"

"Natalie's message was '3121,' and then a series of what I believe are coordinates: 'G-7, G-8, G-9, F-7, and F-6.'"

"And what did the guys in the house say back to her?"

Flea gulped audibly. "They said: 'Standby for orders.'"

"Fucking hell, Natalie. What kind of shit have you gotten into?" Vincent whispered.

The three fell silent as the front door to the blue house opened. The strangers came out and started to leave the way they had come.

There were still too many unanswered questions.

Vincent knew what he had to do. He waited until they were a safe distance away before standing up.

Elise's clammy hands wrapped around his wrist and pulled him back down. "What are you doing?" she whispered in a high-pitched squeak.

"We have to go after them. We need to find out who they are."

Flea shook his head so hard, Vincent thought it would pop off. "Absolutely not. This is insanity!" Flea hissed.

"There's no time to argue; they're getting away. You can either stay here or come with me." Vincent didn't wait for a reply and hurried down the sidewalk, doing his best to stick to the shadows. When he reached the end of the street, he heard Elise and Flea fall into step behind him.

"Don't you dare go without me," Elise said very seriously. "We're in this together."

"I am coming as well, but I want it to be known that you, Vincent Li, are a colossal fool for doing this," Flea added.

Vincent felt a swell of courage with his friends backing up his insane spur-of-the-moment decision.

Together, they stalked their unsuspecting prey deep into the city. The gentle rain picked up into a growing storm, the pelting water and fast winds working in their favor to conceal them.

They followed the strangers to a high school campus, devoid of any green, but surrounded by Oakwood's concrete jungle. Vincent stopped the others at the outskirts of the school when he realized there were armed guards patrolling the border. The people they had followed passed by the guards without incident, disappearing under a large mural of a roaring panther.

Out of the pan, into the fire, Vincent thought. He made a slow circle around the school, scoping out the details; most of the buildings looked to be in disuse, but nearly a third of them had the faint glow of candles behind the windows. He counted at least fifteen guards patrolling the school as well. Their weapons weren't small handguns either—they were packing automatic rifles, clearly not fucking around.

Flea tugged at his pant leg. "Vincent, this is too dangerous. We have to go back." His robe clung to his body and he looked pitiful, shivering in the cold.

Vincent shook his head and blinked rain from his eyes. "We didn't come this far to leave without answers."

"I am never listening to one of your feeble ideas ever again, mark my words," Flea replied, teeth chattering.

Elise, to her credit, remained quiet and followed Vincent without complaint. He wondered if she was as curious as he was, or too afraid to do anything but follow his lead.

Vincent stopped outside a fenced area lined with compact faculty offices; he caught sight of the group from the blue house, hurrying toward the only room with any light.

He turned to the others. "I'll go ahead and see what I can find out."

Elise nodded stiffly. "Be careful."

Vincent nodded back, then turned his gaze to the office. He waited for a nearby guard to disappear around a corner before running up to the fence and hopping it. He could make out a conversation happening inside as he crept up to the office's window.

". . . what did she say?"

The person speaking sounded familiar, but it was hard to fully make out with the rain pelting so hard against his ears.

"There are three thousand one hundred and twenty-one people on the island now," a woman replied.

"He has more than enough," another man said. "Kojo will summon the thunderbirds any day now."

The rain started coming down in heavy sheets, making it nearly impossible to hear the rest of the conversation. Vincent craned his ear, but it was no use. It was like a thousand tiny drums beat all around him.

He was so close. He just needed to know a little more! In a fit of frustration and careless daring, Vincent peeked his head up to the window. Nothing could have prepared him for what he saw next.

Six people stood around a table. The woman and two men from the blue house were there.

Next to the woman was Roach, face grim. He had slimmed down considerably, but it was undeniably him. "We can't wait around anymore. We gotta act now, boss."

Across from Roach was Gil, deep in thought. "Fine. We'll let Natalie know tomorrow night."

Standing closest to the window, his broad back to Vincent, was a familiar specter.

Vincent's jaw dropped, his brain stopped, and he froze. A whirlwind of confusion, surprise, delight, and fear coalesced in his chest.

Dante motioned to Roach. "Get the necklaces."

Roach unlocked a cabinet in the corner and took out a

wooden box, setting it in the center of the table. Vincent vaguely remembered seeing this box before, back at the apartments with Gil.

Dante lifted the lid and a pale glow washed over everyone in the room.

Inside the box were a handful of glowing silver necklaces. Kojo's necklaces.

"They're—they're glowing? What the hell?" Roach stammered. "But how?"

"Son of a bitch! A Gatekeeper is nearby," Gil growled.

Dante spun around, and for a brief moment, the two brothers locked eyes. Dante gasped. "Vincent?"

Gil saw Dante's expression, then looked out the window; his eyes became hateful slits. "What are you waiting for? Get him!"

The sound of a door banging open brought Vincent back into the moment, and he sprinted back to Elise and Flea, vaulting the fence.

Elise stood up, alert, as he barreled toward them.

"What's going on?" Flea asked.

"Run!" Vincent roared, waving his arms wildly.

Elise picked Flea up in her arms and they sped off into the night, legs pumping hard.

Chapter 25

Vincent's legs ached and the cold air burned his lungs. The metallic taste of blood was thick in the back of his throat, and his ears were dull points of throbbing pain, protesting the freezing conditions around him. But none of it mattered.

Dante's alive. He's been alive this whole time, and now he's working with Gil.

Vincent didn't want to believe it. Where he should have felt only joy at seeing his brother back from the grave, he only felt revulsion and betrayal. After everything Gil had put them through—*why?*

And Gil was planning something big against Sanctuary, scheming like the slimy bastard he was. Anger ballooned inside Vincent. He felt like a pawn being toyed with by that man, and never in his life had he felt such a strong, primal instinct for revenge.

"Vincent!"

He came to a sliding stop over the wet pavement and looked back at Elise.

"What happened? What did you see?" Her tiny voice barely carried over the storm.

Vincent started shivering—or more precisely, he belatedly realized how badly he was shaking. Slowly, his rational brain caught up to him and wrested control of his body back. He took quick stock of their surroundings and picked out a nearby gas station, smashing its windows with the butt of his gun, then clambering inside.

Elise set Flea down and wrapped her arms around her body, rubbing herself for warmth; her hair was plastered in thick clumps across her face, and she looked absolutely miserable. Flea lifted the corner of his robe and began to wring the water out, and a moment later Elise did the same with her hair.

"Dante's alive," Vincent said bluntly.

Elise paused, bent over, and gave him a confused look. "That can't be right."

Vincent nodded. "I saw him. Dante is alive. He's fucking alive!" It felt surreal hearing himself say it.

"Didn't the ghouls take him? How could he have possibly survived that?" asked Flea.

Elise clamped her hands over her mouth. "Oh my god. Why did you make us run? If he's really alive, we have to go back and get him."

"It's not that simple." Vincent stalked to the counter and grabbed a pack of cigarettes off the shelf. His shaky hands fumbled trying to pull one out and light it, but he didn't speak until he had one going. He took a steadying puff and waited for his nerves to mellow before saying, "I saw Gil too."

"You can't be serious," Elise whispered.

He nodded. "Even Roach was there."

"We've been going out with scavenging parties every day. How has no one stumbled upon him? There were so many people at the school, there's no way!"

Vincent's jaw tensed. "Those coordinates Natalie relayed tonight . . . how much do you want to bet those are going to be the designated scavenging areas tomorrow?"

Elise sucked in a startled breath. "You don't think?"

"She must have been warning Gil every night so he could avoid bumping into anyone the next day," Vincent said. "She always knows the scavenging coordinates beforehand."

"So, Natalie and Gil . . ." Elise's sentence trailed off as she came to the sickening realization.

"They've been working together this whole time," Vincent said. "Natalie never busted us out. Gil let us go."

Flea looked up at him. "What of Dante? Is he Gil's prisoner?"

"I wish that was the case," Vincent murmured.

Flea shook his head, confused, but the horror on Elise's face showed she understood.

"They're working together?" Elise said, whimpering. "No . . . no, no, no."

Vincent clenched his eyes shut, ashamed.

"That can't be right," she said. "There has to be another explanation! Dante would never work with a man like Gil."

"I know!" Vincent roared. He saw her shrink away, frightened, and a part of him felt terrible for it. "Just let me think. I need to think." He rolled the cigarette between his fingers, losing himself in the smoldering glow at the tip.

The mystery extended beyond Natalie, the scope of complexity so beyond his understanding he had no idea where to start. A low grunt of frustration escaped Vincent's lips, and he tapped impatiently at his head, trying to squeeze some sense from it.

There was one name that seemed to connect everything since the day the first Gate opened in Oakwood. Kojo had a hand in all this, he was sure of it. Something else nagged at his thoughts. A word had popped up. Vincent remembered hearing it before, but until now it had just been another nebulous thing the Catastrophe had brought with it.

Thunderbirds.

Vincent put out his cigarette on the counter, then turned to Flea. "What do you know about thunderbirds?"

"Thunderbirds?" he echoed. "They are fictitious monsters used to frighten children on Terra Mater into good behavior. Why do you wish to know about thunderbirds of all things?"

"Humor me."

Flea shrugged. "Where do I even start? Every culture has their own variation of it, so the details vary wildly. Some say thunderbirds are no bigger than you, other say they are as big as a house."

"Is there anything that's the same between all the different versions?" Vincent asked.

Flea pawed at his jowls. "You are correct. A few details remain constant. Let's see . . . thunderbirds are very rare beasts of magic with the ability to create powerful storms by beating their wings, hence the name. They are so rare, in fact, that they only exist in a pair—twins, to be precise. Once they fully mature from their eggs, they fly out across the world, bringing with them lightning storms and floods that destroy anything in their wake. They only stop once they are killed, at which point they disappear from the world, only to be reborn later." Flea shrugged. "That's the gist of it. As I said, though, it's only a story meant to scare children."

Vincent regarded the storm raging outside. Thunder boomed and lightning illuminated a swell of water gurgling through the street.

Elise followed his gaze through the window and asked, "Vincent, what aren't you telling us?"

He told them what he now knew.

"That's impossible," Flea said. "Thunderbirds don't exist."

Elise said nothing, her eyes unfocused, lost in her own thoughts.

"I'm just telling you what I heard," Vincent said with a slight shrug.

Flea paced in an angry little circle, shaking his head. "Well, then, this *Kojo* is a fool. There is simply no evidence they exist."

"Just a few months ago you didn't even know you could travel to a different world through a Gate," Vincent said.

Flea faltered. "That's different. I knew it was theoretically possible, but thunderbirds? That is preposterous."

"Let's pretend they're real," Vincent said. "Could someone open a Gate for them to come into our world?"

Flea stopped pacing and regarded him with crossed arms. "For argument's sake, let's assume they do exist. If the stories are even partially true, then thunderbirds would possess immense magical properties, hundreds of times more powerful than a sorceress. If they tried going through a traditional Gate, their innate energies would destabilize it and cause it to collapse. It would never work unless the Gate was being fed even more power."

"So it *could* be done," Vincent said.

"As I said, it would require an immense power source, something no single person could achieve. Not even a sorceress could create a Gate of that magnitude alone." Flea sighed. "But yes, it *could* be done."

That's all Vincent needed to hear.

By the time they made it back to Sanctuary, daylight had begun to pierce the rain clouds, dulling the smothering rain into a light mist. Vincent, haggard from traveling all night, ran up to the blockade and banged on the trailer.

"Let me in!" he said, panting. "Come on, Conrad. Wake the hell up and let us in!"

A doughy face popped out over the ledge. "Vincent? Elise? How the hell did you two get out there?"

"Just lower the ladder," Vincent said.

Conrad peered at Flea. "Did you guys take him out for a walk or something?"

Vincent gulped down a big breath of air. "Conrad! Ladder!"

"All right, all right. No need to yell about it."

A second later, a metal ladder slid down the side and Vincent scrambled up it, Elise and Flea on his heels. He walked briskly past Conrad and the other guards.

"You going to tell me what's going on?" Conrad asked.

"No time to explain," Vincent snapped. He slid down the ladder on the other side and hurried toward his house.

When Natalie opened her front door, she wasn't prepared to have a gun shoved into her nose. Vincent grabbed the startled woman by the collar of her shirt and pushed his way inside.

"What the hell is going on?" she shouted, backpedaling to keep up with him.

Vincent shoved her into a chair and pointed the gun at her face. Without looking back, he said to Elise, "Close the door."

Natalie watched her close the door, then turned her eyes up to Vincent. "You better start explaining yourself," she said.

"Don't make me laugh, Natalie. You're the one who needs to start explaining."

She gave him an imploring look. "I don't know what's got your undies in a knot, but can you stop waving that thing in my face? It's making me real nervous."

Elise put a soft hand over his. "Don't forget we're just here to talk."

Natalie nodded, her hands up in peace. "We're all friends here. Let's just talk . . . whatever this is, out."

Hearing her say that felt like needles in his ears. Vincent

shrugged Elise off, and he pulled his eyebrows together into a furious glare. "You bitch, Natalie. Did you really think we wouldn't find out eventually?"

"Vincent!" Flea said reproachfully. "Such language is unnecessary."

"I don't know what you're talking about," Natalie said.

Vincent trembled, fighting back the urge to do something violent. Elise, in contrast, looked despondent, her shoulders sagging and her arms limp at her sides.

"Why are you helping Gil?" Vincent asked.

Natalie's eyes fell to the floor and she sighed. When she turned her face back up, she had the look of a person who knew the jig was up. "I'm sorry, guys. I truly am."

"God damn it, Natalie! Why?" he wailed.

"I had to," she said. "It was never anything personal. I like you two, really." She paused to consider her next words. "There's a bigger picture you're not seeing here, though. You got to believe me. I would never have done this unless I had to."

Vincent saw what might have been genuine regret, but he had no room for sympathy of any kind. All the years spent in Oakwood came back to him, pumping through his veins, hardening his body and heart.

"I trusted you. We all did." He shook his head, cursing his own gullibility. "We saved your life. Doesn't that mean anything to you?"

Natalie looked away.

"That's what I thought."

Elise wiped her eyes with a sniff. "What are you going to do with her?"

"First, you're going to tell us everything you know," Vincent said, jabbing his gun at Natalie.

"I can't," she replied, her expression suddenly stoic.

"Tell me what Gil's planning!" Vincent yelled. "Why is he so interested in Sanctuary?"

Natalie's face was a blank, unreadable slate.

"We should tell George about this. About everything we've learned," Elise said.

"Not until I know what's going on," Vincent replied. "Not until I know why my brother is working with them."

"It doesn't matter," Elise said. "Whatever is happening, we can't deal with it alone. We need help. We need George's help."

"I wouldn't go running to him if I were you," Natalie said.

"And why not?" Vincent spat.

Natalie became tight-lipped again.

He lowered his voice to a dangerous whisper. "What aren't you telling us?"

"Maybe she's just trying to confuse us?" Elise suggested.

"Is that what you're doing?" Vincent asked Natalie. "Quit fucking with me and cut the shit."

Something flickered in Natalie's eyes, and she kicked out, hitting the old wound in his leg. He cried out, and in the same instant, she sprang up and grabbed his hand. Elise let loose a shrill scream as they wrestled for control of his gun.

Vincent might have stood a chance, but he hadn't accounted for how much the cold weather and rain had dulled his reflexes. Natalie twisted his wrist back and pried the gun from his stiff fingers; before Elise realized what happened, Natalie had Vincent's gun pointed at them.

"Don't move a fucking muscle," Natalie snarled. "I really don't want to hurt either of you, but I will if you don't give me a choice."

"Please don't hurt us," Elise begged.

Natalie's eyes softened. "Oh, honey. I don't want to." She motioned to the gun at Elise's waist. "Lower it to the ground nice and slow, then slide it on over."

Vincent's lip twitched angrily, but there was no other choice. Elise did as she was told.

Natalie slipped Elise's gun inside her jacket, then waved to the wall. "Vincent and Flea, to the wall. Elise, you're coming with me."

"What? Why?" Vincent protested.

Natalie knitted her eyebrows together. "Do it now!"

Flea's arms shot up in surrender as he scurried to the wall, and Vincent gave Natalie a nasty look before joining him.

"Come on." Natalie took Elise's hand and led her away.

Elise looked back as they went through the front door, her gray eyes pleading to Vincent for rescue.

Come on, think! Think! He frantically searched his pockets for something to use, but he only had a flashlight and map. His thoughts were going in desperate circles when his fingers wrapped around a bottle. Vincent pulled Flea's potion from his jacket pocket, suddenly remembering he had it; he looked at the brown sludge inside. "What exactly does this Armoring Potion do?"

"It will make your skin tougher than rock without all the

stiffness," Flea explained. "I had to substitute some of the ingredients, so your results may vary."

"Could it stop bullets?"

Flea's eyes opened in understanding. "Ah, very clever, Vincent." He scratched his head thoughtfully. "You know, I'm not entirely sure. However, I am more certain than not that it would protect you from gunfire."

"Here goes nothing." Vincent popped the top off and threw the potion back like a shot of alcohol. He immediately dropped to his knees, a pained grunt escaping through gritted teeth.

It felt like a hundred-pound ball had been dropped into his stomach, stretching it to painful proportions. He howled, but as quick as the sensation had come, it went away. When he opened his eyes, he noticed a strange, cracked quality to his hands. They were a gravelly shade of gray, scaly and dry, and when he moved his fingers it sounded like stone scraping against stone. Vincent stood up and admired his body, stunned by the rapid transformation.

"Vincent, this is no time to be admiring the genius of my work. Natalie is getting away!"

Flea's voice focused his attention back on rescuing Elise. With a long battle cry, Vincent charged out the front door, his feet pounding like heavy boulders.

Natalie turned around at the sound, curiosity and shock crossing her face. Her eyes widened, and she pointed her gun at him.

For a fleeting moment, Vincent realized how stupid it was, charging a loaded weapon; he threw his arms over his face, screaming his doubt away and propelling himself forward even harder. Through the crack in his arms, he saw the muzzle of Natalie's gun flash in quick succession. Instead of pain, he felt light pinches over his arms and body as the bullets plinked off his skin harmlessly.

Natalie had only a moment to say "Oh shit" before he bowled into her midsection. She flew across the street and hit the ground hard.

Elise fell to the side and scrambled back a few paces, hyperventilating at the sight of him. Vincent offered a rocky hand to her, and she looked at it with something that danced between terror and curiosity. "Vincent? Is that you?"

"Yeah." At least his voice was still normal.

"What happened to you?"

"Armoring Potion from Flea."

She gave a humorless chuckle. "Of course. An Armoring Potion. That explains everything."

Vincent pulled Elise up, then turned to the sound of uneven footsteps hurrying away. Natalie, a ways up the road, looked back, ashen-faced; she saw him watching and quickened her pace, half-limping in her escape.

"Are you going to let her go?" Elise asked.

"Yes." He didn't want to, but he noticed movement in the homes around them, obviously drawn by the gunshots. The last thing he needed was for a scared group of idiots to lynch him, thinking he was some kind of rock monster. Vincent took Elise's hand and hurried back into the house with Flea.

Chapter 26

Vincent shut the door behind him and called for Flea.

His face popped out from behind a nearby table. "Forbidden arcana, you're alive."

Vincent motioned at his craggy exterior. "How long am I going to be like this?"

"Probably only a few minutes more," Flea said, stepping into view.

"What do you mean *probably*? You don't know for sure?"

Flea shrugged, unperturbed. "Normally my Armoring Potion would last fifteen minutes, give or take a few depending on your size. However, as I already explained to you, what you drank wasn't my original formula. I had to improvise some of the ingredients—couldn't find any golem dust, you understand." He circled Vincent, looking him over with a scrutinizing eye. "Everything seems to be in order. The initial test trial has been a success."

"Test trial?" Vincent barked. "I was your guinea pig? What if I'm stuck like this forever?"

"Don't fret," Flea said calmly. "I ran the numbers and there's only a seven percent chance that could happen, given your physiology. By the way, do you feel any pain? Perhaps some nausea? What about your vision? Can you see everything all right? In very rare cases, blindness has been reported."

Vincent lurched toward him with his arms outstretched, struck by a sudden urge to strangle the little bastard, but stopped himself with an irritated growl. "Once this potion's effect wears off—and it *better* wear off—I'm going back out there to find Gil."

"Are you mad?" Flea said. "He has a veritable fortress, complemented by his own army."

Elise sounded her agreement. "It'd be suicide."

"Natalie's getting away even as we speak," Vincent said. "There's only one place she's going, and once she gets there, Gil might get spooked and vanish. He's managed to stay hidden this long, who knows when we'll get another chance like this?"

"We can't go running after them blindly," Elise protested.

"I'm not asking you guys to come with me. I'll do it alone," he said, picking at his tough skin, anxious to go.

Flea chortled in disbelief. "He *is* mad."

Elise grabbed him by the shoulders and forced him to look her in the eyes; they were alive with energy, a miniature storm swirling around her pupils. "You're not going out there, Vincent."

He jerked away from her. "He's got my brother, Elise."

All the muddled thoughts of Kojo, Gates, and thunderbirds were blasted away by a single, clarifying thought: he had to get Dante back. Vincent saw Elise standing before him, defiant and unmoving. It was maddening. Didn't she understand how important Dante was? How dare she try to stop him?

Vincent suddenly didn't care that he was still a stony creature and made a run for the door. Dante was slipping through his grasp with every passing second.

Elise forced her body between him and the door, and pushed him back. "No, Vincent!"

He moved without thought and shoved her aside. "I've lost Dante once already, I'm not doing it again." He managed a couple steps before Elise lunged onto his back, toppling him over. "Get off me!" he yelled, easily throwing the lighter woman off him.

But Elise was infuriatingly persistent and pounced back onto his chest. "I won't let you!"

"Get the fuck off me," he growled.

She grabbed his head and forced him to look at her. "I don't want to lose you, too!" she cried, fighting hard to stop her upper lip from shaking.

"What?"

"I've lost everyone else, I'm not going to lose you," Elise said. "You're so stupid! Why do you always think you have to do things alone? I want to get Dante back just as bad as you, so let me help." She pointed at Flea. "Let *us* help you."

Elise leaned down and pressed her forehead against his. A familiar sensation rippled down his body and set him at ease, and he was suddenly exhausted. "Are you done?" she asked.

Vincent closed his eyes and took a deep breath. "Yes."

Elise stood up with a nod and offered him her hand. As she helped him to his feet she said, "There's no way you can go back alone. Gil's dangerous, his people are dangerous. Even with me and Flea there, we wouldn't stand a chance of reaching Dante safely. Especially now that he's on guard."

Vincent shook his head, thinking clearly again. "You're right. So what can we do?"

"We force a stalemate with Gil, and then he'll have to talk to us peacefully," Elise said.

"How do we do that? We have no leverage, nothing to threaten him with," Vincent said.

"Not alone we don't, but if we approach him with a big enough army he'll have to use diplomacy or risk an all-out battle. It's our best bet for getting Dante out without any bloodshed."

"That's a great idea and all, but you're forgetting one tiny detail: we don't have an army."

"The scavengers of Sanctuary," Elise explained. "Most of us have been trained with guns, and a lot of us have even fought creatures before. It's the closest thing to a standing army this place has. We'd just have to convince George to help."

"What makes you think he'll help us?" he asked. "Dante doesn't mean anything to him. He's got no reason to risk his, or anyone else's, life."

She took his hand and squeezed. "Maybe not for Dante's

sake, but Gil's planning something that involves Sanctuary. We might not know the specifics, but George knows what kind of man his son is. I'm sure we could make a strong case that it's a threat he can't ignore."

Vincent smirked, pleasantly surprised she had come up with such a shrewd plan. "Are you suggesting we *use* George? That's sneaky, some might even say dirty. What'd you do with the real Elise?"

"It's mutually beneficial for both parties to go after Gil." She shuddered, a guilty expression on her face. "I just hope that nobody gets hurt in the process."

Vincent couldn't care less who got hurt, so long as they got Dante out, but he didn't tell Elise that.

Flea cleared his throat pointedly. "I hate to bring this up, but Natalie said not to trust George."

"She could have been lying to get us to lower our guard," Elise said.

Vincent wasn't so sure. Natalie's warning tickled the part of him that was suspicious of everything, and it had created a powerful itch.

George seemed like a standup guy. He was smart enough to keep everyone in Sanctuary alive, he was organized, he was a good leader—all things befitting a former Police Chief—but that was the problem. Vincent had said it before, and he still believed it: nobody was that squeaky-clean.

Vincent racked his brain for some detail about George he might have overlooked, but the only thing he could turn up was their visit to the police station. There had been a pile of unopened letters waiting in George's office. An important guy like him probably got mail that couldn't be ignored for too long, and George didn't seem like the type of person to procrastinate. Vincent remembered one letter being postmarked ten days prior to the Catastrophe.

Why would the Police Chief ignore his mail for so long? Vincent sighed wearily. He was probably just overthinking things. And to be frank, there was the more important task of convincing George to help save Dante, at hand.

Something clinked against the floor, and he looked down at a small slab of rock. He checked his hand, where a patch of bare skin showed beneath his craggy exterior.

"Ah, your armored skin is sloughing off, just as I predicted." Flea walked up to him and shook his pant leg, causing chunks of gravel to fall around his shoe. "Elise, would you give me your assistance in shaking Vincent out?"

Elise and Flea spent the next ten minutes peeling off pieces of hardened skin; it didn't hurt and was oddly satisfying, like Vincent was molting and refreshing himself. When it was all done, he stood in a pile of rubble, relieved to find himself no different than before he drank the Armoring Potion.

With Vincent safe to be seen in public again, the three hurried home and changed into dry clothes. Vincent instructed Flea to prepare more potions while he and Elise set off to talk to George.

When they reached the bank, Vincent didn't bother knocking and barged in. He heard the murmurings of an agitated conversation from the back and found Conrad talking with George about something.

Conrad scowled at Vincent as he entered George's tiny office. "Speak of the devil and he will appear." He pointed a thick sausage finger. "That's the guy I was telling you about, George. He got off the island somehow, and I'm beginning to think he's the punk who started the fire, too. It's time to take the kid gloves off. If we don't start enforcing the rules, people are going to think they can just come and go as they please. We'll start losing people. Hell, we might have lost one already."

"Did someone go over the blockade?" Vincent asked.

"Natalie did. It looked like she got out of a bar brawl or something," Conrad said.

George massaged his forehead, looking exhausted and thinner than usual. His eyes were dark, sunken pockets, giving him an almost skeletal look, and Vincent wondered when he had last slept.

George reached behind his desk and sprayed himself with cologne, then regarded Vincent. "Someone started a fire at the bridge last night. Now Conrad tells me you and Elise showed up this morning, *outside* the blockade. Natalie has apparently run off. And I'm pretty sure I just heard gunshots. Is there anything I'm missing here?"

Vincent glanced at Conrad. "Can Elise and I talk to you alone?"

"What's so important that you need to talk in private?" Conrad snorted. "George, we need to start planning. If we don't secure Sanctuary, we run the risk of losing everything we've built here."

George's eyes glittered like dark jewels in his head.

"Conrad, did you forget who you're talking to?"

"N-no, of course not," he said.

George motioned out the door. "Then please wait outside, won't you?"

"But George—"

"I don't like repeating myself, Conrad." George betrayed no hint of a threat, but he didn't have to. His unsettling calm got the message across, loud and clear.

Conrad bowed himself out with a curt "Yes, sir" and shut the door.

George motioned at the chairs in front of his desk. "Tell me what's going on."

Elise nodded a go-ahead to Vincent, and he said, "I know where Gil is."

George's usually intelligent eyes looked at him with a dull sheen. "Is this your idea of a joke?"

Vincent kept it short and stuck to only the facts, leaving out his own theories about Kojo summoning thunderbirds into the world. He didn't want to sound completely crazy. George's face grew increasingly dark, dangerous lines marring his features as Vincent retold the events of the past week.

When he was done talking, George was silent, his thick fingers laced together over his mouth in a contemplative silence. "Vincent, if you're lying to me about any of this . . ."

"He's not," Elise said.

"I have no reason to," Vincent added. He squirmed uncomfortably in his seat. It felt like George was passing judgment on them.

"You should have come to me with this sooner," George said, grave.

"I'm telling you now, aren't I?" Vincent said.

George grunted and looked down at the table. "What is my son planning?"

"A lot of the scavengers have been trained with guns. If we group up and go to Gil, we might be able to scare him into talking things out," Elise said.

George showed his approval on his face. "Fight fire with fire."

"So you'll do it?" Vincent asked, maybe a little too eagerly.

George studied him carefully. "Is there something you're not telling me?"

"What? No, I've told you everything," Vincent replied. "I'm just concerned about Sanctuary."

"If Elise said that, I would have believed it, but you?" George smirked. "Don't make me laugh, Vincent. I'm no idiot."

Vincent's face burned hot like a kid caught red-handed, doing something shameful.

George leaned back into his chair, suddenly disinterested. "We can't go after Gil with the scavengers."

Elise gasped. "But you just said—what about Gil? We can't leave him alone out there."

"Do you think Gil is going to be scared into submission by a ragtag group of frightened scavengers?" George shook his head. "None of them are trained for this kind of situation. I'd be sending them to their deaths." He got up from his chair and stood to his full height, his imposing presence looming over them. "Could you lead me to Gil's hideout?"

"I could, but you just said you weren't going after him," Vincent said.

George's lips peeled over his teeth, the gesture slow and reminiscent of a predator reveling in an impending kill. "I only said we can't use the scavengers." He called for Conrad, and the pudgy man opened the office door. "Gather my followers here, and let them know this isn't a drill," George commanded.

"Of course." And then Conrad was gone.

George turned his attention on Vincent and Elise, his eyes sparkling with renewed life. "Go home and rest. In two hours, I expect you both to be back."

"What's happening?" Elise asked, barely squeezing the question out.

"I'm going to put a stop to Gil's plans," George said, moving around the desk alarmingly quick.

Vincent and Elise jumped out of their seats and were practically chased out of the bank by George. His hulking frame stopped in the doorway, and he focused intently on them as they stood in the empty parking lot.

"Two hours," George repeated. "Don't keep me waiting."

Chapter 27

Elise was the first to voice her thoughts when they walked through their house's front door. "Was I the only one who felt really uncomfortable being in the same room with George?"

Vincent felt a shudder go up his neck, and he shook his head. "In my whole time being here, I've never gotten a vibe like that from the guy. It was like talking to a completely different person."

"Do you think we can we trust him?"

He growled his frustration with the whole situation—it was question after question. Vincent rubbed his throbbing temples and took a seat on the living room couch. "I just don't fucking know, Elise."

She sat next to him and the cushion caved between them, making their bodies lean into each other. "Things are really messed up, aren't they?"

"Yeah."

"Is Sanctuary safe anymore?"

Vincent spurted out a quick laugh. "What do you think?"

She propped herself over her knees, cupping her face in

her hands and looking glum.

Flea came into the room. "What happened? Were you able to convince George to help?"

Vincent nodded at the dog. "We're heading out to confront Gil in a couple hours."

"Oh my . . . do you suppose it will become violent?"

"I'm hoping for the best, but always preparing for the worst," he replied, standing up. "Elise, Flea, get a bag ready. Bring clothes, some food, anything you think we'd need to survive out there alone."

Elise grabbed his hand, stricken. "Are you suggesting we leave Sanctuary?"

"Not yet, but if things get out of hand, we're gone."

"You cannot be serious," Flea said. "How bad could the situation get?"

"Sanctuary is nearing the bottom of the barrel. I can feel it in my gut," Vincent said. "Can you have a bag of your most useful potions bottled and ready to go?"

"Of course I can."

Vincent nodded. "Get it done, Flea."

"Vincent, I don't want to leave Sanctuary," Elise whispered.

He gave her a reassuring smile. "We'll be fine either way. I'll make sure of it." He didn't add the second half of his thought: *If we're lucky.*

They went upstairs and packed. When Vincent finished, he collapsed on top of his covers and closed his eyes, too exhausted for anything else.

Two hours later, Vincent and Elise found themselves back at George's bank, where a small gathering had formed. About thirty men and women milled about in the parking lot, conversing quietly among one another. He recognized a couple faces from around town, but most were people he never would have given a second glance. Every one of them, however, carried an arsenal of weapons that included pistols, submachine guns, grenades and flash bangs. Some even had riot helmets and bulletproof vests.

More surprising than this hidden army's existence was their general demeanor. It wasn't one Vincent would have expected from people about to confront an opposing force. He couldn't detect any traces of fear or anxiety, emotions he was swimming in himself. In fact, they looked eager.

A tight knot formed in Vincent's stomach.

George stepped out of the bank in full SWAT gear. He wore black fatigues, over which was a heavy vest and padded plates; a helmet protected his head, and he carried a metal riot shield over his back. In his hand was a heavy-duty shotgun, and a bandolier of grenades completed his intimidating look. He was going to war. There was no doubt about it.

Conrad emerged from the crowd in similar attire and approached George. "We're all here and ready. Just give the order," he said.

George pulled down his face mask and nodded his understanding. He searched the crowd and found Vincent and Elise lingering in the far back, then beckoned them over.

Vincent swallowed whatever misgivings he had and led Elise forward.

"I appreciate punctuality," George said to them as they approached.

"Where did you find these people?" Vincent motioned to the crowd, which had formed into tight ranks without any direction from George.

"They live here," he replied.

"What are they supposed to be?" Elise asked quietly.

"Sanctuary's defenders," George said. "The world is a dangerous place now, so I handpicked these people and trained them to be just as dangerous."

The answer made Vincent uneasy. If George had trained an armed force right under everyone's noses, what else was he hiding on the island?

"Where are your guns?" George asked.

"Natalie took them when she ran off," Vincent explained.

The big man frowned, then reached behind him and unholstered two handguns, planting one in Vincent's hand and the other in Elise's. "You don't want to be caught in a gunfight emptyhanded," he said.

Vincent eyed his weapon, looked to "Sanctuary's defenders," and then looked at George. "We're not trying to start a fight, remember? We just want to talk to Gil."

The corner of George's lips quirked up, and he put a heavy hand on Vincent's shoulder. "Of course that's the plan." He turned to his private force with a raised fist, made a swirling motion in the air, and they fell into uniform groups of six. "Take me to Gil, Vincent."

They marched for the bridge, drawing stunned gasps and looks from the whole town as they passed through. A few people approached George, but he repelled them with a stiff glare that made it apparent he wasn't in the mood to answer questions.

Once they crossed the bridge, George made Vincent and Elise take point. It was a silent journey without even a whisper of conversation. The only sound was that of feet marching in robotic unison behind Vincent, making him feel as if a hungry machine slowly pursued him, trying to wear him down.

Vincent eventually stopped on a lonely and deserted street, the main entrance into the high school at the end of the road.

"Is this it?" George asked.

Vincent confirmed the same panther mascot he had seen last night. "Yes."

George dropped a dark visor down from his helmet, obscuring his features behind the black plastic. "Remember the assault formations I taught you," he said to the group behind him. "Keep within calling distance of each other and communicate."

With that last order, George raised his shield and walked forward. His army followed suit, flowing around Vincent and Elise like they were a stone in a stream.

Elise's hands clamped painfully around Vincent's arm, and she huddled into him for protection. "What have we done?" she asked, eyes darting among the attack force surrounding them. "What did we start?"

"Just stay close to me," he croaked. Vincent waited until they were the very last ones, then proceeded into the school with his gun drawn and ready.

The high school campus was empty of human life; however, crates of food and various supplies had been left in the open, as if abandoned in a hurry. Vincent wondered if Gil was already gone, and a tiny part of him hoped that was the case.

George's people swept the halls with trained efficiency, moving swiftly through classrooms and shouting "Clear!" intermittently. Vincent noticed the hallways connecting the main buildings were dangerous chokepoints, forcing everyone to clump up, ripe for an ambush. As they passed through them, Vincent and Elise gripped each other tightly, their eyes nervously scoping out any signs of danger.

They came upon an elongated courtyard with tall buildings flanking either side, creating a faux gladiator arena. Windows opened into the courtyard for invisible spectators to watch, and the sky overhead rumbled its approval, momentarily ceasing its rain.

George pumped his shotgun once. "Get ready," he whispered, calm and authoritative.

Vincent watched the others adopt a more aggressive posture with their weapons, and then fan out in both directions. They moved with startling efficiency, each one taking up a predetermined spot in a formation Vincent wasn't part of. Before he knew it, he and Elise were standing alone behind George.

At the opposite end of the courtyard, a lone man stepped

out from behind a door, an assault rifle resting arrogantly over his shoulder. "You aren't as clever as you thought. You made a mistake coming here," Gil said.

Vincent held his breath, expecting a rebuttal from George, or even a cursory exchange of words—at the very least some kind of acknowledgment between father and son.

Instead, Gil leapt behind cover as bodies popped up from the open windows around them. Vincent's heart leapt into his throat, and he tackled Elise back as a hailstorm of bullets peppered the courtyard.

Hundreds of miniature explosions echoed in the enclosed space, bits of concrete and dust shot up in tufts, and bullets ricocheted around their heads. George threw his shield up and retreated into a door on his left as his soldiers covered his escape and acted as meat shields. Half his force went with him, while the other half fled into the opposite building.

Vincent hoisted Elise up and pulled her through a door on their right, his only concern being to get the fuck out of the open. He and Elise fell into the far wall, as far from the exposed windows as possible. Through the door he saw they had left behind at least five of their own, now bullet-riddled corpses.

Gunfire became a constant, dull drone in his ears, punctured by men and women yelling commands at each other.

Elise screamed as a spray of bullets cut a jagged line over their heads, showering them in dust.

Vincent put his arm over her shoulder and forced her flat

on her stomach with him. His eyes fell on a man ahead of him. "What the fuck are we doing?" Vincent yelled.

The man looked to be in his forties, with peppered hair and the beginnings of wrinkles on his face. He cast Vincent a glance and said, "They're above us! We're going after them!"

Was Dante one of the people firing on them?

A second thought occurred to Vincent, more chilling than the last.

What if Dante was killed in this gunfight?

Panic swelled in Vincent's chest, squeezing the air from his lungs. *This isn't what's supposed to happen! This isn't how it was supposed to go!*

The man seemed indifferent to such worries and darted ahead with everyone else. Vincent tightened his hold around Elise's hand and followed after them. George's force charged up a wide set of stairs at the end of the hall and were greeted by bullets at the top.

A woman leading the charge was hit in the face, and a spray of blood shot out behind her head as more bullets pelted her body with soft thuds. The others fell behind cover on either side of an arched entryway. Someone unpinned a grenade and threw it around the corner; there was a short scuffle and panicked voices yelling for retreat, but they were cut off by a small explosion that rocked the building.

Agonized screams filled the hall on the other side, and then a voice yelled, "Push forward!"

Vincent stayed back while those around him surged ahead as a cohesive unit. He dared a peek around the corner and saw them making steady progress against a well-armed, but dwindling, opposition. When Gil's people were culled down to a few remaining men and women, they got up and fled down the hall, shooting wildly over their backs. George's soldiers finished them off in cold blood, then pressed onward. Across the courtyard, George led a similarly victorious charge in the building parallel to theirs.

Vincent crossed the hall, stepping over a countless number of bodies along the way. Stomach acid tickled the back of his throat, but he forced himself to check every passing face, with their glazed-over eyes. Thankfully, none of them were Dante.

Vincent and Elise ventured down a set of stairs to where the fighting was thickest, in an abandoned cafeteria square. Gil's forces had barricaded themselves in on one side, and George's did the same on the other, reenacting their own version of trench warfare. Vincent was far from a military expert, but even he could see that Gil was steadily losing the fight. He prayed that Dante was smart enough to get out before it was too late.

He led Elise to a safe spot of cover behind a wide pillar, then wiped beads of sweat from his brow and peeked around it. His eyes zeroed in on Gil, shooting desperately through a busted window leading into the cafeteria kitchen.

Both sides took potshots at each other and more of Gil's fighters dropped. From his vantage point, Vincent saw Gil's fierce façade crumble; a man standing next to him took a bullet to the forehead, instantly dying.

That was the last straw for Vincent's past tormentor. Gil

threw his rifle down and turned away from the window, disappearing into the kitchen.

Vincent made a mental note of the kitchen's location relative to the building, and then spotted an exit behind him. He tapped Elise on the shoulder, beckoning for her to follow him out.

Once outside, Elise stopped him and asked, "What are we doing out here?"

Vincent looked down a walkway on their left, which would hopefully lead to the back of the cafeteria. "Gil's trying to run, and I'm not letting that fucker get away." Before Elise had the chance to argue, he took off, leaving behind the sounds of gunfire.

When they rounded the back of the building, they saw Gil fly out through a door and fall to his knees.

"Stop!" Vincent called.

Gil's crazed eyes turned on him. "Fuck you!" He scrambled to his feet and ran, panting.

It wasn't hard to keep up. Gil was tired, a wounded and harried animal at the end of his rope. As they gained on him, Gil abruptly spun around with a gun aimed at their faces.

Vincent threw his body to the side and bowled himself and Elise behind cover.

Gil squeezed off three shots before his gun clicked empty. He shouted his disapproval, then threw it away in disgust and took off again.

Vincent started to get up, but he heard Elise stifle a strained whimper. He looked back and saw her clutching her leg, where a dark spot of red was forming. "Oh fuck," he gasped.

Elise rolled up her pants with a painful wince and showed off an ugly hole in her right calf, the same spot Vincent had been shot months ago.

"Are you all right?" Vincent asked, momentarily forgetting all about Gil.

"Yeah," she squeaked. "I think I'll be fine." She grunted and sucked rapid breaths through her nose.

"What do you need me to do?" he asked.

"Go get Gil!" she snapped.

"But what about your leg?"

Elise forced a brave smile. "I'm a big girl. I'll be fine. Don't let Gil get away!"

A resurgence of fury flooded his body, filling every fiber with an intense urge to hurt Gil. Vincent nodded his understanding and continued the chase. He dug into a hidden reservoir of energy and caught up to his adversary, floundering across an open basketball court. Gil saw him and redoubled his efforts to get away, but Vincent closed the gap between them in seconds.

Realizing there was no escape, Gil turned around, a nasty sneer on his face. "You're just full of surprises, Vincent." He threw his arms out. "So what now?"

Vincent drew his gun on him.

Gil guffawed at the sight. "What are you going to fucking do, Vincent? We've been in this situation before. You don't have the balls to shoot me." He spat at Vincent's feet. "You fucking bitch, go back to Sanctuary where you belong and play house with Elise. You're useless for anything else."

Vincent stared down the sights of his gun, and for a brief

moment he wanted nothing more than to end it right there. Gil had given him every reason to, and if he was being honest with himself, he had fantasized about killing this man on many sleepless nights.

"That's what I thought." Gil turned and began to limp away.

"You shouldn't turn your back on a loaded gun," Vincent said. He squeezed the trigger once.

Gil howled and dropped onto his side, clutching at a blooming wound in his leg. "Motherfucker!" he cried. "What the fuck did you do to me?"

"That felt good," Vincent said. The overwhelmingly vengeful part of him wanted to do it again, to revel in Gil's pain. He walked up to the man squirming on the floor and pointed the gun down at his face.

Gil stopped long enough to look up, terrified. All the smugness had left his face. "No, don't! Don't kill me," he cried.

"Why not?" Vincent asked.

"I know things." Gil reached down his shirt and held up Kojo's necklace, the dull lump of silver hanging from it spinning lazily. "And I have this."

"Why would I want that thing?" he demanded.

"Because it—"

The hairs on Vincent's neck bristled, and he sensed a presence behind him. He spun around, stopping short of squeezing the trigger when he registered who was standing there.

His brother had a gun of his own, but held up his arms

in a peaceful surrender. "Hey, little brother, how about not pointing that thing at me?"

Vincent hesitated, but decided to keep his gun trained on him. "Why are you working with Gil?"

Dante frowned. "I know, I got a lot of explaining to do."

"I saved him," Gil said eagerly. "I saved your brother, I did that!"

Vincent gave Gil a vicious kick to the chest that sent him sprawling on the floor with a pained gasp. "You shut the hell up!" He turned back to Dante, but despite his heart being overjoyed to see him alive and well, his brain told him to be wary. "So he saved your life and you think that's enough reason to help him and Kojo summon the thunderbirds into our world? Have you lost your fucking mind?"

Dante pressed his lips into a thin line, looking morose.

"I'm right, aren't I? That's what all this has been about," Vincent said.

Gil barked a quick laugh. "You idiot. You really have no idea, do you?"

Vincent turned on him, his hand pulled back to strike again.

Gil cowered, doing a poor job of hiding his murderous snarl under a mask of feigned innocence. "I'm sure you have a lot of questions . . . I've got the answers."

Dante took a step forward. "Don't you say a damn word, Gil!"

Vincent jabbed his gun at his brother. "Don't get any closer," he warned.

Gil chuckled darkly. "It's over. Don't you fucking get it,

Dante? George won. It's every man for himself now, and I don't plan on dying."

"You're a goddamn coward! If we give up now, he wins. We can't let him win," Dante said. "Too many lives are at stake."

"The only life I care about is my own," Gil said.

Vincent looked between the two, thoroughly confused.

"I won't let you," Dante said. "We still have a chance if we can get to the Gatekeeper."

"Will someone start making some goddamn sense?" Vincent hollered.

Gil turned his eyes on Vincent. "Listen to me, kid. Tell George I have information he needs, and that I'll give it to him on the condition he spares my life and lets me join his crew."

Dante stormed toward them, startling Vincent.

"Stay back!" Vincent ordered, but his brother ignored him. "Dante, I'm warning you."

He flashed him a dark look and said, "Move aside, Vincent." He shouldered past him and aimed his gun down at Gil.

Vincent sucked in a sharp breath. "No, don't!"

Dante pulled the trigger.

Gil collapsed on the ground, a small trickle of blood oozing from his forehead and an expression of surprise frozen to his face.

"Why did you do that?" Vincent asked in a low whisper.

Dante shook his head, grim. "I really didn't want to, but he left me no choice."

Vincent grabbed Dante by the shoulder and forced his brother to look at him. "What's happening here?" he asked, a sick feeling of dread curling around his insides.

Dante looked past him at the school. "I really hoped it wouldn't come to this, but we're out of options now that Gil and his people are dead." He kneeled beside Gil and ripped the necklace from his corpse, stuffing it into his pocket.

"Dante, talk to me, please," Vincent implored.

His brother grabbed him by the shoulders and spoke slowly, urgently. "There's no time to walk you through this, Vincent. George is going to be here any second. When you get back to Sanctuary, whatever you do, keep Elise alive. Trust no one. I'll come find you."

"I don't understand."

Dante gave him a doleful, lopsided grin. "I'm counting on you." He then took off running.

Vincent stayed there, dumbfounded, until Elise's voice snapped him out of it. He watched her limp toward him, George and his remaining army trailing behind her.

Elise practically fell into him and threw her arms around his neck. "Thank god you're okay. I was so worried!"

Vincent hugged her back, Dante's words haunting his thoughts: *"Keep Elise alive."*

George went straight to Gil's body and checked around his neck and, when he didn't find anything there, checked through his son's pockets.

That's strange, Vincent thought. *Why is he looking for Kojo's necklace?*

When George realized it wasn't on Gil, he stood up with

an irritated huff and regarded Vincent. "Did you take anything off his body?" he asked.

Vincent shook his head numbly.

"A damn shame," George muttered. He didn't give Vincent a second look and turned to the people gathered around them. "Back to Sanctuary, everyone. We're not done yet."

Vincent hung back with Elise, leaning heavily on him for support, and watched George march back to Sanctuary. He looked down at the corpse by his feet.

"You didn't do this, did you?" Elise asked, more a statement than a question.

Vincent shook his head, unable to shake the feeling something big was coming on the horizon.

Chapter 28

Vincent had expected to have some answers at the end, not a clusterfuck of questions. He knew he was missing something glaringly obvious. It felt like someone was holding a nebulous picture right in front of his face; he could make out tiny details here and there, but he couldn't take a step back to see the big picture and make sense of it all.

Vincent's eyes flicked over to George. The ex-Police Chief was also hiding something, of this he was sure.

"... *keep Elise alive. Trust no one. I'll come find you.*"

What was Dante's cryptic warning supposed to mean? Who could he trust, and was someone coming after Elise? She limped alongside him, resolute, using his arm as a crutch. The thought that someone would want to hurt her made his lips involuntarily peel back in a snarl.

Elise, sensing him staring, turned her face up to his and frowned. "Is something wrong?"

He shook his head and forced his expression into something more neutral. "No, I'm fine."

"You're a bad liar." Her eyes crinkled into a knowing smile, and she quickly added, "It's all right. I've accepted that it's just the way you are, and I wouldn't want it any other way. You wouldn't be you otherwise."

"You're not so bad yourself, tougher than I expected." Vincent motioned to her lame leg. "How's it feel?"

Elise shrugged and said, "It's not so bad. And look, it's in the same spot Gil shot you. We're twinsies now!"

"Please don't call us that."

She wrinkled her nose at him. "I'm calling us twinsies and there's nothing you can do about it."

Vincent grinned. "I guess we both have things about us that'll never change."

When they made it back to Sanctuary, it occurred to Vincent that he had run, walked, stalked, and even dodged bullets for the past twelve hours—with almost no rest in between. His body was paying for it. His muscles and tendons ached, and each step inflamed them further until he was practically crawling over the bridge.

At the top of the blockade, George motioned for Conrad. "Take a few of my men and guard this bridge. No one gets off the island, understand?" he said to him.

Vincent cocked his head, confused, as George and his people funneled back into the island. Conrad approached him, waving his gun menacingly. "You heard the man. Get back into Sanctuary."

"I heard him, but I don't get it," Vincent said. "Is he worried people are going to try and leave?"

Conrad smirked, all traces of his usually jovial demeanor gone. "It's none of your business. Now move before I lose my patience."

Vincent glowered at the pudgy man. "Who the fuck do you think you are? You can't order me around."

Conrad held up his assault rifle and waggled his eyebrows. "You want to run that by me again?"

Elise took Vincent's arm and pulled him away before the situation escalated any further. After they climbed down the other side, she said, "I don't like it. This whole place gives me a bad feeling now, Vincent."

As they walked down the road, Vincent observed the line of armed guards now sitting atop the cargo trailer. He had always thought the island was the perfect fort because of its one, defensible bridge. Only now did he realize it went both ways: it was also the perfect prison.

Flea was pacing nervously in the front room when they got home. He sighed with relief. "Forbidden arcana, you made it back finally. I was beginning to worry."

"Relax, I'm not dumb enough to get myself killed," Vincent said.

Flea snorted. "*Not dumb?* That is a dubious statement at best."

"I might kill you one day, Flea."

He turned his nose up haughtily. "There's no need to get offended by it. I am merely stating my observations."

Vincent eyed the little dog, realizing he was the shape of a fat little ball, perfect for punting across the room.

"Vincent," Elise said pointedly. "Don't even think about it."

He gave Flea one last glare, and then sat with her in the living room.

Elise propped her leg up on the coffee table and carefully rolled up her pants, showing off a nasty smear of sticky blood.

Flea gasped. "What happened to you?"

"Gil shot her," Vincent answered.

"It looks worse than it actually is," she said. "Flea, could you get me the first aid kit from the bathroom?"

He scurried off and came back moments later with a little white box. "What happened out there?" he asked, handing it over to her.

Elise opened it and began setting out the necessary supplies to patch herself up. "Yeah, what did happen out there? I showed up after the fact."

"Dante killed Gil," Vincent said.

She froze momentarily, a bottle of iodine in her hand. "Are you serious? How do you know?"

"I was standing there when it happened," he explained. "He just did it before I could even react. He was saying a lot of things all at once, so I'm not sure what to make of it. What I do know is that he didn't want Gil talking."

Flea pawed at his face. "About what, I wonder?"

Vincent shrugged. "Gil was trying to barter for his life by trading information with George."

"Did Dante mention anything that stuck out to you?" Elise asked, while methodically cleaning her wound out.

Vincent paused, contemplating if he should tell her the last thing Dante said, but decided against it. That was the last thing Elise needed to be worrying about right now. "No."

"What do you think we should do?" Elise asked.

"Yes, what now?" Flea chimed.

When did I become the decision maker of the group? Vincent thought. He scratched at some stubble on his chin, and the answer to their question came to him with alarming urgency. "We need to get the hell out of Sanctuary. Now."

Elise nodded reluctantly. "I figured you'd say that." Her eyes turned to him with a sudden fierceness. "But I'm with you all the way."

Vincent stood up, feeling hopeful. "I'll go get our bags and think of a way around the guards at the bridge," he said.

The words barely left his mouth, when a loud boom came from over the house. White light flashed through all the windows, blinding them amid a hundred crashing cymbals, and the house shook as if hit by an earthquake.

Vincent, Elise, and Flea all fell to the ground with startled screams while glass shattered throughout the house and loose objects fell from their places. The phenomenon lasted a full minute before the quaking stopped, and the powerful light receded, replaced by a sudden thunderstorm. Rain poured through the broken windows and lightning flashed every couple seconds, the day outside now darkened by storm clouds.

"What was that?" Vincent yelled. The wind whistling into the house made his voice tiny and insignificant. He jumped to his feet and ran to the front door.

A force of nature greeted him outside. Rain fell so thick he could barely see the house across the street, and the trees in their yard bowed against the winds cutting across the island. Elise and Flea joined him at the door, shielding their faces against the elements. A sudden vacuum threatened to suck them out of the house, but reacting fast, Vincent snatched Flea's robe as the dog tumbled out the door with a surprised yelp. He yanked the dog close to his body and tucked him under his arm.

"Up there!" Elise shouted.

Vincent followed her finger and saw a beam of iridescent light shooting up into a pool of shimmering water in the sky. A vortex of black clouds swirled around it, alive with tendrils of lightning coursing through it and roaring thunderously like a caged beast fighting to break free.

Vincent had a split second to admire the spectacle when his body weakened abruptly, sapped of all its energy. He wobbled in place, then stumbled back into the house and crashed into the floor, sending Flea tumbling away.

Elise fell by his side, screaming his name, but he barely heard her. His vision swam and darkened around the edges. Looking to his side, he saw Flea try to stand and fail.

"Something is draining our energy," Flea mumbled.

Vincent focused on Elise's panicked face, and he dully wondered how she was still standing, unaffected.

"What do I do?" she begged.

Flea pointed a weak finger up the stairs. "Bring us the Resiliens Adjuvant . . . in room . . . yellow bottle."

Elise darted off, leaving Vincent alone on the cold floor. Rain sprayed through the open door, soaking him, and he tried to crawl away, but his eyelids grew heavy. So heavy, so tired. He shut his eyes, welcoming the much-needed sleep.

Glass touched his lips and a cold sludge crawled down his throat. It was sour and not entirely unpleasant. Somewhere in the background, he heard Elise's muffled cries. A tiny prick of heat formed in his stomach, barely discernable, and began to expand.

A warmth filled Vincent's body, the sensation indescribably comforting, like sitting in front of a cozy fire during winter while drinking hot cocoa. His eyes fluttered open to his strength returning, and Elise's fuzzy outline sharpened over him.

"Did it work?" she asked hesitantly, a bottle of yellow liquid in her hands.

Vincent sat up on his elbows and felt a rush of blood to his head. "What the hell just happened?" he said, groaning.

Elise hurried over to Flea and fed him the mystery drink.

A moment later, he came to with a rousing bark and said, "Thank goodness you found the Resiliens Adjuvant." Flea grabbed at his head and shook the last bits of grogginess out. "And thank goodness I'm a genius and prepared the concoction correctly."

Vincent stood on strong legs. His energy waned still, though considerably slower. "What's happening, Flea?" he shouted over the thunder, which seemed to be never-ending.

Flea took the bottle from Elise and stuffed it into his robe. "Someone's opened a Gate," he said seriously.

"Are you shitting me?" Vincent went back to the door and, to his horror, saw the pool in the sky had grown significantly larger. "That's a Gate? It's massive!"

Flea appeared behind his leg, gripping onto it for dear life and squinting against the raindrops pelting his face. "It's feeding off the island," he explained. "More specifically, it's feeding off the energy of those living on the island, literally sucking out their life force to grow larger. My potion is providing us protection against it, but it will only work for so long."

"What's going to come through a Gate of that size?" Elise asked.

"Thunderbirds," Vincent said, as sure as the fear he was feeling.

"That's ridiculous. Thunderbirds don't exist," Flea said, though he didn't sound confident. "However, a Gate of that size begs the question: what manner of creature could require one so large? Not even a dragon would need a Gate of this magnitude."

Vincent turned back into the house. "We got to get out of here!"

"Wait a moment," Flea said.

He whirled on the pug. "Wait for what? I don't want to be around when some sort of super creature comes through that thing."

"I understand, and I am in full agreement," Flea said, wringing his hands. "*However . . .*"

Vincent didn't like the sound of that one bit.

"That Gate out there will continue siphoning the energy

from the area until there's none left."

Elise kneeled beside Flea. "What does that mean?"

Flea gulped. "It means that everyone on the island will eventually die unless someone stops it."

Elise gasped into her hands, then turned to Vincent. He knew that look.

"No, absolutely not," he said. "This isn't our fucking problem."

"There are thousands of people on Sanctuary," Elise said.

"It doesn't matter. The only ones I care about are standing here with me. Besides, we don't even know how to close a Gate."

Elise bit her lower lip. "There's got to be something we can do, though. Can't you stop it, Flea?"

"Not without preparation. And that's if we were talking about an ordinary Gate." He pointed up. "That thing in the sky is an entirely different beast."

"That settles it." Vincent went to the stairs. "It's time to go."

Elise stamped her foot. "I'm not going! If you and Flea want to run away, that's fine, but I won't abandon the people here."

Flea hung his head, then nodded, as if coming to an understanding with himself. "Sorceress Epoch did not enchant a coward."

Elise and Flea stood together, their minds made up.

Vincent wondered if he could knock her out and carry her away, but realized it would be impossible given his physical state. A crazed laugh bubbled up as he accepted defeat and imminent death. He could be like the heroes in his fantasy books, though. That wasn't so bad, was it? There were worse ways to go out. A facetious thought occurred to him: if he died today, he wouldn't be able to finish the books Elise had gotten him. That'd be a real shame.

"So? Are you going to leave?" Elise asked.

Vincent rubbed his temples and blew a deep breath through his nose. "You give me such a headache sometimes, but you know what? Fuck it. Let's close that damn thing in the sky."

Elise's shoulders slumped in relief. "I knew you'd do the right thing. You're a good guy, Vincent."

He waved her comment away, then turned to Flea. "All right, you're the magical dog. How do we stop this?"

Flea took a tentative step toward the door, muttering to himself while shaking his head at some thoughts and nodding at others. When he looked back, there was a glimmer of the cockiness they had grown accustomed to. "Something must be channeling all this energy from the people into the Gate, a conduit of some kind. I can only surmise it's happening at the base of that beam of light."

"Are you saying there's a real chance of stopping this?" Vincent asked.

"I may be able to disrupt it, or redirect the energy back." Flea hurried upstairs and came back with his staff, brandishing it triumphantly over his head. "I am the greatest wizard to have ever existed. I can do anything!"

Vincent exchanged smiles with Elise, then picked Flea up.

Flea pointed straight ahead. "Onward steed! To victory!"

Elise made to follow him out the door, but Vincent stopped her. "You have to stay."

"Why?" she demanded. "I can't stand around while you two are out there risking your lives."

He pointed out her leg. "You can barely walk."

"I'll be fine. It doesn't even hurt anymore," she said heatedly.

"Don't be stupid," Vincent snapped. "You'll be a liability if you come with us. Someone opened that Gate, and whoever it was isn't going to be happy with us when we try closing it. The last thing I need is to have to babysit you, too."

Elise pursed her lips. "Don't tell me what to do!"

Her fire reminded him of Grandma, and he felt a pang of guilt having to tell her no. His brother's warning to keep her alive echoed in the back of his thoughts, but even if he hadn't said anything, Vincent still didn't want her getting hurt. It was safest if she stayed here, out of harm's way.

Elise took a step forward, so he pulled out his gun. "What are you doing?" she asked, eyes narrowed to slits.

"I swear to god, I will shoot you in the foot if that's what it's going to take."

"You wouldn't dare," Elise said.

"Wouldn't I?" Vincent's expression hardened. "I don't want to be here, but I am, aren't I? We all have to make our sacrifices, and yours is to wait because it's going to give us the best chance of success."

"But, Vincent—"

"We're wasting time!" Flea shouted. "We must act now!"

Elise opened her mouth, but hesitated, realizing Vincent was right. She limped forward and pulled them into a tight hug. "Try to come back in one piece, you hear?"

"You really don't have to tell me that," Vincent said. He gave her a brash smile and darted into the storm. He heard Elise call his name, but didn't look back for fear of losing his nerve.

Chapter 29

The elements lashed at Vincent's unprotected body, whipping his clothes around him and beating against him relentlessly. The wind felt like a physical wall, blowing so hard he had to lean into it to stop from toppling over, and the rain sent a torrent of water gushing over his feet. Vincent had never felt so insignificant before in his life, so helpless to the whims of Mother Nature.

"Vincent, look out!" Flea shouted.

He looked up in time to see a thick tree trunk barreling down the street at him; it was moving too fast, and he had one of those moments where he could see everything happen in slow motion, but was unable to do anything about it. He blinked, and the next moment the tree was upon him, only a few feet away from crushing his body.

"Shit!" Vincent threw his arm up, bracing for the impact.

There was a dull *wump* as the trunk hit an invisible barrier before his face; the bark splintered with a loud crack and broke in two, each piece spiraling off to opposite sides.

One piece went into someone's living room, and the other continued its haphazard race down the street. Vincent watched concentric circles radiate out from the tree's point of impact and realized he was encased in a clear dome.

"What is this?" he asked. His voice bounced back, loud, as if speaking from inside a glass jar.

Flea let out a breath and the sounds from the raging storm came back in full clarity.

Vincent looked down at the dog in disbelief. "Did you do that?"

Flea lowered his staff with a nod, looking bewildered. "I conjured up a shield."

"I thought you couldn't do magic?"

"I-I don't understand it. I simply reacted and my magic worked." Flea sniffed the air. "The magical energies are flowing properly . . . but why?"

They weren't able to ponder the question for long. An ear-piercing screech came from the skies; Vincent cried out in pain and clamped his free hand over his ear as the sound persisted. He looked to the clouds and saw a massive shadow circling behind the Gate's rippling waves. The shadow disappeared from view along with the drawn-out scream, and a moment later, a massive bird pushed its head through. It thrashed violently as if stuck, screaming its disapproval. Vincent's heart screamed with it, terrified, yet awestruck and entranced by the sight.

It was big. The head alone was the size of his old seafoam-green house, and he could only assume the rest of its body was equally huge. Smoky feathers of blacks and grays adorned its neck and head, blending with the dark clouds around it. Its eyes were brilliant balls of blue energy, literally sparking and crackling, and two whips of lightning trailed over them like long, erratic eyebrows. The giant bird struggled harder, squeezing a bit more of its body through.

It felt like watching a growing crack in a window. Vincent was helpless to stop it and knew the bird would eventually break through the Gate. The monstrous creature howled its rage and pulled its head back, disappearing from the sky. In the same moment, lightning forked down from the clouds, stabbing Sanctuary with impunity. Vincent shut his eyes as one of the lightning bolts hit the house next to him, showering him in an explosion of dirt and grass. When he opened them, he saw the house in flames and a zigzagging scar of uplifted land from the lawn into the street.

"What was that?" Vincent asked, all thoughts of Flea's sudden resurgence of magic gone from his mind.

"I-I-I don't know. Its power, did you feel it? Oppressive and crushing." Flea gulped. "Whatever it is, we can't let it through the Gate."

Vincent squared his shoulders, admitting to himself what Flea couldn't. That was a thunderbird. He fully understood the stakes now. It went beyond the island. If the creature broke free into their world, it would wreak havoc upon the remnants of humanity. He pressed on, harder and more determined than ever.

Even before reaching the source of the Gate's power, Vincent had a strong inkling of where it was coming from.

So when he finally found it, he wasn't surprised to see the spot where George's bank used to be engulfed in pulsating light. From where he stood, he could feel a rushing, tingling sensation over his body, and heard a thrum of power coming from it.

"The Gate is being channeled from in that," Flea confirmed.

Vincent heard gunshots nearby and saw George stumble out from behind a row of tall bushes. The large man blindly fired a gun over his shoulder at unseen attackers, then lumbered into the home closest to him.

Vincent dove behind some cover as Dante and Roach came into view soon after; they made a straight line for the house George disappeared into, and moments later, more gunshots could be heard from inside. *What have you done, Dante?* Vincent thought angrily. He sprinted to the house, readying his gun for a fight.

The front door swung wildly and banged against the frame as he went up the front steps. He grabbed onto it and took a cautious peek inside. The house was dark and empty.

Vincent slipped through the door and set Flea down. "Be ready for anything," he whispered. A trail of water by his feet led deeper inside, and he swallowed his fear before following it.

The muffled chaos from outside seeped through the walls, acting as an eerie backdrop to the whole situation. Vincent listened for any signs of a struggle, but got nothing. The lack of action was more unsettling than if he had walked in on a full-blown gunfight. There were four people wandering these darkened rooms, and the house was only so big. Something should've been happening.

The trail of water led Vincent into a living room with a series of sliding glass doors on the far wall. Lightning flashed through them, shining light over someone on the floor.

Vincent's hands shook more than he liked to admit as he inched toward the body. "Flea, can you magic me some fire?" he whispered.

Flea tapped the foot of his staff against the floor, and a bright flame burst into existence, floating a couple inches over the tip. He brandished the flame over the body.

Beneath its glow, George stared up at the ceiling, his glassy eyes reflecting the fire. A thick pool of blood had collected around his body, and his entire chest had been turned into a lumpy, shredded mess of meat. Someone had made damn sure he was dead with what looked like shotgun blasts; bits of buckshot stuck to the peripherals of the wound.

Vincent looked away in disgust, overwhelmed by the smell of it more than anything else. George's chest cavity exuded an odor belonging to a rotting carcass in the sun. "Fucking hell." His eyes fell upon a set of bloody shoe prints leading away from George's body; he followed it through the connecting kitchen and into the dining room on the other side.

There, he found his former illicit business partner, Roach, sitting alone on the floor. The man turned his eyes up to Vincent, wheezing sloppily, his hand clamped tight over his neck. Blood spurted out between his fingers with every labored breath.

"Long time no see," Roach said. His voice gurgled grotesquely and made Vincent cringe.

Vincent crouched in front of him. "Christ, what happened to you?"

Roach lifted his hand, showing a weeping gash across his neck. "One of his bullets grazed me, got me in a bad spot."

Vincent looked around for something to try and triage the wound.

"Don't bother," Roach said. "I'll be dead soon."

Vincent thought he should be furious after everything Roach and Gil had done, but he could only feel pity. He shook his head with a sad sigh. "I wish I had a cigarette to give you or something."

"It's all right." Roach hacked up blood and it dribbled down his chin. "I guess I deserve this. I went along with Kojo's plans because I was too scared . . . of what would happen if I didn't. I knew what I was doing was wrong, but I'm a piece of shit, you know? I thought helping Gil stop the thunderbirds would make up for it, but you can't clean shit. Shit is shit no matter how much you try to clean it . . . I'm just a sparkly piece of shit." He laughed weakly. "Sparkly shit . . . that's kinda funny, huh, boss?"

Vincent shook his head, thinking he misheard the dying man. "Did you say Gil was actually trying to stop the thunderbirds?"

Roach took a shuddering breath and said, "Yes. He was the only one . . . willing and able, but make no mistake about it, he was an evil son of a bitch—just a means to an end. Gil knew if he didn't stop Kojo . . ." He paused and took another deep, rasping breath. "Everyone was going to be in trouble, himself included, if the thunderbirds made it to our world."

"So then you know how to close the Gate?"

Roach jerked his head up and down. "Dante's going to get the Gatekeeper. She can close it."

"Who's the Gatekeeper?"

Roach's head lolled to the side, limp.

"No!" Vincent shook him, desperate. "Who is it, Roach? Tell me! Roach? Roach!" The full weight of Roach's body fell into him; he let the corpse fall to the floor and scrambled away from it, mortified.

A necklace popped out from Roach's shirt. Vincent carefully removed it from his neck and held it up, letting the dull lump of silver dangle before him. He had seen this thing so many times. Why was it that sometimes the silver glowed and other times it didn't?

Something clicked in his head, but before he could act on his revelation, a deep voice said, "You have something of mine."

Vincent and Flea spun around to George's mangled corpse standing over them. His face was hidden behind a wooden mask that resembled an old man; wrinkles were etched beside the eyeholes and white hairs hung loose beneath a small smile. Vincent's mind struggled to make sense of what he was seeing. His eyes told him it was George, but his mind said people don't survive with all their organs pulverized in their chest.

George's arm shot out in a blur and snatched Flea's staff out of his hands.

Flea reached for it with a cry of protest. "Give that back!"

George snapped the staff in two in his huge hand, extinguishing its magical fire in the process.

Flea's voice petered off into a frightened squeak in the dark.

"What an odd day it's been," George said, his voice muffled behind the mask. "First Roach pretends to be the hero and attempts to kill me, and now I find an enchanted dog has been hiding right under my nose. Tell me, who's your sorceress?"

"The g-greatest sorceress to ever exist," Flea stammered. "Sorceress Epoch! And y-you would do well to leave before I blast you to smithereens, you foul beast!"

"Interesting . . . very interesting," George drawled, moving a step forward.

"I will not warn you again!" Flea shrilled. "I will use the full extent of my magic!"

"You don't have to play games." George pointed to Flea's broken staff. "You can't do anything without it. I'm impressed, however, that either of you are still standing. You must have brewed some Resiliens Adjuvant. How did you manage that here on Earth?"

Flea puffed his little chest out. "I am the greatest wizard alive and nothing is out of my reach."

"Of course you are."

Vincent shook himself out of his daze and drew his gun on George. "What are you, really?" he demanded.

"I'm George Garcia. Isn't that obvious?"

"Don't fucking play games with me!"

George chuckled chillingly. "You're resourceful, I'll give you that." He clicked his tongue nonchalantly. "The real George Garcia died before the Catastrophe. I killed him because I needed his body to make this charade work, and I have to say, it's worked perfectly."

Vincent recognized the mask finally, even obscured in the shadows. "You're Kojo." He didn't wait for a response and unloaded his gun into George's body.

The big man flinched as each shot burrowed into his head and body, but when it was over he remained standing, much to Vincent's dismay.

Kojo ran a big hand over his mask, feeling the new holes the bullets left behind, and grunted a sound of disapproval. "I don't like it when people damage my mask, Vincent. I really, *really* don't." His hand shot out and grabbed Vincent around the neck in a throat-crushing grip. "Don't make me angry. I don't like getting angry . . . Do you know why?"

Vincent punched back weakly, the effort futile.

"It's because anger makes one act irrationally. It is a primal instinct, a stupid instinct, and it is the tool of the weak." Kojo ripped his necklace from Vincent's other hand, then threw him to the floor. "Lucky for you, I learned to control my fury a long time ago."

Vincent scrambled away, coughing and clutching at his burning throat.

Kojo looked down at himself and heaved a sigh. "Look at this body. It's useless now." He turned to Roach's corpse with a grimace. "This will have to do until I find something better." He kneeled over him, then took his mask off and placed it on Roach's head.

The skin around the mask bubbled unnaturally, liquefying into a thick paste; it sucked the wooden mask down into it, then re-formed into Roach's face. To Vincent's bewilderment, Roach blinked and sat up as George fell over, lifeless.

"What is even happening right now?" Vincent whispered to Flea.

The dog whimpered pathetically.

Roach took the necklace from George's dead hand while rubbing at the oozing cut on his neck, as if working a crick out of it. He stood up and headed to the front door.

"Where are you going?" Vincent called.

"My job is done here," he replied. "The thunderbirds will be coming through the Gate soon, and there's no one left to stop it. As much as I want to stay for the fireworks, I have appointments elsewhere. There's always work to be done." A vindictive smile flashed across his lips. "Enjoy your last moments, Vincent. Make peace with whatever god you believe in."

Roach left, whistling a cheerful tune.

"It's over, then," Flea said, turning his somber face to Vincent. "Without my staff there is no hope of me closing the Gate."

"You can't, but there's someone else who can."

"What? I don't understand."

"Come on, there isn't much time!" Vincent picked Flea up and fled the house.

When Vincent burst through his home's front door, he found it empty. "Elise, where are you?"

No one answered.

His stomach dropped. *Am I too late?* He took the steps three at a time and prayed she was hiding upstairs. Vincent turned the corner into the hallway and came face to face with Dante, coming out of Elise's bedroom.

"Where's the Gatekeeper?" Dante asked, looking strained.

"She has a name," Vincent said.

"We don't have time for games. Where's Elise?"

Vincent shrugged. "I don't know. Are you even sure she's in the house?"

Dante pulled Kojo's necklace out, showing off its pale white glow. "Where is she?"

"I'm not helping you until you give me some fucking answers, Dante. What's a Gatekeeper, and how is it they can close Gates?"

"I don't know the specifics of how it all works, but Gatekeepers are people with special powers. Something about them disrupts Gates and forces them to close."

"How is that possible?" Flea asked. "I've never heard of such a thing."

"It's very possible," Dante said. "What do you think was going on in the month leading up to the Catastrophe? Kojo was rounding up all the Gatekeepers he could find and killing them so that they wouldn't interfere with his plans. Thing is, he missed Elise because she came into town late. She was supposed to be our ace in the hole. Natalie was watching over her to ensure her survival until she was needed."

"Forbidden arcana," Flea whispered. "Elise closed the Gate at City Hall. It makes sense now."

Vincent got a bad vibe from his brother, from the way he said Elise's name like she was an expendable tool. "Why keep me in the dark about all this?" he asked. "I could have helped."

"No, you wouldn't have," Dante said, a pitying look in his eyes.

"What the hell are you talking about?"

"The effort from closing a Gate of that magnitude would kill her," Flea said, stepping between them and literally growling at Dante. "You intend to sacrifice her."

Vincent's heart stopped. "What do you mean it would kill her, Flea?"

Flea spoke over his shoulder. "When a Gate is closed, it creates a brief magic vacuum. If you don't properly accommodate for this, it will pull energy directly from the one who closed it. Do you recall how winded Elise was when the Gate at City Hall closed? Imagine that, multiplied by thousands. Elise would never survive such an ordeal."

Vincent didn't want to believe Flea's words, but the silence from Dante confirmed it. "You heartless motherfucker. You can't be serious."

Dante slashed the air with his arm. "I never wanted it to come to this, but it's the only way. If she doesn't close that Gate, everyone on the island dies, and then more will die wherever those thunderbirds go!" He took a tentative step forward. "One life, for many."

Vincent couldn't even look at his brother, the sight of him repulsive. To even consider his plan felt vile and heinous, a betrayal to Elise, Grandma, and himself. "You stay away from her," he seethed.

"We can't be selfish little kids anymore, Vincent. We have to consider the greater good."

"What you're contemplating is murder, plain and simple."

"I know, and I accept that burden."

Vincent yelled over his shoulder, "Elise! If you're still in the house, run! Get as far away from here as you can!" A sound came from the kitchen downstairs, and he ran to the banister. "Go! Just go! I'll find you!"

"What the hell are you doing?" Dante said.

Vincent looked back and saw his brother storming forward. Flea scurried off to the side, clearing the hall for the brothers.

"Get out of the way," Dante snarled.

Vincent charged with a drawn-out roar. He threw a wild haymaker that his brother narrowly sidestepped. Dante blocked his next punch and tackled him into the wall. Vincent felt the air pressed from his lungs, but recovered and kicked Dante off, then followed up with a swift punch to his midsection.

Dante stumbled back as Vincent struggled to regain his breath. He realized Flea's potion was wearing off, and he was losing the little energy he had left, fast. "Give me the Resiliens Adjuvant!"

Flea pulled the potion from his robe and threw it to him.

Dante came at him like a bull and swung a heavy fist into his back; Vincent buckled under the hit and missed the catch. His brother saw his wanting eyes on it and, in response, crushed the bottle under his shoe.

"No!" Vincent wailed, watching the liquid spread over the floor. He dragged himself up and threw himself onto Dante.

His brother caught his weight with ease. "It's over!" he yelled, pinning Vincent against the wall. "Stand down!"

Vincent kneed his brother in the side, but it did nothing. "How come the Gate isn't draining your energy?" he asked, gasping.

"The necklace protects against it," Dante replied.

Vincent noticed a gun wedged under his brother's belt loop, and snatched it out in a last-ditch effort. Dante was faster and swatted the gun from his hand. It flew off to the side and clattered to the floor, useless. Vincent threw a few more punches, but he may as well have been hitting him with pillows. With his energy sapped, he had nothing left to give. Dante roared and tossed him aside.

"Stop it!" Elise screamed.

At the end of the hallway, she stood in a standard shooting stance with Dante's weapon trained on him—Vincent was proud to see no shakiness to her form.

Dante took a step, but Elise fired a warning shot at him without hesitation. He froze and threw his hands up. "Okay, okay. I hear you loud and clear. Let's just talk."

"Is what you said true? I can close the Gate?" Elise asked.

Dante nodded.

"And the other part—the part about me dying. Is that true, too?"

He nodded.

"Don't listen to him," Vincent said, shaking the cobwebs from his head. "Don't . . . just go. Go now . . . while you can."

Elise's shoulders sagged. "Am I really the only one who can stop it now?"

Flea crawled to her feet, fighting to stay awake like Vincent. "You'll die . . . you fool."

She locked eyes with Vincent, her stormy pupils swirling with life. "What should I do?"

Vincent pushed himself up on shaky legs and leaned into the wall, frustrated with his unresponsive body. "Don't be fucking stupid," he slurred, barely getting the words out. "You go. Live."

"If you do that, you'll be condemning us all to death," Dante said. "Could you live with yourself, knowing that? I don't know what Vincent's taught you these past months, but you aren't like him."

Vincent's eyes bulged, furious. He knew what Dante was doing, appealing to her good side. The part of her that was infuriatingly kind and made up her whole being. Vincent revved his brain, trying to think of a rebuttal to make her see things properly, but his brain blew smoke.

Lightning flashed and thunder boomed through the house. The thunderbird in the sky screeched, and then a second screech joined it. Didn't Flea say thunderbirds always came in pairs?

Dante spoke with renewed urgency. "It's now or never, Elise! Vincent's going to die if you don't do this."

Vincent saw the wheels turning in Elise's head, and never before had he been so scared, so absolutely terrified. The thought of her throwing away her life in exchange for his own was too much to bear, like a crushing vise over his heart.

"Please, Elise," Dante implored.

Shut up, Dante! Shut up! Vincent's mouth didn't relay the message. He was on the floor, a helpless bystander trapped in his own body.

"Will it hurt?" Elise asked, choking the words out around a sob.

"I don't know," Dante said.

Elise dropped the gun and put a hand to her mouth, a distant and forlorn expression on her face. She swallowed down another sob, then nodded. "What do I have to do?"

"Nnngh," Vincent said.

Dante looked from him back to Elise. "Go to the bank and walk into the light. You'll see a dagger there. Just take it."

"It's that easy?"

"It's that easy," he said.

Elise blinked hard and tears rolled down her cheeks. "Okay," she whispered. "I've made up my mind."

Vincent willed his fingers to twitch. His vision blurred, hot and wet, and to his horror, she left. Just like that, she was gone. No flair, no words. Just gone.

Dante walked back to his little brother and cocked his head so they could look each other in the face. His expression was stony. "I'm sorry, little brother. Someone had to do it."

Vincent's thoughts were a dull, raging scream. His eyelids became too heavy to hold up and everything went dark.

***

"Where is she? Where's Xifeng?"

"Daddy!" Dante tore himself from an older woman on the far side of the maternity ward lobby and ran into Bo's arms.

Bo picked up his son and focused on the woman approaching him. She wore a long white coat over blue scrubs, a doctor. "Which room is Xifeng in? She's giving birth to our second child," he said, beaming. He tickled Dante's stomach. "You'll have a brother or sister soon."

"I wanna brother!" Dante squealed.

The woman rubbed a weary hand down her face and blew out a low breath before speaking. "Are you her husband?"

"Yes, that's me. My name is Bo Li. I was at work when I got the call." He fidgeted in place, anxious to be at his wife's side. "I'm sorry I'm late. I got lost on the way here . . . the signs, I have difficulty . . ." He shook his head with a laugh. "It doesn't matter. I'm here now. Take me to her, please."

The doctor grabbed the attention of a nearby nurse and whispered into her ear. The other woman nodded and went to take Dante from him.

Bo pulled away. "What're you doing?" He saw something

in the doctor's face that rooted him to the spot. "What's going on?"

The nurse tried taking Dante again, and that time he let her.

"No!" Dante squirmed in her arms. "I want Mommy and Daddy!"

The doctor waited for them to disappear into a side room, and then placed a gentle hand on Bo's shoulder. "You might want to sit down for this."

"Sit down for what?" he shot back. "Tell me what's going on. Take me to Xifeng! Right now!"

"Mr. Li, please. Listen to me." The doctor sighed. "Your wife passed away."

Bo only managed a faint sound in reply.

"There were complications during the birth."

"Complications?" he echoed, the word an annoying gnat, buzzing in his ears. "You can fix complications. You're a doctor, that's what you're supposed to do."

She shook her head. "Xifeng died half an hour ago."

The fluorescent lights were suddenly too bright to bear and threatened to burn his eyes to unseeing coals. His strength left him like water flowing down a drain, and he slumped to his knees.

Xifeng was dead. She had died alone while he was lost in the city, lost because he couldn't read the street signs, lost because the words danced around like they always did. What if he had been here sooner? Would she have survived? Would his presence have helped? No, instead she died alone because of his stupidity. He was so *stupid* and *useless*. Bo's throat went dry. Did she live out her final moments feeling abandoned? Did she hate him, did she die cursing his name?

"What have I done?" Tears poured freely down his cheeks. "How could I have done this to you, Xifeng?"

"No, no, no. It wasn't your fault," the doctor reassured.

Liar! he thought viciously.

"Before she passed, she said she wanted the boy to be named Vincent."

Bo looked up in a daze. "What do you mean?"

The doctor smiled, as if what she was about to say was a condolence. "She gave birth to a healthy boy. She said she wanted to call him Vincent because it means 'to conquer.'"

He looked at her mouth, at the sickly-sweet smile that meant the news was a bittersweet lining. Vincent was the name of the thing that took his beloved Xifeng from him. It disgusted him, he hated it. The name tasted like ash in his mouth and made him sick.

Chapter 30

Vincent stirred awake to something slimy trailing over his face.

"Wake up, Vincent. I promise I'll keep doing this until you do."

He cracked one eye open with a whispered groan and saw Flea sitting on his chest, mid-lick. "What the hell are you doing?" he asked, hoarse.

Flea hopped off his chest. "I have been trying to rouse you from your slumber for the past hour. You taste awful, by the way."

Vincent sat up and blood rushed to his brain; he gripped his head and waited for the feeling to pass before opening his eyes again. "Where's Dante?" he asked.

"He was gone when I came to."

"How long were we out?"

"I believe an entire day has passed," Flea said. "The sun is rising again."

Vincent heard birds chirping, noting with a sinking

feeling how quiet it was otherwise. He pushed himself onto his feet and made his way outside, moving only as fast as his tired legs would allow. Outside, the sky had calmed to a light fog, and there was no Gate. What remained of Sanctuary was covered in a dewy sheen, glittering under the few rays of sunlight that managed to penetrate the cloud cover.

Vincent knew where he had to go, but his whole being told him not to. Flea appeared beside him, a sympathetic look on his wrinkled pug face.

Flea put a hand on his leg. "We should go look."

Vincent nodded numbly, and the two headed for the bank. Other survivors of the incident began to wake around them, bleary-eyed and confused. A few pointed to Flea while whispering to each other in fascination; the wizard had chosen not to hide his identity anymore and walked upright. Nobody bothered them otherwise, perhaps seeing the look on Vincent's face and understanding he was in a bad place.

What remained of George's bank and the surrounding area was a smoldering crater of blasted earth and debris. A single body lay face up in the center, floating in a puddle of murky brown water. Vincent lunged in, splashing frantically, slipping and falling over the uneven footing beneath him. Flea waited patiently by the water's edge, looking gloomy with his ears pinned down.

Vincent practically fell onto her, but he felt cold and lifeless skin under his fingers. He stumbled back as reality came crashing down. After a contemplative silence, he mustered up the courage to approach her again. Elise looked past him to the sky, unblinking, her gray eyes muted and dull. Her hair clung to her face in dirty clumps, and her blue-tinted lips were parted slightly, as if trying to say one last word.

Vincent was hit with an overwhelming sense of how undignified she looked. Rigid and dirty, with no one to remember her but himself and a talking dog. Nobody on this fucking island even knew the sacrifice she had made for them. He brushed her hair to the side and wiped smudges of dirt off her pale skin, but it was pointless. Elise was dead.

Vincent pulled her close and bent over, suffering silently as his senses blotted everything else out.

When his body could give no more, Vincent waded to the edge of the dirty pool with Elise tight in his arms.

Flea sniffed loudly and wiped his sleeve against his eyes. "It was probably painless," he said. "With so much power moving around, it was probably over before she even realized."

"Is that supposed to make me feel better?" Vincent asked dryly.

"I don't know."

As Vincent stepped out of the water, something glinted by his waist and caught his attention. He looked down and saw a crystalline dagger clutched tightly in Elise's hand. "That's Kojo's dagger," he said, a wave of fury dispelling any coldness in his body.

Flea pried it from Elise's hand and sniffed the blade. "This must have been the conduit used to channel the energy into the Gate. I've never seen this type of crystal before. It would be interesting to study."

"Give me it," Vincent demanded. He set Elise down, then walked a few paces away. He screamed and threw the dagger into the concrete, smashing it into a million pieces.

Flea looked taken aback at first, but then nodded his approval.

Vincent shuffled back to Elise's body and picked her up.

"What will you do with her?" Flea asked.

"Give her a place to rest."

By the time Vincent finished, the sun was beginning to set behind him. He stood atop a small cliff overlooking the bay. His hands were raw and blistered, caked in dirt from the tireless work he had done over the last seven hours.

Before him was Elise's unmarked grave.

Vincent wiped the sweat from his brow, then threw the shovel over the edge of the cliff; he listened for the splash before turning his eyes to the sunset. The fiery ball burned a swath of reds and oranges across the sky. It was beautiful, actually. He couldn't remember the last time he had looked at one.

"I think I understand it now," Flea said.

Vincent regarded him with a grunt.

"The reason I couldn't use my magic was because of Elise." He snapped his fingers and created a flame over his thumb. "Simply put, she breaks—broke—magic. That explains why she could close Gates; she simply scattered their energies with her presence. If I had to postulate further, I would say that's why she was unaffected by the draining properties of the Super Gate."

"Super Gate, huh?"

Flea nodded. "That is what I'm calling it."

Vincent wondered if working out complex ideas was Flea's way of coping. He reached for a bottle of whiskey by his feet, unopened and beckoning for him to drink. Vincent unscrewed the top and lifted it to his lips, but stopped short. He looked through the amber bottle at the distorted view of Elise's grave.

I need to remember this.

Vincent tipped the bottle over and let the dirt drink the whiskey until there was nothing left. He then tossed the bottle into the bay without even a hint of regret.

Standing in the dying light, with only Flea for company, Vincent reflected on how very alone he was. Everyone he ever cared about was gone, and the vastness of the new world felt endless. It was almost enough to make him want to lie down and die.

But he couldn't. He had a mission. Vincent lit a cigarette between his lips, then threw on his backpack. "I'm going to look for Dante," he told Flea.

"What will you do when you find him?"

"I don't know."

Flea twiddled his fingers nervously. "May I come with you?"

Vincent blew out a breath of smoke and chuckled. "You sure you want to stick with me still? I'm only looking for trouble. You realize this, right?"

"That's precisely why I must go with you. What kind of wizard would I be if I allowed my foolish friend to walk into danger alone?" Flea folded his arms, daring Vincent to argue otherwise.

"We're friends?"

Flea's fierce expression wavered. "Aren't we?"

Vincent hummed thoughtfully. "We've been through more shit together than most people go through in a lifetime. I'd say that makes us *best* friends."

Flea's ears perked up, and his tail fanned back and forth happily. "Why, of course we are!"

Vincent motioned for him to follow. "Come on, then. Let's get the hell out of here."

They set off together with no particular destination in mind, so long as it put distance between them and Sanctuary.

Learn more about upcoming books at:

www.OLEggert.com

www.goodreads.com/OLEggert

www.facebook.com/theOLEggert

www.ingramcontent.com/pod-product-compliance
Lightning Source LLC
Chambersburg PA
CBHW030654120726
47905CB00001B/201